The Oreo File

A Novel

By Carol Van Strum

Jericho Hill Publishing
Alfred, New York
14802

This is a work of fiction. Names, characters, places, and incidents are the product of the author's imagination or are used fictitiously. Save for historical figures, any resemblance to actual events, locales, or persons (living or dead) is coincidental.

Published November, 2016 by
Jericho Hill Publishing
Alfred, New York
14802

Cover Design & Artwork by Bobbie Halperin

Table of Contents

Acknowledgements

I am deeply grateful to the Lincoln and Benton county (Oregon) historical societies for gathering and preserving what little is known of Lew Southworth ("Nigger Lew") and keeping his memory alive. Many thanks also to Nikko Merrell, Precious Bódle, and Beth Mitchell for guiding wayward penguins on their long trek from the lost kingdom of WordStar; to Bobbie Halperin for another glorious cover; to Peter von Stackelberg for believing; and to Jordan, Julie, and Kiki for unflagging faith in an Agéd Parent.

Dedication

To dear and distant friends:

Lynn Jeffress, poet and muse, who made it happen

and

Rosalind Peterson, indefatigable fighter, who makes caring fun,

And to my blessed, unruly family, wherever you are.

"To much of the public, an Oreo is simply a black cookie sandwich with white cream filling. In the African-American community, however, an Oreo is used as a racial slur to insult blacks who "act white" or identify as such. The racial name Oreo is controversial because many blacks recount being called the racial term for doing well in school or speaking proper English, not because they didn't identify as black. In short, these African Americans were singled out as sellouts simply for excelling academically and in other areas. Many blacks find this term hurtful, for they are proud of their African-American heritage."

– Nadra Kareem Nittle (racerelations.about.com)

Prelude

During the final hours of the 20th Century, the explosive boom of a calving polar ice shelf ushered in the new millennium unheard and unheralded. The iceberg was the size of Rhode Island and extended more than a thousand feet beneath the ocean surface. Carried eastward on the circumpolar current around Antarctica, it would slowly drift northward for more than a decade before breaking up. Most of its inhabitants would vanish in the first weeks of its frigid journey.

There were thirty-one penguin chicks initially, furry bundles of thick down over plump bodies amply fortified with fat. Abandoned on the vast ice shelf by their parents when they became too big to feed, the chicks huddled together to preserve body heat, calling vainly for their parents' return. Until their waterproof, insulated adult plumage grew, allowing them to swim after food in the frigid water, they would live on accumulated body fat, unaware that their ice island was moving steadily farther from their ancestral rookery.

Within the first weeks, more than half of the population took to the water as their plumage matured and hunger drove them to seek food. One by one they plodded and tobogganed to the water's edge, peered uncertainly at the icy ocean, and dove in, never to return. Most would fall prey to seals, orcas, or starvation; only four would survive two years of solitary wanderings to make their way back to their birthplace and find it gone.

The twelve birds remaining on the iceberg eventually matured and also dove into the ocean, but instead of swimming away to a solitary fate, these late-bloomers returned from their forays, shooting out of the water in great vertical leaps onto the ice and greeting each other with boisterous wing slaps and raucous calls. Perhaps an abundance of predators in the region discouraged travel; perhaps their floating home drifted beyond some magnetic or geologic trigger for instinctive behavior. Or perhaps the oddball they followed, whose unorthodox moves enhanced their survival, had tuned in to changing environmental signals. Whatever the reason, they stayed with the vast iceberg as it moved erratically east and northward, adapting to its shifting environments with new social behaviors and learning patterns.

For nearly a year, all twelve birds thrived, until the iceberg faltered, trapped by pack ice during the fierce Antarctic winter. Cut off from open water and their food supply, the penguins huddled in the lee of wind-swept ice structures until hunger drove them into the incessant storms. Following their dogged leader, they trudged and slid northward over miles of pack ice to open sea, where a hungry troupe of Weddell seals quickly reduced their number.

Diving deep and fast, eight penguins escaped the carnage and continued north, away from seals and pack ice. Fishing, swimming, riding out storms on occasional ice floes or icebergs, they moved out of Antarctic waters into bewildering cross currents and pockets of barren, lifeless sea. An upwelling of fertile, frigid water off of Peru saved them from starvation, drawing the birds farther northward in a food-rich current.

On the day the Twin Towers fell in distant Manhattan, six penguins crossed the equator in the wake of an American cruise ship, feeding on bacon rinds and other unfamiliar delicacies tossed overboard from its galley. Only one person saw them, a near-sighted woman from Passaic, New Jersey, who told her fellow passengers she had seen a litter of dolphin puppies with the cutest yellow cheeks.

Chapter One

The big project for the year in seventh grade is writing your autobiography. All about your life since you were born, and your ancestors, and the people who made a difference in your life, and what you see yourself as in the future. You're supposed to stick photographs in, and it's all supposed to mean something.

I wonder if everybody else made up shit like I did. You know, gave 'em what they want to hear, like how a fake dad made such a difference in my life. All the time I'm dishing up this crap, I'm thinking what would happen if I wrote the real story. So I start another file to write about the people who really did make a difference. Jeez, I couldn't show my face around this town again if they knew.

—The Oreo File

If you missed baseball practice, you sat out the next game. That was Coach's rule. Nothing else could have dragged Brad to school that morning.

He had slept through the worst of the storm the night before, only dimly aware of monster waves pounding the cliffs below the house and hundred-mile-an-hour winds driving fusillades of rain against the windows. Some time before dawn, the eerie stillness of the storm's aftermath woke him. The inside of the house was pitch dark, the blackness outside the windows just fading to grey. His light switch clicked uselessly when he hit it, and the rattle of the old fridge had stopped. Somewhere, power lines were down.

Brad closed his eyes and pulled the warm quilt over his ears to shut out the silence. He couldn't go back to sleep. What if the whole world had blown away and their house was the only thing left? He got up and stumbled through the debris of his room into the dark kitchen.

By feel, Brad found the tin of matches and lit the emergency candle stuffed in a wine bottle on the table. He split kindling and lit the stove. At least he could fool the storm and wake his mother up to fresh coffee.

If he'd found his jacket right away that morning, he thought later, the day might have gone differently. He was cold, and his t-shirt had the clammy chill of old laundry, which it was. Not finding his jacket on its peg by the door, he took a flashlight from the silverware drawer and hunted through his room. Originally a pantry off the kitchen, his room was small, its floor buried somewhere, Brad assumed, beneath irregular mounds of clothing, books, sheet music, rusted Tonka trucks, and ancient Lego constructions. He scanned the surface with the flashlight, spotting his math book gone missing since Sunday and the elk antler he'd been meaning to mount on the wall for a clothes hanger, but no jacket.

The stove was hot by now, spreading warmth and the fragrance of steeping coffee throughout the large room that served as both kitchen and living area. Colorless dawn light filtered through the windows, but Brad kept the flashlight on, still searching. He was hanging over the back of the couch when Sal tapped his shoulder. He jumped and dropped the flashlight. His sister grinned, pointing to the frayed khaki field jacket hanging over the back of a kitchen chair. Sal shrugged into her own windbreaker and slipped out the kitchen door. Brad put on his jacket, damped down the stove, and followed her out.

The windswept shore pines around the house still dripped from the storm. A dense belt of pine and spruce muffled sound from the highway. Brad gulped huge lungfuls of storm-washed air. From the back step he watched Sal on the trail out to the headland, her orange stocking cap bobbing jauntily. Beside her, dwarfing her tiny figure, ambled a brown horse with a pelican dancing for balance on its back.

The horse, Joe, had wandered onto the lawn of the cancer ward in Portland where Sal had been dying four years ago. Allowed to stay after no one claimed him and his presence brought such joy to a doomed child, Joe had become a pampered pet of the whole hospital. When Sal miraculously recovered, the doctors and staff had chipped in for a horse van to send Joe home with her. The first time Sal was strong enough to hike down to the beach with Brad, they had found the pelican washed up with a broken wing and brought it home for their neighbor to set. Sal named her Bertha. Bird and horse followed Sal everywhere; Brad had developed a wholly unscientific theory that they kept her alive. He zipped his jacket and trotted after them, past wind-gnarled pines and wiry dune grass to where the continent ended in a spill of massive, jagged boulders that held back the Pacific Ocean.

Brad jogged past the horse and caught up to Sal on a flat slab that hung over the cliff like a balcony. The sun wasn't up yet, and the ocean looked slick and melted, like a mylar sheet over something heaving to escape. Salt spray dotted Sal's orange cap. Seagulls dive-bombed the waves, screaming, and a line of black cormorants skimmed the swells, heading for open sea.

Something moved on a ledge below Brad and Sal, just above the surf. In the spray from a big wave, Brad saw what looked like four stone butlers standing in the foam. The mist cleared, and one of the butlers bowed formally to another. Brad could see clearly now what they were, but it made no more sense than stone butlers did.

"Jesus H. Christ, what the hell are they?" he whispered.

"Penguins?" Sal said. "But – in Oregon?"

She slid from the boulder and hopped down the cliff, rock to rock. Bertha followed, flapping awkwardly. Sal scrambled onto a rock tilted against the ledge where the penguins stood; she crouched there, watching them. Bertha waddled after her and watched them, too. The penguins stared out to sea, oblivious of their audience. After a few minutes, Bertha shook herself and took off, flapping heavily and then gliding northward before folding her wings to plop into the water for breakfast. The penguins still didn't move. Sal climbed back up to Brad, grinning.

"What the hell are they doing here?" he said. From long experience, he believed Sal knew things he'd never comprehend. Dogs never barked at her, wild things didn't fly or run away. It was, he thought, just one of a zillion things he'd never understand.

"Where'd they come from? Escape from a zoo? Fall off a ship? Or what?"

Sal shrugged and shook her head.

"How did they get here?" he persisted. "Swim? All the way from the South Pole? Isn't that where penguins live? Will they stay? For good, I mean? Make nests or whatever they do? But why here?"

Sal laughed, interrupting his barrage. "I don't know! I don't know! I think they're waiting for something. That's all. Aren't they beautiful? Aren't they? Wow, wait'll Mom sees them!"

They looked at each other and bolted for the house. When Sal started wheezing, Brad hoisted her onto Joe's back. They raced into the yard, skidding in the mud by the old Subaru that Brad and Molly had made from two junkers. Molly was loading her gear into the trunk. She looked up when Sal shouted.

"Mom! Penguins! Come and see!"

"That's nice, hon, but not now."

Molly straightened, one hand on the trunk lid to shut it. Sal slid off Joe's back onto her shoulders.

"Mom, they're real. Real live penguins, right here on the cliff! C'mon!"

"Sure, and there's a unicorn in the garden, too." Molly shook Sal off and started to close the trunk.

Brad lunged for the trunk lid, tossing a lunch bag and climbing boots on the ground and grabbing Molly's video camera.

"Brad, put that back! I'm late!"

"Hey, I saw them, too, Mom. Penguins, just like Mr. Popper's. You gotta see 'em!"

Molly tossed her boots and lunch back in the trunk and reached for the camera. "Okay, okay, so there's penguins. But I'm late!"

"Mom, you gotta see 'em first. There's been murelings here forever, but never penguins. It's your big chance! C'mon, I'll carry it for you...."

"Murrelets, not murelings," Molly said, and Brad knew she believed them now. She shook her head and took the camera. "Brad, I can't. It may be my big chance, but today's the murrelets' only chance. The restraining order ends today. Howie's meeting me there as soon as it's light enough to film the nest."

Brad gave up and helped her repack the car. Sal chewed her lip, her fists clenched at her sides. Molly gave her a quick hug.

"Look," Molly said. "The nest's only a half hour drive. Howie can run the tape to Portland, and I'll stop back here to see your penguins, get a few shots in before going to Florence."

Sal nodded and stood with Brad, watching the Subaru turn through the trees to the highway. By the time school started, Brad knew, their mother would be a hundred or more feet up a tree filming a seabird no one had ever noticed until biologists found its nest in old-growth forest miles from the ocean. Then she'd be filming a crafts fair in Florence, a commissioners' meeting up north, a bridge repair or other event for the local TV news. A really big story like the penguins, though, she could feed to the networks. Maybe they'd hire her; she could buy a real car with a defroster that worked.

Sal tugged at Brad's sleeve. Back to reality.

"Brad? We could just skip school, couldn't we?"

Brad turned toward the cliff trail, then stopped. "No. I got practice today."

He plodded through morning classes by rote, with no recollection of their content. His notebooks sprouted sketches of penguins, and as usual when concentration eluded him, he saw in pages of text only patterns of thirds and fifths, hearing chord progressions instead of words. The announcement at the end of algebra class freed him at last: baseball practice was canceled, the field still under a foot of water from backed-up storm drains.

Brad looked at the clock. One-fifty. Sal's grade-school bus dropped her home at two-thirty. He dumped his books in his locker, keeping only his unfinished writing project, and grabbed his jacket. Slipping out the janitor's door and past the dumpsters, he skirted the bushes concealing the kids' smoke hole. Muffled laughter and whiffs of marijuana smoke sifted through the leaves. Brad checked his pocket for his mom's grocery list and broke into a run. Sal wouldn't wait for him, and he didn't blame her.

He raced through back streets to the main drag. There was just time to buy Molly's shampoo and toothpaste and meet the county bus, which would get him home just minutes after Sal.

The official bus stop was at Low Gap Road, a quarter mile past their driveway, but today the driver had to stop at Brad's turnout anyway, honking at a huge satellite van that was backing into position among a crowd of other news vehicles. Brad leaped out of the bus and started running. The penguins! His mom had done it! He raced up the driveway, dodging more vehicles, and stopped short. The yard in front of the house was filled with people and cameras that swung toward him like dinosaur snouts.

"Is that her boy?"

"No way. Wrong color."

"What's your name, son? You her neighbor?"

Brad ignored them, looking for Sal or Molly. The Subaru was not in sight. Nor was Joe, or Bertha. Someone shoved him.

"By that bush for a close-up. Right there."

"Isn't there a girl?"

Nobody mentioned penguins. Brad looked again for Sal or his mother. A bald man with a microphone and earphones on his head pushed him again, jabbing a white card at his shoulder. Brad shoved back.

"What's going on?" he asked. "Who do you want?"

"Who are you?" The man turned away, not waiting for an answer, then glanced back. "This is Molly Matthissen's house, isn't it?"

Brad lunged for him, knocking the white card to the ground. He jerked the man's mike and earphones off. "My mom!" he yelled. "Where is she? What happened?"

The reporters were suddenly quiet, looking at each other but not at Brad. A red-haired woman carrying a spiral notebook took Brad's arm and led him away from the cameras.

"I'm sorry," she said, but Brad didn't think she meant sorry for him. "We – they – all thought you knew. Your mother's in jail, charged with murder."

"Murder!" Brad laughed. He thought of Molly, carefully carrying earwigs out of the house and catching mice in live traps. "You gotta be kidding. Who the hell would my mom murder?"

The woman looked at her spiral pad. "A man named Borstal. Howard Borstal. An FBI agent…"

"Howard? Uncle Howie? FBI…?" Brad choked back another laugh. "What kind of joke is this? What the fuck is going on?"

"He was your uncle?" The woman started scribbling in her spiral pad, and the cameras moved in on him, all the reporters gabbling at once.

Brad bolted. He charged though the crowd and ran for the back yard. Sal swung the kitchen door open as he landed on the porch. He dove through it and skidded into Joe's tail. The horse lifted his head from a bowl of granola on the table to look at him, then turned back to the food. At the sink, Bertha perched on the dish rack, dipping her head under the running tap and spattering water across the room. Sal slammed the door and wedged a chair under the knob. She sank to the floor and Brad crouched next to her, out of range from the window.

"Brad, who are those people? And where's Mom?"

Chapter Two

Right off my autobiography's in trouble on account of having no ancestors. Uncle Howie says no problem, 'cause we're all related through DNA. He gets out some history books and says take your pick. He really gets into it, too, which is what's cool about him. We hooked up Daniel Webster with Queen Victoria and Dred Scott and John Audubon and some other dudes in a family tree would make anyone proud. Howie came up with the best one, and not from any history book. This was old Nigger Lew. Honest to god that's what he called himself, and he was for real, even if he's no more my ancestor than Queen Victoria. Back in the 1800s Nigger Lew was the only black man living here on the coast, a slave who bought his freedom and homesteaded land along the river, by a creek he named Darkey Creek, after himself. That's all Howie remembered, but I liked Nigger Lew for an ancestor right off. Howie says there's a lot more about him at the Historical Society, so we can fill in more details on him later.

—*The Oreo File*

Molly Matthissen was arrested on the day before her son's thirteenth birthday. It was the third impossible thing to happen before breakfast.

The briar patch where she crouched, taut and poised to run again, offered concealment at a stiff price. Blackberry stems the diameter of broomsticks spiraled upward around her, their monster thorns jabbing her legs, back, and arms. Woven among the green new growth, last year's dry, brittle stalks cracked and rattled at the slightest motion. Molly closed her eyes, the better to be invisible, and listened hard.

The briar thicket covered an overgrown mound, the decayed root mass of a giant fallen a century or two ago. The hollow left when the roots were torn from the soil had created a small plateau on the steep slope of Cook's Ridge. High above her, dawning sunlight streaked sideways through the rain-soaked canopy, dappling the forest floor and massive fir trunks in steamy, shifting patterns.

She had never been here so early in the spring, and never at dawn. During the blistering droughts of summer, the half-mile hike through a moonscape of burned-over logging debris had often led her and the kids to this sanctuary of cool shadow, rich with scents of mulch and fir resin and bizarre fungal eruptions.

It was no such sanctuary today. The reek of chain oil, sawdust and blood brought on waves of nausea. Breathing through her sleeve as quietly as possible, Molly froze, listening for any sound of pursuit. Even the forest was silent, as if in shock. In the distance she heard crows calling, and then, faint and far, the welcome sound of sirens. Fear held her back, ready to run again, until she heard voices.

Molly made sure there were more voices than the three she dreaded before she dared move. She scrabbled out of the briars and brushed stickers from her arms, feeling naked without her camera.

When the first uniforms appeared, she ran toward them, overwhelmed with relief. Until she saw the guns.

Then a blur. She was thrown to the ground, her arms yanked behind her, steel cuffs snapped over her wrists. Fir needles stabbed her cheek and filled her mouth. A heavy foot pressed her neck further into the dirt and a voice chanted familiar words that meant nothing. Only one image meant anything at all: the glimpse as she fell of three loggers behind the police and ambulance crew, nodding eagerly at a fat man in a brown suit.

Her mouth and nose clotted with damp mulch and fir needles, her lungs frantic for air, Molly replayed the image and gagged on her own incredible stupidity. She willed the boot to press her face harder into the blessed, fecund darkness, to grind into oblivion the shame at what she had done, the guilt for what she had not.

The boot lifted suddenly. Rough hands hauled her to her feet. Her eyes burned, blinded by dirt, eyelids pierced by fir needles. The hands shoved her and she stumbled. Her brain spun in oxygen-starved pinwheels.

"Hey! She can't breathe!"

The voice seemed far away and rippled, like a warped record. Tentative hands swabbed her nose and mouth with a cloth. Involuntarily she gulped in air, still reeling.

"Don't move. I mean, don't blink."

Gentle as it was, the cloth ground as much dirt into her eyes as out of them. Calloused fingers plucked fir needles out of her eyelids, and through the grit she looked dizzily into two brown, bewildered eyes. Behind the bewilderment, she thought she saw something else. She tried to tell him what she'd done, but her throat rebelled against the dirt and she threw up all over him instead. The other cops laughed.

"Sorry....so sorry," she rasped.

"Don't speak a word of it, ma'am. Don't speak a word."

Caged in the squad car, her tongue still trying to dislodge bits of mulch, she wondered briefly if he was part of a good cop/bad cop routine. Much later, after the strip search, the prodding and poking, the long hours in the barren interrogation room, she realized he hadn't appeared again. Whatever he'd actually meant to say, his curious choice of words struck home as no repetition of formal Miranda language could.

Don't speak a word of it, ma'am. Don't speak a word.

She chanted the words in her head while first one, then another detective team cajoled, lied, yelled, and wheedled in their zeal for a confession.

Don't speak a word. It was the only advice that made sense. She stared in silence at the detectives, at their coffee cups and take-out bags from McDonalds and Taco Bell. Her throat hurt, and her mouth was dry. She concentrated on her tongue, trying to pry dirt from her teeth, and kept silent. They had said an attorney would be appointed to represent her. She would wait.

At first, expecting a lawyer to turn up any minute, waiting was easy. She needed to tell someone what she had done, and quickly, so they could act before it was too late. After four or five hours, no attorney had arrived, and she silently despaired.

An attorney has been called, they had said. Then he was on his way. Then for no given reason a different attorney had been assigned. Then the new attorney was on his way; she could make a recorded statement now and they would play it when he arrived. She stared at them, saying nothing. By this time she knew no attorney was going to arrive, and she wondered how many hours or days they could keep this up. More to the point, how long could she continue to hold her bladder? And why, if the detectives were so absolutely convinced of her guilt, did they need any confession?

Against such puzzles she struggled and succeeded in partitioning her mind, shutting down all memory functions until further notice. From this point on, only the immediate present existed, placing her as actor/observer in a rather boring charade.

One thing she observed, the most consistent thing, was that all of her interrogators were overweight; several qualified as grossly obese. Each time they entered the room they carried styrofoam cups and take-out food, eating and slurping between questions. They never offered her anything and she was hesitant to ask, unsure whether asking for food or water or a bathroom would be giving up her right to remain silent. Tuning out their questions, she studied with morbid fascination their mouths and jaws working over every bite. The repulsive details kept her own hunger at bay. Not one of them, she thought more than once, could run half a block without getting winded. Shouldn't police, of all people, have to stay in shape?

A second thing she observed was how hungry and tired she was, how close to falling apart and sobbing uncontrollably, though not for the reasons the cops would think. To quell her weakness, she began closing her eyes during their questions and focused on designing birthday cakes for Brad. She rejected one design after another before settling on a shield shape, a field of green with a violin at center point. What else? A bow crossed over a bat, a mitt, a treble clef, a baseball. She shifted them from one point to another and finally smiled to herself at the result. The smile seemed to anger the detectives more than her silence.

Between interrogations, they cuffed her hands behind her back and left her alone in the stuffy, windowless room for what seemed longer and longer time-outs. They had taken her watch but she could judge the time crudely by how many times she could sing all seventeen verses of "Barbara Allen" to herself. The room was featureless, except for a formica table, four plastic lawn chairs, and a large mirror on one wall that she presumed was one-way glass. Smells of old paint, grease, and cigarette smoke clung to every surface, despite the No Smoking sign on the door.

When the fourth, or was it the fifth, interlude dragged on so long she lost track of how many times she'd completed "Barbara Allen," Molly stood up to relieve her aching shoulders. They were so obviously determined to break her down, so confident of succeeding. She wished she knew the law; how long could they keep her from seeing an attorney? She walked around the room twice, once on tiptoes. On the third round, she stopped abruptly at the mirror and pressed her face against it. The room beyond was small and dark, and behind her own reflection she could make out a startled face staring at her; beyond the face she saw the digital time display on a deck of recording equipment.

The detectives returned moments later, carrying styrofoam cups and plastic-wrapped Danish. As before, they didn't offer her anything, but they also as usual unlocked the handcuffs. Molly sat down.

"I wish to make a statement," she said.

The officers stared at her, then at each other, pleased. One of them switched on the tape recorder and spoke into it, glancing at his watch and recording his name, the time, and another repetition of the Miranda warning. He nodded to Molly. She coughed and began speaking, clearly and rapidly.

"My name is Molly Matthissen and yes, this statement is made under duress or coercion. First, Officer Davidson's recorded statement that the time is ten thirty-five is not true. The correct time, as of a few minutes ago, was two forty-seven. I have been in police custody since approximately eight o'clock this morning. During that time, I have not been allowed to speak to an attorney, I have not been permitted to make a phone call, and I have been allowed nothing to eat or drink. And during this time a succession of grossly overweight officers have brought in soft drinks, coffee, six milkshakes, four McDonald's burgers and fries, two Taco Bell enchilada plates, a box of donuts, and at least seven vending machine Danish, which they have consumed while questioning me."

Officer Davidson's hand reached for the tape recorder, but stopped when Molly went on.

"My statement is this: I am hungry. I am thirsty. I demand to see an attorney. I need a bathroom immediately, and I suggest Atkin's diet be required for your entire force."

Davidson slammed his hand on the recorder's stop button and the two officers waddled from the room so fast they forgot to handcuff her again. They also left a nearly full milkshake and an unopened Danish on the table. Molly ripped open the Danish and ate it. It tasted of sugar and Elmer's Glue and could have been preserved with embalming fluid, but she was too hungry to care. She hesitated only a moment over the milkshake, concluding the officer was so fat he was probably impotent and unlikely to have AIDS. She took the lid off and drank the entire shake without the straw.

Pissing off the cops was probably not a good idea, she thought, but the food, bad as it was, was worth whatever they threw at her next. Which better be soon, or the milkshake cup would have to double as a toilet. The door opened before she resorted to that expediency, and two presumably female cops handcuffed her again before leading her from the room. The shorter one was square-shaped and solid, what Molly's neighbor would call the brick shithouse model. The tall one had enormous breasts jutting from a cinched-in waist, a Barbie on steroids.

Both had cell phones, pagers, radios, handcuffs, chains and other gear dangling from waistbands and pockets. They led her without speaking down a hallway to a heavy door with wired glass in it. Inside was a barred cage with a steel gate that opened only when the glass door behind them was shut and electronically locked by unseen operators. Past that was a guard station with a bank of TV monitors, then another hallway flanked by steel-barred cells, most of them empty. The shorter cop unlocked Molly's handcuffs and shoved her into a cell halfway down the hall. She heard the door clang shut, but had eyes only for the toilet in the corner.

It wasn't much of a toilet, simply a large steel cylinder rising from the concrete floor, capped with the plastic lid of a Sherwin Williams paint bucket. A printed sign taped on a pipe behind it read, "Toilets flush at 6 a.m. and 6 p.m. ONLY." Scrawled next to it in tiny ball-point script was, "And pigs can fly and cops don't lie." From the smell and concentrated contents when she opened the lid, the last flushing – if ever – must have been weeks or months ago. Even this was not as daunting as removing the one-piece orange jumpsuit they'd issued her. They had taken all her own clothes, even her underwear. She pulled open the velcro fasteners and crouched over the toilet, naked to the knees, aware of the blinking red light of a TV monitor mounted over the barred door. Trying not to touch any portion of the foul toilet, she peed recklessly into the muck, holding her breath.

Finished at last, Molly glanced around the bleak cell. The outside wall was taken up by steel and concrete slab bunk beds with split plastic pads for mattresses and a single blanket rolled up at one end. No pillows. High up on the wall, a slit window of opaque green glass, no bigger than a VCR tape, reflected the flickering fluorescent tubes hanging between a network of huge duct pipes on the ceiling. A broad, jagged crack bisected the wall behind the beds; pinpoint spears of sunlight pierced through in places. Tributary cracks spread in algae-covered deltas across the wall and the concrete floor, converging on a drain grate in the center. In the corner at the end of the bed nearest the alleged toilet, a dented steel shoebox affair dangled off one bolt under a handle less faucet, which dripped a stream of brown liquid into the box and out the broken drain pipe onto the floor.

Naked and shivering, Molly studied the room again, struck by the ultimate horror. There was no toilet paper.

Chapter Three

My sister Sal is nine years old. She has blue eyes and no hair and fifty-three scabs and a blood blister. I know, because we counted them. She's always getting scraped up, see, and once when she tore up her arm on barbed wire and it was bleeding all over, I told her what a neat scab it was gonna make and how I'd give her a penny for every scab. So we counted and I owed her 85 cents, counting old mosquito bites, which was kind of cheating but I didn't care because it stopped her crying. She gets double for a blister and a nickel for a blood blister. I'm gonna go broke before she's ten.

Sal's real name is Cassandra, can you believe it? But I called her Sal from the day she was born, short for Salamander, 'cause that's what she looked like, a salamander. I always liked salamanders, especially newts when you pick 'em up off the road after a rain. Something about their feet, so small with perfect little fingers and toes, and the way their elbows stick out, and the always coolness of their skin, and the way they sit on your hand and look at you, like they know something you'll never find out no matter how big you are. That's the way Sal looked at you, full of some secret from before time, and she didn't look like any of the other babies, she was so wrinkled and small and skinny, with real little hands, and she had these ridges on her neck, up behind her ears, that they said were left from having gills. She had this hole in her heart, too, not a hole really so much as a three-chambered heart like a newt instead of four like people have, and they had to fix it with surgery when she was still so tiny.

—The Oreo File

Mac McCrae tossed tools and gas cans into the back of his pickup and hung his chainsaw on the sideboards. Behind him, the last of the crew were snuffing smokes and drifting away from the watchman's trailer. The sharp beeps of the yarder high up on the ridge had started up again; its cables whined, dragging logs up the uneven slope of the hill. On the hillside opposite, a chainsaw started up. Mac ignored it. He swung himself into the cab, raised a hand to a choker-setter trotting past, and headed in low gear down the rutted track.

Only once before, when his son was born six weeks ago, had Mac ever left a job site early. Futilely, he punched from one radio frequency to another, trying to find a local news station, but the signals were too weak to penetrate the folded ridges and hills of the Coast Range. He switched off the radio and drove a little faster than the rough road allowed, trying to make any kind of sense of what the watchman had told him. The old man's only entertainment was a police scanner that he kept on day and night. When the crew broke for lunch and gathered by the trailer for the watchman's ever-brewing coffee, the old man had sought Mac out.

"Hey, this woman, Molly Whatsername, Matcherson? Ain't she your neighbor, Mac?"

Mac nodded, waiting. The old man jerked his head toward the trailer, where the scanner squawked intermittently.

"Says they busted her this morning. Killed some FBI agent up Fisher Creek."

That was all the watchman knew, and nothing more had come over the scanner during lunch break. Mac swung the truck off the logging road into a trail so overgrown with berry thickets and alder saplings it was invisible to any but a native eye. Mac had grown up in these hills; he and his brother had camped and played commando in its secret places, and every creek, trail and fold in the mountains was home. The truck lurched down the ridge, flattening briars and saplings. The shortcut shaved off two miles of switchbacks, bringing him back to the logging road at the bottom. Another side road led through a sunlit meadow of swordfern and salal into a vast swamp that he and his brother had called The Frog Farm. Were the zillions of frogs still there? Mac didn't stop. He ground the truck into four-wheel drive, churning mud over the windshield. Molly would be counting on him.

She had moved in next door four years ago, her and the little black boy she called her son. No one knew anything about them, which didn't stop rumors that the kid was retarded, the mother some gangster's crack-addled whore. Gossip to fill time between game shows, Mac's wife, Sara, had said. She dragged Mac next door to meet them. Molly was thinner then, with the haunted, fierce look of a cornered animal. Brad was eight or nine, tall for his age and quiet until he picked up that fiddle of his. Molly drove an old Valiant that had no reverse gear; every day she and the boy drove off, him to school or riding with his mother to a hospital in Portland where his little sister was dying of leukemia.

That much Mac and Sara had found out on that first visit, and it was enough for Sara. She took them into her generous heart, sharing whatever meals they'd accept, offering to keep the boy after school and take him to his violin lessons when Molly was in Portland. Sara had been on autopilot since her miscarriage a year earlier, and Mac secretly worshipped Molly and Brad for bringing Sara back to life.

The boy, Mac had concluded quickly, was not retarded, but simply too quiet and serious for a kid that age, with a stiff courtesy toward Mac that bordered on hostility. The first break in his reserve had come when Mac brought home a road-kill deer to skin and cut up for the freezer. The kid had watched his every move, pouring out questions – where had he found it, how could you tell it wasn't spoiled, what was that floppy thing under the stomach? Mac showed him how to separate the backstrap, slice up steaks, roll a roast, and wrap everything airtight for freezing. A few weeks later, Brad collected his own road-kill and proudly presented Mac and Sara with a neatly wrapped stack of meat.

The second opening had come when Brad turned up one day with an encyclopedia volume and asked Mac if he'd ever played baseball. Mac never questioned why a quiet black kid who played violin like an angel and scrounged highways for road-kill should want to play baseball.

"Yeah, some," he said. "In high school. And Okinawa, just pickup games. Been a while, though. Wanna play?"

He dug his old catcher's mitt and bat out of a trunk in the garage, and found more mitts at a thrift shop. After work he and the kid would hike down to the beach and throw and bat until dark. He started going to Brad's Little League games, astonished at how nasty and downright cruel the kids were to each other. The only thing resembling team spirit was their frenzy of insults and cat-calls at their own team's fouls or blunders.

The first time Brad struck out, his teammates jeered more viciously than ever. Mac heard the word nigger and was on his feet, ready to run down and smack some heads together. He stopped when he saw Brad's reaction. Tucking the bat under his left arm like a violin, the kid walked back to the bench and stood at attention in front of the team, no expression on his face at all. The jeering faded. He nodded and sat down next to the center-fielder, their best batter, who first shifted uncomfortably, then smiled, flattered, when Brad asked him something. The next time the team booed another kid's blunder, Brad stood and held his cap over his heart. One by one, the whole team silently followed suit.

Mac downshifted for a steep curve, still grinning at how a black, fiddle-playing ten-year-old, without a word of anger, had brought together a bunch of rude white brats into something remarkably like a good-natured team. Brad's ringing call, "Yo Yo Ma! Yo Yo Ma!" became the team's standard cheer for a good play. When Mac asked him what it meant, Brad gave one of his rare smiles.

"One of the best cellists ever lived," he told Mac. "But don't tell them, okay?"

Their conversations seldom ranged beyond baseball and butchering, but the Secret of Yo Yo Ma cemented something between them. And then, against all odds, Brad's sister had come home, miraculously cured, or as the medics said, in remission. She arrived riding high in the cab of a van carrying Joe the horse home with her. To this day, Mac blushed to think of his shock meeting this slip of a girl.

"My god, she's white," he told Sara.

"Of course she is. So's her mom, in case you hadn't noticed."

"But … Brad …"

"Mac, don't you remember anything?" Sara laughed. "Brad's adopted. Sal's her natural kid."

"Oh, yeah." Of course he'd known. But gossip dies hard.

What surprised him even more than Sal's color was the change she wrought in Brad. Overnight, the kid seemed to shed a thousand-pound load. His rare smiles became commonplace, and the classical music he played began shifting in midstream to lively jigs, reels, hornpipes, folk tunes accompanied by Sal's lilting voice. He helped Mac build a fence and shed for Joe, as usual asking questions about every join and hinge. Afternoons he spent with Sal, polishing Joe like a Model T and combing his mane and tail. Then the two would sit on the porch with the Wall Street Journals Brad collected from the bank for kindling. They took turns reading stories to Joe, often laughing wildly. Not a great reader himself, Mac wondered at Brad's choice of the Wall Street Journal, but didn't really care enough to ask why. What mattered, he thought, was hearing the kid laugh.

When Molly took full-time work with the local TV station, Mac saw something else emerge in Brad: a fierce protectiveness toward Sal. Whatever Sal did, Brad was never more than a few feet away, even when Sal discovered the ocean and took to it like a duck raised in the desert. Brad had told Mac once how the ocean creeped him out, all those sharks and jelly fish lurking in its depths, but he spent hours immersed in it now, paddling along with Sal.

Even in the safety of home, Mac noticed, it was a year or two before Brad would leave Sal alone with Molly's news partner, Howie, or even with Mac himself. Something freaky to do with the kids' dad, Sara told him. Molly had asked her and Mac to sign a paper agreeing to adopt the kids if something happened to her. She'd given them a fat envelope of court papers that Sara kept with her cookbooks, but Mac had never opened it.

Mac slammed on his brakes. In front of him a doe stood in the logging road, legs poised for flight, ears alert, staring at the pickup. A few yards behind her, a fawn wobbled on spindle legs. Swearing, Mac waited. Sara was taking their new baby for a checkup this afternoon, so if Molly was arrested, even by mistake – and it must be a mistake, he thought – Brad and Sal would come home alone to the fallout. Mac swore again.

One of the unspoken rules of road-kill dining was you never deliberately hit a potential meal. The doe turned and walked slowly down the road ahead of him, turning every few steps to look at her fawn, which followed in jerky half-steps. Mac stayed well behind them in low gear, stopping often, until the doe turned off into the brush and the fawn wobbled after her. Mac plowed on, speeding up finally onto the paved county road, then gunning the pickup on the coast highway. He wiped grease and sawdust from his watch. One-thirty. Damn. Home was another hour away, and he couldn't remember what time Sal's bus dropped her off. He floored the accelerator.

* * *

Brad pressed his back against the kitchen door, adding his weight to the chair Sal had wedged under the knob. Sal sat beside him, stroking the shaggy hair over Joe's rear hoof. Brad felt her shoulders tremble. Outside, the gabble of reporters' voices rose and fell, their footsteps on the porch shifting as they moved, trying to see through the curtained window. Someone pounded on the door again. Sal turned to Brad, her face white.

"They'll break it down," she said. He put his arm around her and leaned harder against the door.

Joe lifted his head suddenly from the bowl of granola and whinnied. The noises outside stopped.

"Jesus, there's a goddamn horse in there," a voice said.

Joe whinnied again, greeting the sound of a cranky pickup crunching up the driveway next door. Sal wriggled free of Brad's arm and lifted the curtain to peer out, Brad beside her. The pickup door banged and Mac bounded over the fence into the yard. His huge figure was breaded with grease and sawdust, from Stihl Chainsaw cap down to muddy caulk boots. Ignoring their questions, he charged through the reporters, shoved several off the porch, and planted himself in front of the door.

Smelling fresh meat, the cameras started rolling again. Reporters surged toward the steps, yelling questions.

"Your name?"

"Are you her neighbor?"

"Get those kids out here, will ya?"

"Hey, you're a logger. How's it feel living next door to an ecoterrorist?"

Mac stared at them. Like he'd stare at a swarm of yellow jackets, Brad thought. Mac took off his cap and scratched his head, knocking hunks of sawdust loose. His mouth opened slightly, his tongue bulged against his cheek. The reporters went silent, pens and mikes poised, waiting for his answers. Mac tilted his head toward them and spit a large gob of tobacco onto the nearest microphone. Reporters and equipment backed away.

Sal pulled the curtain wider to let Brad see. Mac stood on the porch, shifting his weight from one boot to the other, clots of mud cracking onto the floorboards. Still he said nothing.

A reporter piped up, hesitantly, "Say, uh, mister...."

Mac swung his big head toward the voice, his jaw working again. The man's voice trailed off. The red-haired woman with the steno pad took up the challenge.

"All we're asking is..."

A red flush spread through the grime on Mac's neck. He grabbed a shoved and tapped it on the porch, his foot tapping with it.

"Uh-oh, Mac's gonna lose it," Sal said.

Mac stepped off the porch. He pounded the shovel hard against the step, and scooped up a mound of fresh horse shit. The crowd backed off, tripping over their gear and each other. Mac herded them with the shovel, out of the yard and around the house. Brad heard doors slam and motors start, gears grinding, tires crunching gravel. Sal pulled the chair from the doorknob, and together they maneuvered Joe out the door and down the steps. Sal leaned against the horse, shaking. Brad thought she was crying until she giggled.

"That's one interview they won't put on the air," she said.

Chapter Four

Sometimes things happen that have nothing at all to do with each other, but you connect them because they happen at the same time. And then because you're the person they happened to they end up connecting anyway. It's spooky. Like the day I dropped the bed frame on my big toe and it made this big, swollen blood blister with the nail busted half off. It was so gross I couldn't stop looking at it, thinking I'd go through the rest of my life with this disgusting toe, and that same day the doctors told us Sal had leukemia and wouldn't have any rest of her life at all. For that whole year she was sick I kept looking at my big toe, watching the nail slowly grow back and the black part disappear, and when it was almost a regular looking toe again I had this secret sureness that Sal was going to make it, too. And she did.

The day we found out she was gonna live was the same day Mom got her job and we met Howie. We liked him right off, he was so different from my fake dad or anyone else. For one thing, he likes to sing and plays the guitar like Norman Blake, and he knows more songs than I ever thought there were, some of 'em so scuzzy he won't sing 'em if Sal's around, but he can make me laugh just humming them. He's how I found out about fiddle tunes and how cool it is to play with backup, sometimes we're up half the night playing old reels and jigs and hornpipes. He asks your opinion on everything even if you're a kid, and he listens like even your dumbest questions are so important he has to stack maps and dictionaries and encyclopedias all over the table to find the answer. Sal really liked him, too, because he made her laugh and showed her how to clean Joe's hooves, and when he builds Lego castles or plays pirates or card games with you he gets into it just like it's for real.

> *Sal liked him so much she asked Mom once why he couldn't be our dad, and Mom looked kind of funny and sad and said no, but he sure made a good uncle. That's how he got to be Uncle Howie.*
>
> —*The Oreo File*

Joey Wire sat under a rhododendron in the old lady's yard behind the funeral home. From a bulging pocket he drew some grubby cigarette ends scrounged from the smoke hole. He wiped the dirt off them, and snapped off the filters. He crumbled the tobacco from the butts onto the book in his lap, pulled a pack of rolling papers from another pocket, and constructed a somewhat lumpy cigarette. He lit up and peered for the umpteenth time through the board fence at the kids hanging out under the portico back of the funeral parlor.

It was the usual bunch of dropouts and losers, Joey saw, smoking weed and talking big, laughing and jabbing each other to prove what cool dudes they were and what a good time they were having. Except when someone died, the funeral home was vacant, the only place in town that wouldn't boot them out or call cops on them. The RIPs, they called themselves, for "Rest in peace, man," meaning something was happening, usually booze or crashing a party or getting together afterward to brag about how wasted they'd been or which of them got laid. They were the closest the Oregon coast had to a gang, and a sorry excuse it was, Joey thought. Sometimes he'd bring them a pack of Camels or Marlboroughs, or hotwire a rig for them to get themselves in trouble with, but he seldom hung out with them for long; it was more fun to watch in secret, and even that grew boring after a while.

He'd thought Brad might be headed this way. Joey had followed him from school after the announcement canceling baseball practice, but lost him in the market, where Joey was sidetracked by antibiotics in the pet section. He felt in a side pocket for the slim box of aquarium-use-only tetracycline tablets and glanced down at his book, a pad of hall passes marking his place. The ground was wet, and he had things to do. He put out his cigarette and carefully stuffed the end behind his ear before getting up.

Crossing the yard, Joey slipped up to the back door of the old lady's house, with its crude plywood cat door cut at the bottom. A fat tabby with tufted ears stared at him from the window ledge. Joey nodded at it, remembering how thin and ragged the cat had looked a year ago, when he'd first used the yard as a spy hole. The old lady hobbled around with a walker and never left the house; Joey rarely caught more than a glimpse of her, but he'd seen the pitiful scraps of leftovers she put out for the cat. From one of his bulging pockets he drew out four cans of Iams, stacking them neatly by the door. If you're going to borrow – he never thought of it as shoplifting – you might as well get the best. The tabby was proof of that, Joey thought. He nodded to the cat again and left the yard, clutching his book against his chest.

* * *

Molly sat on the cracked mattress of the lower bunk, holding the tray a guard had shoved through a slot in the cell door. The flimsy plastic tray held a sandwich, a half-pint of low-fat milk, two folded paper towels, and a wrinkled, brown wedge of apple. The sandwich was shrouded in clear plastic. Rorschach blots of mold coated the surface of the bread, and the ham or whatever meat product it was had a greenish, iridescent sheen. Molly's stomach growled, and against all judgment she tore open the brittle wrapping. The smell instantly silenced her stomach. She drank the milk, which was surprisingly cold, and slowly ate the apple. The two paper towels she placed carefully under the folded blanket, a treasured stash of toilet paper.

Except for an occasional, half-hearted gurgle through the pipes overhead, the drip of the leaky faucet, and the sporadic hum of a distant elevator or the muffled clank of doors, the building seemed deserted. The incessant snoring of the only other inmate, invisible in a nearby cell, was irrationally comforting. Cold moisture seeped into her jumpsuit from the mattress. Molly stood up. Water from last night's storm had puddled on the concrete slab of the bunk and saturated the spongy foam of the broken mattress. Water still oozed from the cracked concrete wall in a gleaming stain that spread from the watermarks of previous leaks. Shoving the tray and moldy sandwich through the slot in the steel bars, Molly paced slowly and carefully over the rivulets in the floor and chewed small bites of apple, every swallow a minor triumph over the oppression of waiting for something – anything – to happen.

Brad and Sal, she knew, would be okay. Mac and Sara would make sure of that. The desperate ache for her children was less for their sake than for her own, masking a deeper turmoil of grief and rage too raw to indulge or even acknowledge. Molly shook off this insight and forced herself to chew another bit of apple. The security door at the end of the corridor banged open, and she heard voices.

"….only two in this unit. She's down this way…watch your step. There you are."

The brick shithouse guard led two women up to the cell door. One was middle-aged and dumpy, overfilling a flowered print dress, a sweater over her shoulders. The other was taller and rail thin, wearing a plaid skirt and matching jacket. Both wore high-heeled shoes; the tall one chewed gum. Secretaries or clerks, Molly thought. They stared through the bars at her in lurid fascination. Molly stared back.

"She still hasn't talked?" the dumpy one asked.

"Nah," the guard said. "Your tough ones don't, you know."

The dumpy woman shivered dramatically. "Ooh, look at her arms. There's blood… "

The guard shrugged, sorry to disappoint her. "Her own. Resisting arrest. A real wild one."

The tall woman nodded. "Well, I mean, just look at her hair, you can tell."

The guard stepped on the sandwich tray and laughed. She kicked it aside and shepherded the women back to the security door, which slammed shut on their giggles and excited chatter. Molly set the last shred of apple carefully on the edge of the tilting sink and sat down on the Sherwin-Williams toilet lid, looking at her scratched arms. Spitting on her hands, she wiped the smears of dried blood from the worst scrapes, then ran her fingers through her hair, straining out clumps of dirt and fir needles.

Twice again during the afternoon, one guard or another led tours of courthouse employees in to stare at her. Hearing them approach, Molly folded her arms across her chest and sat on the Sherwin-Williams throne with her back to the visitors, listening to their titillated laughter and complaints.

"Hey, we can't see. Make her turn around," a man's voice whined.

"Not without backup," the guard answered. "This is maximum security, remember."

The final entrance of the long afternoon was not another tour guide, however. The two original guards dragged a thrashing woman down the corridor, opened Molly's cell, and dumped her on the floor.

"Company for you," the Barbie guard said.

The two guards left, laughing. Molly stared at the woman on the floor. Her back was arched painfully, her arms flailing, legs twitching. She was barefoot, and apparently the cops had given up trying to get her into a jail jumpsuit, leaving her in a tailored blouse and panties, no skirt. The woman's head twitched back and forth, her eyes seeking Molly's, pleading with her. Molly stepped back from the flailing arms, trying to make sense of the faint sounds coming from the woman's mouth.

"Par…par…par-park…"

Molly stared. Was the woman drunk? No, she thought, a drunk would pass out before losing such control. She leaned closer.

"Park? They arrested you on a parking violation?"

The woman tried to shake her head no, and slammed it against the floor. One ear started bleeding, scraped by filthy concrete, and her hair, unleashed from a French braid, swirled in grey coils about her restless head, mopping algae from the floor.

"Park … med …meds!"

Molly gazed at the thrashing figure, the vibrating hands clutching each other. From a long ago childhood she remembered a school librarian, the trembling fingers attempting to date stamp a book.

"Parkinson's Disease? Is that it?"

The woman sighed loudly and managed a nod. "B ... b ...bracelet ... meds..."

"They took them away from you? Your pills?"

The woman nodded again. Her head snapped sideways, her body suddenly rigid. "Help. Toi ... toi.... " Her hands scrabbled uselessly at her panties.

"Toilet? Oh my god," Molly said. She helped the woman upright, holding her under the arms while trying to pull the panties off and drag her to the toilet. They didn't make it. Just as she managed to slide the panties down, the woman convulsed and seemed to explode, shooting a stream of diarrhea in all directions with her gyrations. She folded against Molly's arm finally, quivering and barely conscious. Molly set her down carefully on the cleaner end of the lower bunk.

"Don't mind the noise," she said. "I'll get help."

Molly stood up and faced the TV monitor, which she assumed also had a microphone. She put two fingers in her mouth and whistled. It was a whistle a neighbor once had accused of shattering windows, a whistle her kids had proved could hurt eardrums half a mile away. In the confines of the jail, the sound rebounded and intensified, an unbearable, piercing note that simply wouldn't stop. The snoring inmate down the hall awoke and screamed, then banged furiously on the cell bars, adding to the din. Molly drew breath and let fly again and again. Doors banged in the hallway and guard station, and two cops charged Molly's cell.

"Hey, you, stop that!" One yelled.

Molly yelled right back, pointing at the woman crumpled and trembling amid streams of shit. "Get a doctor. Now. Immediately. I mean now!"

The two guards stared dumbly into the cell, then laughed.

"Doctor, hell," one said. "She needs AA."

Molly lowered her voice and spoke with forced enunciation. "For your information, she is not drunk, and she is not on drugs. If you had done your job, you'd have read the bracelet she wore saying she has Parkinson's Disease and how to contact her doctor. You would have found her pills in her pocket and helped her take them. Because you didn't do your job, she could die in the next few minutes, and believe me, I will testify to your negligence. And if you don't get a doctor quick, it'll be worse than negligence. It'll be cold-blooded fucking murder."

The two cops looked at each other. The shorter one fumbled for the radio clipped to her belt.

Chapter Five

I never had this thing with animals like Sal has. Except for my dog Winston. He was this big old golden retriever my mom had before me. She says he must've always wanted a puppy of his own, 'cause when she brought me home from the clinic he thought he'd died and gone to heaven with his very own baby. She has all these pictures of a fat brown blob – which is me – sleeping on Winston's paws, with his furry ear flopped over me like he's listening to every heartbeat. He was my best friend all the time I was growing up. When he was killed was the worst day of my life. I still have nightmares sometimes of him running to me with his ears flying in the wind and that truck skidding around the bend off the pavement, tossing Winston like a rag doll, and him lying there by our driveway whimpering and bleeding from his mouth and then just being dead forever, and my fake dad not even coming out of the house when I screamed, not even afterward when mom and I buried him and had a funeral so Sal would know he was gone. Sometimes when I think of him it's like I have a hole in my heart like Sal did when she was born and I can't ever love anything like that again.

—*The Oreo File*

Brad and Sal stood on the look-out stone and stared at the ocean. Mac had shooed them out of the house while he made phone calls, and they'd raced for the cliff as if the reporters and news had never happened. The tide was coming in. A few seagulls swooped lazily over the waves, and on the beach to the north, sandpipers raced the wave line. From the sandstone cliffs below the highway, orange beaks of oystercatchers popped in and out of nest holes like wind-up toys. Brad looked again at the ledge where the penguins had preened and bowed this morning. The ledge was empty. As they watched, a wave surged over it and receded in a rippling quilt pattern of foam.

Brad scanned the tumbled rocks of the headland quickly, looking for any sign or shadow of penguins. Nothing. Studying again the vacant ledge, he felt hollow himself. Howie. The reporters had said he was dead. Brad fought a wave of nausea. Sal clung to his jacket suddenly.

"Brad, is it true? About Howie?"

"Mac's finding out," he said, but even as he said it, he knew, and so did Sal. She buried her face in his jacket, shaking with sobs. Comfortless himself, he patted her shoulder. There was nothing to say. Nothing. He stared blindly at the waves, not registering the first bullet shape that shot from a crest and disappeared. Then another followed, and another. He straightened up and spun Sal around, lifting her up to see.

"Sal! They're back! Look!"

He turned Sal in time to see a yellow head submerge, a sleek body shoot straight upwards and dive back into the foam. A penguin leapt out of the water onto a rock below the ledge where they'd preened in the morning. Two more squirted onto the rock, landing on their feet with wings outstretched for balance. A fourth bird sailed up with effortless grace and landed on its predecessor. The row of penguins fell over like dominos. Brad laughed.

Sal gasped and pointed at the water. "Brad, another one! Oh Brad, it's hurt…"

The fifth bird was definitely in trouble. It flopped toward the rock and fell short, sinking completely in the breaking wave and bobbing up again for a moment, looking flat and dead in the foam that was sucked out by the next wave. It disappeared, and they saw it again a minute later, a flash of yellow and a beak poking out of a swell beyond the breakers, paddling in choppy circles. Twice more it tried to land and missed. Sal cried out and Brad grabbed her arm. On its fourth try, the bird got lucky. A big sneaker wave washed it onto the rock and left it there, lying on its side in a puddle of foam.

The other penguins hopped up the cliff to their old ledge and began preening themselves, seeming oblivious to their motionless comrade. They didn't move when Sal tore away from Brad and jumped past them, or when Brad stumbled after her. By the time he reached her, she was struggling to hold the wounded bird with waves breaking over them both. Shouting, swearing, Brad shoved her up the cliff out of reach of the waves. Somehow, he was never sure exactly, he managed to hoist the penguin up after her. Together, they boosted the creature past the other penguins and onto the top of the cliff.

Sal sat with the penguin's head on her lap. Its beak was open, its breath making bubbles of bloody foam around its nostrils. The bottom half of the beak was impaled on a three-inch steel fish hook. Green and orange streamers on the hook's shaft had tangled in the bird's throat, and a snarl of fishline wound tightly around its wing. The wing was more like a flipper, the feathers sawed off and compacted like reptile scales. The yellow patches on its cheeks were bloody, and blood oozed from deep gashes where the fishline cut into the leathery wing.

Sal tried to loosen the fishline. She was soaked, her lips blue.

"Forget it," Brad shouted. "Let's get him home."

Carrying a fifty or sixty pound penguin half a mile is not easy, he discovered. The bird's skin was so loose he could feel the body slipping back and forth under it. It was too compact and inflexible to carry over his shoulder. He made a sling of his jacket, and carried it home with Sal taking the other end, Joe plodding inquisitively behind.

Mac was waiting for them at the house. He'd lit the fire and turned the lights on and filled Joe's manger. A big pot of his wife's venison stew bubbled on the stove, and an apple pie steamed on the warming shelf. When he saw them stumbling along the path with their burden, Mac ran out and took over. He carried the jacketed penguin into the kitchen without even glancing at it and ordered Sal to change into dry things. Brad helped him set the jacket down and unfold it from the penguin. The bird wobbled to its feet and leaned against the sink cabinet, shaking its head and gagging on the streamers wadded up in its throat.

Mac hunkered down and studied the fish hook in the penguin's beak, running his finger along the tangled fishline.

"Be right back," he said, and was gone.

Brad heard Mac's pickup door slam. A minute later, he was back with pliers and wire cutters and went to work. Brad held the penguin across his lap, and Mac started cutting. Brad's clothes were soaked. The smell of Sara's stew filled the house. His stomach growled, and he wondered how long the bird had gone hungry, unable to eat with that wicked hook piercing its beak and streamers clogging its throat.

Mac snapped the shaft of the hook above and below where it went through the beak. He poured peroxide on the piece still left and pulled it out. With needle-nose pliers, he snared the wad of streamers and gently pulled them from its throat.

"Oh, man, this stuff's a real killer," he said, inspecting the fishline.

It took some twenty minutes to snip and unwind the line, easing it out of the skin where it had worked its way through almost to bone. Mac stopped frequently to pour peroxide over the torn skin. With calloused fingers, Mac pried each strand loose, as tenderly, Brad thought, as if it were his own baby. When he was done, the bird lay in Brad's lap, gasping and swallowing air. Sal crouched down and hugged it to her, setting it on its feet. Blood and peroxide fizzed on her clean clothes. She let go, and the bird swayed on its feet. Brad filled a mixing bowl with water and dipped its beak in to rinse it.

Mac gathered his tools and stood at the sink, scrubbing them.

"Well, we done the best we could." He tossed wads of bloody paper towels and cotton balls into the trash. "Lucky you caught him, he wouldn'ta made it long with that stuff in him."

Mac watched Sal lift the bowl, trying to get the bird to drink. It stood a good three feet high, almost up to her shoulder. Mac stared as if he'd never seen it before.

"Jesus Christ. What the fuck is it?"

* * *

Mac brought Sara and Baby Craig over to see the penguin while Brad and Sal polished off the apple pie. They were already full of stew and a whole loaf of Sara's garlic bread. Mac put the sleeping baby in Molly's laundry basket and took the bowl Sara carried.

"Bottom fish. We mashed it up real good."

Sara put an arm around the penguin, while Mac pried its wounded beak open. He stuffed a small fingerful of mashed fish into its throat. It gagged, shook its head, and swallowed, looking surprised. Mac stuffed another bit into its throat, then another. The penguin stopped struggling, opening its beak for more. Mac scooped up fish slurry on a spoon and poured it into the gaping beak. Again and again the penguin swallowed, more and more eagerly.

"Not too much," Sara said. "Wait a bit and then give him more."

The penguin opened its beak, staring hopefully at the spoon. When Mac put the spoon away, the bird walked for the first time, shuffling across the kitchen with its good wing held out for balance. The wounded wing dangled uselessly. By the back door, where the night wind sifted through cracks in the frame, it found an old boot of Howie's and stood on it, its beak in the air. After a few minutes, it tucked its head under its good wing and slept, as motionless and improbable, Brad thought, as a stone butler.

Sara poured cups of hot chocolate and sat down, gesturing to Mac to join her.

"War council," she said. "Tell us what you found out."

Mac filled a bowl with stew before sitting. "T'ain't much. DA's office was closed and the sheriff won't talk to anyone but reporters or lawyers. So I called Molly's boss at the TV station."

Mac slurped a big mouthful of stew and wiped gravy from his chin with his sleeve.

"Mac!" Sara nudged him.

"Yeah. Well, what's his name, Mort? He don't know much more'n we do. There's an arraignment in the morning, should tell us what happened, anyway."

"An arrangement?" Sal asked.

"Arraignment. It's a court thing. They say what you're charged with and – uh – you say whether you're guilty or not."

"So Mort didn't know anything?" Sara said.

"All he has is a press release from the sheriff that spells Molly's name wrong. Says Howard Borstal – Howie – was killed and Molly arrested for murder. And that Howie was an FBI agent."

Brad stared at Mac. "That's what that reporter said, too. But…"

"No!" Sal yelled. Brad didn't know if she meant Howie being dead or being FBI. Or both.

Howie. Brad choked back his own scream. Howie was family. After the long, bleak year when Sal lay dying in Portland, Molly had teamed up with Howie on her first big story for the coastal news station, filming a series on the battle to save old-growth trees for spotted owls. Howie, tattooed ex-Marine, former Forest Service biologist, enlisted Molly in a guerilla media war for the birds. Their treks into the mountains to climb trees and film nests brought them home filthy, scratched, sweaty, and tired, but Howie always had energy left to teach Sal math tricks or play catch on the beach with Brad and Mac. After dinner was best, though, Brad thought. Howie would show Sal string figures or math puzzles while Brad and Molly washed dishes. Then Howie would take his guitar off its peg.

Brad looked at the guitar now, hanging there like always on the wall behind the couch. He caught Sal glancing at it, too. This time last night, Brad was playing fiddle, Howie backing him, the house ringing with reels and polkas, Sal and Molly laughing over the words to "Hop High Ladies." Brad smiled painfully to himself, remembering last winter, Sara huge and pregnant trying to teach Mac to step-dance. Howie's feet tapping rhythms on the floor. Howie and Molly singing Gilbert and Sullivan. Howie asleep under the tree Christmas morning in a gaudy pile of presents.

"Look," Mac was saying. "It don't make any kind of sense, but that's what the sheriff says. Says Howie was undercover, investigating timber spiking and equipment sabotage in national forests."

"No way," Brad said. He looked at Sal. Her face was pale, blue shadows of veins darkening around her mouth and eyes like when she was dying. Her untouched second piece of pie sat in a puddle of melting ice cream. "No way," he said again.

"I don't believe it, either," Sara added, also looking at Sal. "Where did this happen? And how do they know…?"

Mac gulped his hot chocolate. "Fisher Creek," he said, his voice harsh.

Mac went silent. They all knew what Fisher Creek meant to him. Its steep canyons and ridges held the last stands of old-growth timber in the county. It was there Mac had grown up, living with his brother and father in a cabin rented from Fallwell Timber, which had owned much of the county in those days. A logger himself, Mac hadn't said much when Molly embarked on her spotted owl series, but Fallwell Timber and the murrelets had brought him out swinging. His father had spent the last thirty years of his life crippled by a Fallwell yarder without getting a dime from the company, and his brother had been killed in a lathe accident at one of Fallwell's mills. When environmental groups filed a lawsuit to stop Fallwell from logging Fisher Creek's murrelet nesting grounds, Mac had roared into Molly's kitchen with the newspaper and some old photographs.

"That's my home those sons of bitches're gonna cut!" he'd yelled, waving the paper at Molly and Howie. "Me and my brother grew up in that unit!"

Fallwell had rented his dad the old Fisher homestead until he was too crippled to work for them. "Kicked us out and bulldozed the place, the bastards. Turned out they wanted us out anyways, so's they could trade the whole piece off to the feds for some prime timber in south county. Me and my brother knew every tree, every square inch of that ridge…"

That was how the big companies operated, Mac said. They'd cut everything they could haul out and then sell the land for development or trade it to the government for uncut timberland. They hadn't cut Fisher Creek back then because the canyons were too steep for logging in those days, but now modern equipment could clearcut every twig on any slope, no matter how steep. With Fisher Creek, Fallwell had bought rights to cut the last old-growth trees left in the coast range.

Mac was so outraged he called the groups suing Fallwell and offered his services. He dragged Molly across half the state, taking her behind the scenes to film log decks and sawmills, the docks where old-growth logs were rafted together and floated to Japan, and whole hillsides of stumps sliding into rivers where salmon once spawned. He joined Howie staking out groves to watch for murrelet nests, helped him build blinds for Molly's camera work. When the judge wouldn't hold up the Fisher Creek cut without proof the murrelets nested there, Mac took turn and turn about with Howie, watching for the birds to come in at dawn. Finally, last week, they had located an occupied nest tree.

Howie. Brad stared at Mac's face, saw tears there, and felt his own eyes well up.

Sara broke the spell. "Mac, what do they say happened?"

"They don't say. Not yet. Just that three loggers saw it happen."

Mac absently pulled Sal's plate over and started in on her pie. "Some kind of frame up. Gotta be. I mean, Howie FBI? Something stinks." He banged the table with his fork, then noticed Sal's face, streaked with tears. "Oh, sorry, Buckshot. Were you through with this?"

He pushed the plate back at Sal. She shook her head.

Sara put a warning hand on Mac's arm. "What about the bird? Should we feed him again?"

Mac looked at the penguin, still motionless by the door. "Still on his feet, anyway. What do you think, Sal?"

Sal shook her head. "Let him sleep? Will he be okay?"

Mac shrugged. "If we can get food down him a couple days – 'til his beak's healed, and that wing – maybe he'll make it. But what the hell's it doing here, anyway?"

"Dunno," Brad said. "There's four more of 'em out on the spit."

"They were there this morning," Sal added. "We wanted Mom to film them, but…"

Brad saw tears well up in her eyes again. He took the P volume of their old Britannica off the shelf and found a page of penguin illustrations.

"They're Emperor's, I think. Look."

Sal smiled for the first time since dinner. "The emperor's new clothes!"

Brad skimmed the lengthy article. "They're from Antarctica, the South Pole. Wow, some of 'em got to be six feet tall – fossil ones, that is. But it says no penguin species ever live north of the equator."

"Well, we better keep our mouths shut or some goon'll shoot them or stick 'em in a zoo or something," Mac said.

Brad and Sal stared at each other. The thought of what had saved the penguins from exactly that fate was too much to bear. Sal's face paled. In the laundry basket, Baby Craig stirred and whimpered. Sara picked him up.

"I'll stay here tonight," Mac told her. "In case the bird needs feeding. Or something."

"No way," Brad said. "I'll feed him if he wakes up. We'll call if we need you."

Mac stayed until Sal fell asleep. Keeping Molly's tradition, Brad read aloud to her. Instead of the Arthur Ransome adventure she had been reading, he chose a copy of *Double Whammy* that Howie had brought from the library yesterday. The first chapter made both Sal and Mac laugh before she fell asleep. After Mac left, Brad curled up in the armchair in Sal's room and finished the book.

Chapter Six

"The curse of the thermodynamically challenged," Howie says. "DSM Four, Directional Disorders." Meaning me, how I start out one way and end up in the opposite direction. Like last year in the big November storm when I'm trippin' with these older dudes that hang out by the funeral home. R.I.P.s they call themselves. It's been raining ropes for a week and nobody's got wheels, so what's happening that night is they're hoofin' up to Ridgeview Estates, the development up on the cliffs east of the highway, to steal some vodka they saw in a garage there. I don't like vodka but I'm cool, I go along.

The houses up there stick right out over the cliff with decks at the back hanging two hundred feet above the coast highway, so all the lawns and swing sets and barbeques are in the front yards. When we get up to the house there's a dog barking in the garage where they saw the vodka earlier. This blows the whole scene and we're backing off when there's a crunching sound and a loud crack, and the dog yelps. The R.I.P.s are out of there but I'm so dumb I don't even notice they're gone. The street light flickers and the dog yelps again like it's hurt.

Honest to god I didn't think of the house falling down the cliff. I'm just thinkin' of the damn dog, see, and I go bangin' on the door, yelling, but no one comes, so I break the garage window and climb in to the dog. I light a match, only it's not one dog, it's a spaniel mama with a whole nest of puppies. I don't slow down to count 'em 'cause the whole concrete floor's cracking down the middle big time, like the San Andreas Fault. I pitch the mama dog out the window and stuff the puppies in my jacket and dive after her. I'm hauling the mama up the driveway when this man and woman come running out the front door holding two little kids, and at that second the whole house and half the garage just snap off and disappear.

Explaining what I'm doing in their garage at one in the morning ain't an option, so I roll the puppies out of my jacket next to their mama and I'm gone. But then the paper comes out, front page picture of this pile of broken wood and bed frames and soggy drywall at the bottom of the cliff, under a big headline about the Mystery Hero that woke the family up and saved their lives. Oh man, I couldn't look those R.I.P.s in the eye ever again. No way I could explain about the dog, any more than I could about the violin.

"Sometimes what looks like a direction is just an adrenaline rush," Howie says, which I see now is all that holds the R.I.P. dudes together. But at the time I just felt bummed and left out.

—The Oreo File

The 1964 Dodge van was lodged almost miraculously upright against two fir trees, which had been stout enough years ago to stop its fall from the ridge road a hundred feet above. The firs were massive now, and trees and brush had grown up around the van, concealing it even in winter. An alder sapling had sprouted between the body and the bumper, prying the bumper off as it grew. On the rusted, dented sides, Joey could still make out the lettering, DAWSON'S ELECTRIC, an outfit nobody he'd asked even remembered.

The van had been cleaned out when it was dumped; the only thing remaining from its former life had been a coil of insulated wire hanging from the racks that lined the inside. It had been filled with decades of accumulated leaf litter, pine needles and vacant rodent nests when Joey found it. Other vehicles littered the hillside and creek bank far below. For some reason he couldn't fathom, creek and river banks had in olden times been favored graveyards for dead cars. Joey had explored many of them, including a nearly intact Model A buried in silt at the creek bottom, but the Dodge van was the only one useable as a camp.

The van was Joey's winter camp, a convenient half-mile from school and town, nearly invisible, and with a few beads of caulk around the dented doors, fairly waterproof. The slight tilt forward funneled water from the shattered windshield out through the rusted floorboards. Joey lifted the plywood flap he'd installed over the windshield and climbed in, his pockets clanking on the metal frame. He switched on the dome light, wired to a small bank of batteries that he recharged at school or park service campgrounds. A black shadow streaked past him and vanished through the rusted-out steering column.

Joey smiled. The cat had been the original tenant of his camp, a scroungy, feral tom that Joey rarely saw. He surveyed his domain, noting the warm spot left by the cat on the duffle containing his bedding, and emptied his bulging pockets: four more cans of Iams, a charged battery, the tetracycline packet, ramen noodles, a shrink-wrapped hunk of sliced turkey, an orange, a can of Sterno. He placed the book on one of the tool shelves lining the van's sides, on top of a stack of magazines and newspapers scrounged from recycling bins.

With a stick, Joey propped open the plywood over the windshield and set a perforated oil can on the dashboard, placing the Sterno in it and lighting it. Over the flame he placed a battered saucepan and poured in water from a jug filled several times a week at garden hoses up on Ridge Road. While the water heated, he opened a can of Iams and spooned it into a cracked Wedgewood bowl, a recent dump find. After reading the label of the tetracycline packet and trying to guess how many gallons of fish equal one scrawny cat, he opened two capsules and shook them over the cat food, stirring it well and setting the dish on a cardboard mat below the passenger seat.

Joey dropped the ramen noodles and turkey slices into the boiling water, placed a slab of sheet metal on top of the pan, and peeled his orange. He sat on a wooden oyster crate and ate out of the saucepan, reading a 1991 National Geographic story about elephants. His dinner over, the saucepan sterilized by boiling a little water in it, Joey climbed out the windshield to visit the latrine he'd dug into the hillside nearby. It was dark now; headlights from occasional cars up on Ridge Road loomed briefly through the trees. Back in the van, Joey spread out his sleeping bag and pillow, switched on a small reading light, and turned off the dome light. Nestled in his bedding, he finally opened the book he'd carried so carefully all afternoon. Books were too precious to keep here long; the damp softened their pages, bindings came unglued after only a few winter days. He'd picked up this one, a library copy of *Anne of Avonlea*, after some girl left it on a cafeteria table. Eagerly, he opened it and lost himself in the first pages.

Joey didn't look up when the cat climbed in through the floorboards and found the waiting Wedgewood bowl. The bowl was empty when Joey dared to peer over his book. The cat crouched between the front seats, staring at – or through – Joey with its one good eye. The other eye was a swollen, ping-pong-ball-sized bulb of infected tissue and membranes. Joey wondered how long it would take the tetracycline to work, if it worked at all. Well, it was the best he could do. Deliberately, slowly, he lowered his eyes to the book again. Much later, after he'd turned out the light, he felt the steady purring of the cat against his knees, and slept.

* * *

Molly half woke, struggling to breathe. A plume of diesel exhaust tainted the clean, cement-laden air sifting through a crack in the concrete wall next to her head.

She stared at the crack, caught between sleeping nightmare and waking one. The sleeping nightmare made more sense. She'd been running from three huge loggers through an endless stand of old-growth fir, clutching Brad's birthday cake, which slid on its tray and slopped buttercream frosting over her fingers. Behind her the loggers shouted, closing in, swinging mauls that felled the forest like dominos. She ran harder, gasping, and her foot plunged through the naked body of a woman, which exploded in a foaming wave of shit.

Molly sat up and stared at her hands. The fingers were white, the bloodless white of halibut filets. She tucked them under her armpits to warm them, and shivered. The sodden, jail-issue jumpsuit reeked of urine and mildew from the equally sodden mattress.

Overhead, water or sewage lurched through paint-blistered pipes with bone-jarring thumps. Air locks, she thought, low-bid plumbing. Between the pipes, ranks of fluorescent lights flickered incessantly, screaming in soundless frequencies for ballast; one of them was blackened and water-stained half its length. Low-bid lighting.

So this was the new jail, she thought, the county's proud entry in the statewide race to get tough on crime. She tried to remember how many local schools had closed, their buildings condemned for lack of basic maintenance, while county funds drained into this multi-million-dollar flophouse.

Molly rubbed her hands together, trying to restore circulation, and thought of camera angles and voice-overs. Her camera. No, don't go there. Yesterday, amid the cascade of raw terror and then vacant disbelief that had overtaken her, it had been easier to seal off all thoughts of camera, murrelets, and especially Howie, partitioning her mind the way she'd partitioned her hard disk to give Brad his own working space. Now, a single night had eroded the barriers she'd built. She shook her head and moved away from the continuing diesel fumes, only to be assaulted by a worse stench.

On the concrete floor, the wall, and the bunk beneath her, sluggish streams of still-liquid diarrhea were only just beginning to clot, a thin, wrinkled skin forming over the thickest deposits. No one had cleaned up after they carried off the woman with Parkinson's on a stretcher; no materials were provided for Molly to clean it up herself. The smell rose and hung in the air like swamp gas, untouched by a low-bid ventilation system. Gagging, she held her breath and peered down at the floor. No one would believe this without the graphics.

Whatever vehicle had been pumping diesel through the wall finally moved on. Molly moved closer to the crack, imagining a whiff of honeysuckle in the freshening air. She closed her eyes and tried to sleep again.

* * *

Brad finished the book and set the reading lamp on the floor, next to the huge plush owl Howie had won for Sal at the county fair. He stared at the blank darkness of the window, book already forgotten in an unleashed flood of questions. Howie dead? Murdered? His mother a killer? Howie an FBI agent?

Even the questions made no sense. He saw Molly in the cancer ward, reading Freddy the Pig day after day – all twenty-six books – Sal's pale, thin face laughing with a crowd of little bald kids in their wheelchairs and IVs. Molly and Howie singing songs from "The Mikado" while he finished his homework last night. Howie showing string figures and cat's cradle to Sal after dinner. He was going to teach her the kangaroos hopping tonight. Now he never would.

Do FBI agents do cat's cradle? Or stop for every newt on the highway and worry about amphibians disappearing from the planet? Once Howie had rented a movie for them, an old black and white one about two guys who hiked into the mountains with an old prospector to look for gold in Mexico. Brad couldn't remember the title. Howie had played one part again and again, the part where they pack up all their gold, with federales and bandits closing in, and the old prospector won't let them leave until they put the mountain back together. The mountain was good to them, the old man says, so they owe it to the mountain to make it whole again.

Brad fought back tears. Howie. Was it all a lie? Or had Howie been a lie? He looked at the book in his lap. Double Whammy. Mom and Howie. He set the book quietly on Sal's desk and got up, suddenly hungry. Maybe the penguin needed more mashed fish.

In Molly's room, her alarm clock blinked insistently, asking to be reset. Brad ignored it, anxious for the penguin. Sal had put her night light in the kitchen for the bird, "in case he gets scared in a strange place," she said. The penguin hadn't moved, still standing on Howie's boot by the back door, its head under its wing. It didn't wake when Brad opened the fridge for milk and turned the light on to find bread and peanut butter. He switched the light off and sat at the table to eat, wishing the bird would wake up and sit with him. They could eat popcorn and peanut butter and it would tell him about its travels. Patagonia, he thought, maybe it had landed in Patagonia. Or was it Tasmania? He couldn't remember which was which. He fetched a globe from Sal's room and held it under the night light. Patagonia, that was it. The globe was marked with arrows showing the direction of ocean currents. He puzzled over these, wondering how the penguins had managed such a journey, and why. Were there more of them out there off the coast? Maybe these five were part of a whole herd. Flock? What do you call a bunch of penguins?

Brad carried the globe back and sat again in the old armchair in Sal's room, listening to her soft breathing. The thought of Molly locked up in the concrete hulk of the jail turned the peanut butter sour in his stomach. He stared at the salt patterns on the window, the mass of Mac's house next door a black hole against the dark sky. Mac would take them to the arraignment in the morning to find out what the hell was going on. Brad squeezed his eyes shut against the sting of tears.

When he looked again, a light glowed in one of Mac's windows. Brad saw Sara walking back and forth with the baby against her shoulder, her body rocking as she walked. "The Infant Phenomenon," Howie had called Baby Craig. Singing the Infant Phenomenon to sleep, Brad thought. Watching Sara, he fell asleep himself.

Chapter Seven

Thirteen's when your hormones fill up your balls and mess up your brain and get you in trouble. That's what they say, anyway, like they just expect it. Ask me, it's grownups got trouble with hormones, or maybe the wrong ones. I mean, how many thirteen-year-olds you know go around blowing up clinics and skyscrapers, or ripping off stockholders or wiping out all the frogs and changing the climate? Killing off the whole planet, man. I mean, kids just mess up ourselves. Grownups mess up the entire universe. And we're supposed to grow up so we can, too? Don't make me laugh. Peter Pan was on to something, even if there wasn't a black kid among 'em. The Lost Boys, I mean, and they all sold out to grow up anyway. Peter was the only smart one.

—*The Oreo File*

Mac parked his pickup three blocks from the courthouse, unable to get any closer. Satellite vans and news vehicles clogged the street and courthouse parking lot. Reporters jostled with loggers – or people dressed in loggers' suspenders and caulk boots – wearing yellow ribbons and carrying signs. "Boil an Owl for Jesus," "Sierra Club Kiss My Ax," "Jobs Not Birds," Brad read, along with cruder statements. Mac lifted Sal onto his shoulders to plow through the crowd at the entrance. Deputies blocked the doors, ordering people to stand back, the courtroom was full.

"No room at the inn, huh," Mac snorted. "We'll see." He shoved a reporter aside and marched up to the deputies, Brad close behind.

"Dumb Darryl!" Mac bellowed.

One of the deputies turned, his stern face melting into a grin. "Mac

Attack! Long time, eh?"

"What's up?" Mac said. "Thought you and Mary were in Coos Bay."

"Mary's dead," the deputy said. "Cancer. So I come home. These your kids?"

"Oh man, I'm sorry." Mac lowered his voice. "No, not mine. They're Molly's – Molly Matthissen's. Can you get us in?"

Darryl spoke to another deputy and led them inside, up a wide stairway to a hall packed with more people. They passed one at a time through a metal detector and into an even more jammed courtroom. Darryl booted reporters out of front row seats and stayed to talk to Mac through the din of voices. Sal looked around at the crowd and grabbed Brad's hand. Brad had been in court once before, at his parents' divorce hearing. It was nothing like this. Four years ago there had been a big quiet room, a grandmotherly judge, and two excruciatingly polite lawyers talking about his father waving something. The scene today was a madhouse. Cops lined the sides of the courtroom holding riot guns. Reporters and spectators filled the seats, all yelling. A bullet-proof shield surrounded the judge's pulpit, and more cops guarded the altar rail separating spectators from the lawyers' tables. Mac and Darryl finished a shouted replay of old football games, huddled briefly, and Darryl hurried off.

Sal slid over to make room for Mac. "Mac, is this how they always do it?"

Mac shook his head, dislodging sawdust onto his ill-fitting tuxedo. Brad thought it must be his wedding suit; he could smell the mothballs.

"No way," Mac said. "Darryl says word came down Molly belongs to some ecoterrorist group that's going to bust her out." He looked at the riot cops and ran his hand through his hair, dumping another load of sawdust. "Been watching too much TV."

The noise was deafening, punctuated by feedback screeches and static from amplifiers on the ceiling. A court reporter and two cops struggled with microphone wires at the counsel tables, elbowing lawyers aside.

"That's Molly's lawyer, on the left," Mac said. He nodded toward a small, thin man with sparse hair and wire-rimmed glasses, who got up to let the court reporter adjust his microphone. "Court appointed," Mac said. "Low-bid lawyer. Not exactly the brightest bulb in the string."

At the right-hand table, two men sat with backs to the audience, shuffling papers. Next to them a tall, olive-skinned man, black hair shining with oil and glued into a wind-blown parody, sat sideways with his legs crossed, presenting his profile to the room. Not much of a profile, Brad thought, no chin to speak of. "That's the DA himself," Mac said. "Up for re-election, Darryl says. Whole show's just a photo op for him."

A door opened in back of the pulpit, and the bailiff entered, shouting something that quelled the din of voices and brought the crowd to its feet. The judge entered, lifting his black robe carefully to climb the steps to his pulpit. His bloated face glared through the bullet-proof screen at the crowd, spectacles embedded in lumpy folds of skin like ingrown toenails. He spoke into his microphone, triggering a blast of static on the amplifiers. The crowd interpreted this as a signal to sit down. The bailiff answered in another blast of static, and a door on the side of the courtroom opened. The cops lining the walls crouched in combat-ready positions. Brad and Sal strained forward for a glimpse of their mother.

* * *

Breakfast was a plastic bowl of stale cornflakes and a half-carton of milk. Molly picked at the cornflakes and drank the milk, longing for hot coffee. She'd never thanked Brad yesterday for building the fire and making coffee, and today was his birthday. She had little hope of celebrating it.

The milk was cold. Molly shivered in the damp, reeking jumpsuit. Avoiding the shit on the floor, she stretched, on tiptoes rehearsing old ballet exercises. Braving the murky water from the tap, she used one of the precious paper napkins to wipe the worst of the caked diarrhea from her pant legs, succeeding only in distributing it further. The cold water brought on more shivering. Wrapping herself in the blanket, she huddled on the top bunk, face pressed against the cracked wall to catch the fresh air sifting through, and tried to remember verses to "Wildwood Flower."

She was in a shivering doze when they came for her. Three large uniformed male cops along with the familiar brick shithouse model. She wondered where Steroid Barbie was. They cuffed her hands in front of her. Brick Shithouse grimaced in disgust at the fouled pant legs and pulled on latex gloves to fasten steel shackles on her ankles. They led her out of the cell; the chain linking Molly's ankles dragged, snaring the paper jail-issue slippers on her feet. Once through the security chamber, they entered a freight elevator, emerging in a hallway lined with doors. A cop stood by one door, where her escorts stopped and formed a square around her. No one spoke. Molly read the felt-tipped sign taped to the door: DO NOT "ENTER" WHEN COURT IN "SESSION". Quietly trying to untangle the ankle chain from her torn slipper, she pondered the unfathomable intent of those quotation marks.

The door cop's pager buzzed, and he opened the door, standing aside for the prisoner detail. In close formation, the four guards surrounding her moved forward. The bulging belly of the cop behind her shoved Molly's shoulder, knocking her off balance. Peering around the cops, Molly saw the courtroom, the riot squad on alert, the crowd's eager faces, the judge behind his bullet-proof shield. Just as she caught sight of Brad and Sal, the fat cop behind her stepped hard on the tangled shackle chain, twisting her ankle and lifting her off her feet. She heard bones break as she fell, her cuffed hands thrust forward to shield her face. The cop, his foot caught in the chain, fell on top of her. Hitting the floor, Molly's face struck her cuffed wrists heavily under his immense weight, which crushed her lungs. For several moments, she lost consciousness, reluctantly waking to the sound of gunfire and the taste of blood.

Molly felt the cop heave himself off her, but he seemed to leave his weight behind, pressing relentlessly into her chest. She gasped for breath and fluid surged into her throat. A familiar voice spoke softly, close to her head.

"Can you hear me? Are you – are you okay?"

She lifted her head, gazing at him dizzily. The same puppy-dog brown eyes, the same voice that had so long ago, it seemed, cautioned her not to say a word. She tried to speak, but her mouth filled with blood. The bloody, cuffed hands on the floor must be her own, she supposed. A gleaming bone protruded from the right wrist. Her right eye seemed to be out of commission, too; something like warm syrup oozed down her face.

"I called the ambulance," the quiet voice said. "Don't move. Please."

This command she ignored. Fighting sudden nausea and surging waves of dizziness, Molly struggled to her knees and searched, one-eyed, for her children. Brad and Sal were standing on a bench, Sal's mouth open in horror; Molly tried to smile at her. Holding her cuffed hands to her face, she pointed her left index finger toward them and churned the broken mess of her right hand awkwardly in a small circle. Message delivered, she slumped against the brown-eyed cop and passed out.

* * *

Brad and Sal saw their mother fall in time-lapse fragments: the door opening, the four cops squared around her, the filthy orange jumpsuit, Molly straining around the uniforms to catch her kids' eyes. The cops were watching the crowd so intently they lost track of their own feet. The enormous cop behind Molly lurched suddenly and fell. Molly disappeared beneath him in a sickening thump and the clank of chains.

Sal screamed, hurtling toward her mother, Brad just behind her. Instantly, the cops lining the room lifted guns into battle-ready positions; a wall of uniforms materialized at the alter rail, impervious to Sal clawing at them. The judge disappeared, diving somewhere behind his pulpit. A swat team poured in from a door behind the judge, fanning out and aiming guns in all directions. One of them slipped on the bloody floor and fell over the cop sprawled on Molly; as he fell, his gun spat a row of bullets through two windows and a portrait of a dead judge.

The smell of cordite filled the courtroom. The bailiff and court reporter clutched each other under one of the counsel tables. Beneath the other table, prosecutors and defense attorney rolled together in a tangle of speaker wires, sending high-pitched screeches through the ceiling speakers. Reporters and spectators piled on each other under the pew benches, yelling.

Mac pulled Sal and Brad back to their seats, where all three stood on the wooden pew, looking for Molly in the pile-up. Two large male cops and a short female stood over the fat one, lifting him to his feet. He kicked one foot loose from Molly's ankle chain. His face and hands dripped blood. None of them glanced at the inert figure on the floor, blood pooling around Molly's head. Mac's football buddy, Darryl, seemed to be the only cop in the room not pointing a gun. He slipped through the ring of guards and knelt by Molly's head, speaking into a radio and murmuring urgently to her.

"Mom! Mom!" Sal screamed. Brad held her back.

Molly raised her blood-smeared face and slowly lifted herself to her knees. Her undamaged eye found Brad and Sal. She lifted her cuffed hands to make her strange gesture, the naked bone of her right arm spearing the skin above the wrist. Brad didn't understand the message, but Sal stiffened beside him. Molly's face went white and Darryl caught her as she fell.

Brad remembered it all later in slow motion. The four cops standing, looking everywhere but at the figure on the floor, the anxious Darryl cradling Molly's head on his lap. The fading racket as the crowd realized they were not under attack, then the shuffle and thumps of bodies crawling from under the pews. Guards along the walls lowered their riot guns, looking disappointed, and the swat team extricated the judge from beneath his pulpit and hustled him out the back door. Voices of spectators and reporters rose in a barrage of questions. Prosecutors and defense attorney emerged from under the counsel table, dragging tangled wires and sending more feedback screeches through the speakers.

Bedlam. Brad remembered the word from a vocabulary test. Bethlehem hospital, a madhouse. Finally, a nurse barged through the side door, followed by EMTs with a stretcher. In a matter of seconds, Molly was gone.

Darryl gestured to Mac, who herded Brad and Sal after him through the side door. Following a trail of blood spatters, Darryl led them at a trot through a maze of hallways to a freight elevator, which took them to a dingy basement complex with peeling paint on the walls. Still trotting – "to beat the ghouls," Darryl said – he opened a door to the staff parking lot. An ambulance was just pulling out, flanked by police cars. There were no reporters. Darryl grinned.

"First down, move ass," he said, slapping Mac's shoulder and closing the door behind them.

Mac lifted Sal to his shoulders again and ran, Brad keeping pace, until they were out of sight of the courthouse. They were in the truck, breathing safely again, when Sal spoke.

"Mom's camera," she said.

Brad groped for the seat belt behind his back. "Yeah, what about it?"

Sal imitated Molly's hand-grinding gesture. "She was trying to tell us something about the camera! Just before she …." Sal turned to Mac. "Mom – will she be okay, Mac?"

Mac started the truck. "We'll damn sure find out. What's this about the camera? Didn't she have it yesterday?"

"'Course she did," Brad said. "The murrelets, she was filming the nest."

Mac stopped the truck at an intersection and glanced down at Sal, sandwiched between them. "So what did she mean?"

"I don't know," Sal said. "But it's important."

A car honked behind them. Mac turned right and pulled the truck to the curb. "Stay here. Stay low. And keep the doors locked."

Brad watched him run back toward the courthouse, his tuxedo flapping. He released his seat belt and slumped down in the seat until his knees jammed under the dashboard. Outside, the traffic noise built as vehicles left the courthouse en masse; looking upward, Brad saw the top of a satellite van sail past. Sal stared at the dashboard, her face pale, eyes wide, blue veins shadowing her mouth – what Brad called her ghost look. It scared him. He hummed a low C, and after a minute Sal joined him, an octave higher. D, then E, she matched him through the scale. When he started over, she joined him on G and grinned weakly. By the time Mac returned, breathless, they had progressed to E flat harmonies.

"Stay low," Mac said, starting the motor and throwing it in gear. "Damn Oregonian reporter tailed me all the way."

He took back streets toward the hospital, driving in grim silence. Two blocks from the hospital, news vehicles were already backed up. A Life Flight helicopter was settling on the hospital landing pad.

"Screw this. Find out quicker by phone," Mac said.

Sal strained against her seat belt, staring at the distant hospital roof, her mouth silently repeating "Mom, Mom" like a goldfish. Brad tugged her back down.

"Stay down. Grandma Rose'll know what's happening."

Grandma Rose, Mac's formidable mother-in-law, was an R.N. and head of surgery at the hospital. Sal subsided, not reassured.

Mac turned up an alley toward the highway. He said nothing more until bridge and town were far behind them.

"You can sit up now," he announced. "It wasn't there."

"What wasn't?" Brad asked.

"Molly's camera. You sure she had it yesterday?"

"Hey, the murrelets, remember? Of course she had it. I loaded it in the car myself."

"Well, Darryl says it wasn't there," Mac said. "They searched the whole unit, took her Subaru apart for evidence, found the battery pack and a box of blank tapes – but no camera."

* * *

Through one eye, the lid at half-mast, Molly saw moving shapes bathed in lurid, shifting shades of red that kept fading to black. Every part of her seemed to be tied down under the huge weight on her chest. She fought for consciousness against the pressure of tubes blocking her throat and tried to focus on the pen clutched in her left hand. A huge vermillion figure loomed into view, behind it a crimson police uniform. Wrong filter. Fade to black again. Voice-overs in the blackness.

"O positive."

"How many cc's?"

A murmur of angry voices. Then a crisp, authoritative voice taking charge, blessedly familiar.

"Not until I get two signatures you don't."

The vermillion figure, ghost-like, tinged with orange now, held something – red flag? Pink slip? Overdraft? – in front of her.

"All set, hon," the vermillion voice boomed. "Signed and sealed. The kiddies are safe." Then, softer, almost a whisper, "Godspeed, dear. Marge's waiting for you."

Marge? Kiddies? Signed? Sealed? Pain exploded in her head, a supernova of white, searing light, then receded. Safe. Brad. Sal. Safe. Someone tried vainly to pry the fingers of her left hand from the pen, gave up, and strapped down the wrist.

Black again. New sounds: heavy doors opening, wind, a seagull crying, the thump of rotor blades. Urgent voices, urgent feet. Wind. Rotor blades.

Marge ... Margaret? ... Houlihan? ...

Against all restraint and reason, Molly giggled. Hot Lips...

Inside the Life Flight chopper, a young EMT misdiagnosed the convulsive tremor that swept his patient.

Chapter Eight

One of the oldest games in school is something called "Smear the Queer." From first grade on up to high school it's always going on: a mob of kids chasing down a victim and knocking him in the dirt, rubbing his face in it, and when they're really on a roll, breaking an arm or stomping a kidney. In grade school after we moved here I came home every day covered with dirt and bruises 'til I discovered the library to hide in and found out how many books I could read.

In fourth grade, though, there was a new librarian who locked the library during recess. Seemed like the whole school was waiting for me that day, and the principal sent me home after I threw up the dog shit they stuffed in my mouth. I couldn't even tell Mom and Howie what happened, just hid in my room with my head under the pillow. Howie came in with his guitar finally, singing "Nobody likes me, everybody hates me, I'm gonna eat some worms" 'til I threw the pillow at him. We had a monster pillow fight, and then I told him what happened. He listened, playing chords and melodies real soft.

"So what's it mean, smear the queer?" he asked. I told him it means jump on someone you don't like or who's different. Mom called the fat principal, who just said boys will be boys. Like stuffing their mouths with dog shit's okay. Mom wanted to sue the school, but Howie had a better idea. He drags an old mattress out in the yard and teaches me some simple holds and throws, practicing with me 'til I can almost throw him. We go down to the school yard that weekend and rehearse the whole thing. The kid who's always leading the pack is a big fifth-grader named Ronald who can't read and has yellow teeth and a big neck. Howie pretends to be

Ronald, amazing what a good job he does of it, too.

Everything he showed me works out even better than he thought. On Monday recess, I run 'til Ronald's way ahead of the pack, then I slow down near the big wooden jungle gym and swings, so he thinks I'm tired. He yells and comes on, and I stop short like Howie showed me and grab his arm and let his weight carry him over me. He's heavy and moving fast, and the momentum takes him right onto the jungle gym, splayed out and looking surprised. The mob of kids starts laughing. Ronald's so mad he tries to jump down on me and breaks his ankle landing. He crumples up on the ground screaming and the kids keep right on laughing. I walk away and find a teacher and tell her someone fell off the jungle gym and needs help. No one ever chased me again in Smear the Queer after that.

Joey wheeled someone else's bicycle through the press of news vans and cars parked in the muddy lot of Dinkum Donuts, a classically misnamed café set too far back off the highway to attract much tourist trade. Only locals ever frequented Dinkum's, which so far as Joey knew had never produced a single donut. Someone must have clued the media people to its soups, pastries, and off-beat location, Joey thought. He wondered whether the court show was over already or hadn't begun. Someone here would know.

He'd been to school only long enough to learn that Brad was absent, his mom to be arraigned for murder that morning. At the best of times, school offered Joey little beyond free meals, electrical outlets, and a pathetic excuse for a library – a few stacks of moldering books in a windowless, unheated storeroom behind the gym. Food, electricity, and books were readily available elsewhere, and though Joey had never talked to Brad, he never felt quite safe in school when Brad was absent.

Behind Dinkum's, a solitary oversize pickup was parked, its shape so totally encased in half-dried mud that no trace of color showed; only a hand-swiped area of windshield allowed a driver any visibility. Joey glanced at it in disgust. He could never understand what point kids thought they were making when they drove their mud-crusted rigs so proudly about town. He ducked into the back door of Dinkum's and dragged out two large, bulging garbage bags. Heaving them into the dumpster, he noticed three men sitting at the small picnic table near the truck. He stared in surprise. They weren't kids at all, but grown men, decked out in logger's suspenders, plaid shirts, and caulk boots. Take-out containers and cups littered the ground by the table, the wind already picking up ketchup-smeared napkins. The men huddled over something on the table, arguing.

"I don't see nothing. It's blank."

"Fuck, you forgot to press record."

"No friggin' way. I did press it, you could hear it whirring and all."

Joey strolled over and bent to pick up the trash, glancing at the table. The men were peering into the view screen of a video camera, poking buttons. Joey lifted the bottom of his t-shirt and loaded the last of the containers and napkins into it, then leaned over and flicked the cover off the camera lens.

"Lens cap," he said, and headed back to the dumpster, marveling at the stupidity of grown-ups.

Back inside the kitchen, Joey had no time to savor the smells of soup stock, pancetta bacon, yeast, or the rich almond scent from trays of cooling pastries. Geordie, a dark-skinned, red-haired Aussie, was slicing onions at card-shark speed; without missing a slice, he tossed Joey an apron.

"Just in time, mate. Up for bussing tables? Mex can't keep up in there."

Joey slipped the apron over his grubby t-shirt; it hung well below his knees. Harpo, Dinkum's pastry chef, slammed long cylinders of bread dough rhythmically on a marble slab, his feet tapping in counter-rhythms; he winked at Joey through flour-crusted eyebrows. Joey grabbed a tray and a wet towel and shouldered through the swinging door into a roiling sea of customers.

Built almost a century ago as a Grange meeting hall, Dinkum's basic structure was little changed: a large, high-ceilinged rectangular room with leaded windows across the front, the kitchen and bathrooms tacked onto the back. A low platform served as stage and extra seating area at one end; the opposite wall featured a stone fireplace flanked by bookshelves, with a cozy arrangement of tatty armchairs around it. Two round tables, each eight feet in diameter, filled the center of the room, surrounded by constellations of smaller tables, some round, some octagonal, square, or pentagonal. Thick varnish glowed over exquisitely inlaid designs on each table top – birds, dolphins, kangaroos, botanically detailed trees, musical instruments, a map of the New York subway system.

Most of the tables were occupied. Groups of people milled around the coffee carafes and fireplace, talking to each other and on cell phones. Like a macaw among starlings, Mex flitted through the crowd, her blue-black hair piled haphazardly with mismatched combs. A red and gold skirt swirled over tarnished Reebocks. Her beaded, sleeveless top flashed from table to table, to the cash register by the door, off to the kitchen and back again, a coffee carafe in one hand, a tray in the other. Catching sight of Joey, she flashed him a thousand-watt smile that could fill the tip jar on a slow day.

Joey hid the rare surge of warmth and belonging that Mex so carelessly bestowed. His face blank, he trudged unnoticed through the crowd, wiping tables, filling dish tubs with sticky plates and silverware, setting fresh pots of coffee to brew, emptying his pockets into the overflowing tip jar at the register. Quietly, efficiently, he pieced together fragmented takes on what had happened at the courthouse.

Howard. Joey knew him only as Brad's Uncle Howie. Weekend nights musicians from as far as Portland and Seattle found their way to Dinkum's for informal jams that Joey never missed. Having no ear for music was little hindrance to good times at Dinkum's. On the memorable nights that Brad and Howie played, even Joey had felt the awed thrill that silenced all other musicians.

Howie dead? Joey thought suddenly of the cat with its swollen eye and shivered, dumping a tray of dishes into the wash-up tub with a crash. Mex swooped past with a tray of cherry Danish and air-kissed the top of his head.

"Angel!" she sang out. "Angel pudding!"

Despite himself, Joey grinned at her swirling figure. Mex used words the way a painter uses colors, creating her own meanings as she went. "Pudding" he decoded as "you are wonderful and appreciated." Angel was the name they had called him at Dinkum's from the start, before it was even Dinkum's. Four years ago, when what would become the Dinkum's crew had been homeless squatters in the abandoned Grange hall, Joey had come across them struggling to start their rusted, '60s VW bus. He had crawled under the dashboard and rewired a bypass around the dead ignition, returning later to install a new one of dubious but unchallenged provenance. They had called him Angel and never asked for his real name.

None of them used real names, anyway. Geordie was an illegal immigrant using a name from a movie. Harpo, a baker on the run from somewhere in Manhattan, played a harp he'd somehow lugged three thousand miles across the continent. And Mex wasn't even Mexican, she was gypsy – Rom, she'd explained once after singing something in a language Joey couldn't identify – but kids at school had never recognized the distinction. How they all ended up together in a derelict building on the edge of the Pacific Ocean, Joey had no idea; he was only nine years old at the time and never thought of asking, content to share their roof on occasional stormy nights, nurse a secret crush on Mex, and fill up on soups and pan breads cooked in the fireplace. In return, he kept their rig running and street legal.

He had been dozing by the fire three years ago, his stomach full, deaf to the songs and laughter coming from the stage, when a stranger walked in, dripping from the storm. There were no tables or furniture then, just squatters' bedrolls serving as seats by the fire. The man shed his raincoat and sat down next to Joey, who served him a bowl of soup and hunk of pan bread, assuming he was as homeless as himself. The man ate quietly and stared at the lamplit stage, where harp, mandolin, and concertina belted out blues, then music hall tunes. Oblivious to the storm pounding the walls, or the smells of soup and whiffs of marijuana, or his now empty bowl, the man sat transfixed through a final set of Gershwin numbers. He stood up when the trio clattered across to the fire for warmth and Geordie's ever-brewing pot of coffee, and introduced himself as the owner of the building.

"Oh, shit," Harpo muttered. "We're outa here," but the man kept talking.

"I need to see the condition of the rooms," he said.

Only Mex rose to the occasion. She handed a lantern to the man and cupped a candle in her hands to shield the concertina from drips. Like a realtor with a new client, she led him through the building, pointing out stripped wires, rusted plumbing, crudely patched leaks, and the barren but clean kitchen. Geordie and Harpo huddled by the fire, gloomily discussing where they could camp next, while Joey slipped out to inspect the man's car, a sleek Lexus. When he returned, the man was sitting again by the fire, writing in a small notebook.

"You'll need a shower," he was saying. The Dinkum's crew stared at him, stunned, while he made more notes. "Phone. Permits. I'll see to those." He stood up and handed Mex a card. "Right, then. Call me tomorrow with that list. And expect electricians and plumbers within the week."

Three months later, Dinkum's opened for business after a whirlwind of building. Its kitchen gleamed with new commercial ovens, two huge refrigerators, a dishwashing system, a walk-in freezer, and racks of quality cookware. In the dining room, two round tables and assorted chairs, gleaned from restaurant and institutional auctions, shone with new varnish over Mex's magical inlaid tops. A screened corner hid her precious woodworking tools while she finished the smaller tables.

During futile discussions about a name, Geordie had slapped the words "Dinkum Donuts" on a scrap of plywood and hung it over the door as a joke. The name and the sign stuck. Dinkum's soups, breads, pastries, and music quickly attracted a growing local clientele. Within a year, well before the deadline set by the landlord, Dinkum's had repaid the costs of remodeling and hadn't missed a rent check since.

Lugging a tray stacked with clean mugs from the kitchen, Joey found the big room suddenly empty of customers. On the low stage, Mex stood one-legged like a gaudy heron, unlacing her sneakers and kicking them off. Tucking her bare feet under her, she folded up on the stage, staring at the empty room while Joey cleared and wiped tables and swept the floor. Geordie ran totals on the register and took one of the four mugs of steaming cocoa that Harpo carried in.

"Three hundred twelve U.S. dollars in forty-five minutes," he said, reading from a strip of register tape. "And nearly half that again in tips."

Mex shook her head, ignoring the tray of cocoa. She turned toward Geordie in bewilderment, and Joey saw tears in her eyes.

"It … it just doesn't seem right, does it," she said. "Making money on someone – on Howie – dying?"

In Geordie's hand the proud strip of register tape crumpled slowly into a small wad and fell to the floor. A long, hollow stillness drove Joey quietly to the kitchen, where he gulped the last of his cocoa and collected the bag of steamed chicken bones Harpo had saved for the cat. Outside, he tied the bag to his handlebars and glanced back. Through the kitchen window he saw Mex loading mugs and plates into the dishwasher. Tears glinted on her face, but she was no longer crying. She was, he realized, singing. Joey stood, unobserved, watching her. He recognized the words, a song she sang sometimes with Howie, unaccompanied:

> "I'll walk beside you through the passing years
> Through days of clouds and sunshine, joy and tears …"

Frantic suddenly to feed the cat, Joey pedaled furiously from Dinkum's yard. The mud-caked pickup and three loggers were gone. Joey never noticed; he had forgotten they were ever there.

* * *

Penguins are not designed to eat from a spoon. Sara sat on an upturned five-gallon bucket, baby at her breast on one arm, phone tucked against her shoulder, feeding the penguin with her free hand. The bird shook drips from its beak after every spoonful, spattering mashed bottom fish onto cabinets, floor, Sara, and baby. On the stove, a pot of left-over stew bubbled. Gently steaming trays of bacon and huckleberry muffins on the warming shelf made Brad's stomach growl.

A wet blob dripped from Sara's hair onto Baby Craig's diaper. In the doorway, Sal giggled. Mac waved her back while Sara finished her call.

"They just got back. I'll tell them... Okay. Love you."

Brad took the phone receiver, untangled the long cord from a chair, and hung it up.

"Thanks." Sara smiled. "Everyone got hungry at once, and then Mom called – from the hospital."

"We came back to call her," Mac said, taking over the spoon feeding. "Couldn't get near the place."

Sara took the towel Brad offered and moved to a chair, wiping fish gurry off Baby Craig. "Molly's not there now, anyway. Life Flight's taking her to Portland, the university hospital, for multiple surgeries – fractured ankle, ulnus, ribs, and frontal bone, above her eye. Like they dropped her out a window, Grandma Rose says. What happened?"

"A three-hundred-pound robo-cop fell on her." Mac stuffed the last of the fish into the penguin's beak, describing the chaos in the courtroom.

"So there was no hearing?" Sara asked. "No one said what happened yesterday?"

"Never got a chance," Mac said. "I only know what Dumb Darryl could tell. Remember Darryl Denson? He's a county mountie now, moved back here after his wife died in Coos Bay. He says the three eyewitnesses are loggers, didn't give me their names. Their story is they went into the unit early to set up for cuttin' yesterday. Which they weren't supposed to 'cause of the court order, but no matter. They say they found Molly finishing off Howie with a splitting maul and she ran off when they tried to stop her. I know, it don't make no sense, but that's the story. They say they couldn't catch her, so they went back to their rig and radioed for the cops."

"But where was Molly?" Sara asked. "Obviously, the cops found her...."

"That's the crazy thing. Even Dumb Darryl can't figure this one. See, he was already halfway there – the ambulance right behind him – when these guys called nine-eleven. 'Cause an 'unidentified female' – had to be Molly, see – had already called in twenty-five minutes before. All they found at first was these three guys with blood all over 'em guarding Molly's car."

"Molly was in her car?"

Mac piled stew and bacon and muffins on a plate. He shook his head. "No. First off, Darryl and his squad had orders to wait until the chief came with the DA. He said that was weird, the DA never goes on an arrest, makes him a witness or something. Molly was waiting for them right next to Howie. Howie's body, I mean. And Darryl said she ran toward them – to the cops – like she was glad to see them. 'Til they – um – arrested her."

Mac glanced at Sal and skipped the next part of Darryl's account. "Always a bit slow scoping out a play, Darryl was. But give him the ball and there's no stopping him. His brain's in a twist over this one – the DA showing up, three guys all bloody, but Molly don't have a drop of blood on her, and then her camera missing – he don't know what to make of it."

Sara switched the baby to her other breast and reached out for Sal.

"Your mom's going to be all right, Sal. Grandma Rose says University Hospital's the best there is. And Marge is still up there. Grandma already talked to her." She glanced at Brad. "You remember Marge, don't you?"

Brad smiled. How could he forget? Marge was the only black person he'd met after moving here. A nurse with Sara and Grandma Rose at county hospital, Marge had often shared off-duty hours looking after Brad when Molly was in Portland with Sal. She had terrified Brad at first. She was big all over, with a voice to match and a booming laugh that changed channels on the TV remote. What won his heart was her unfeigned delight in his violin. Trained as an opera singer before going to nursing school, Marge brought sheet music of favorite arias to sing with him and taught him voice and breath control. When she'd left for a better job in Portland, he had missed her almost as much as Sara did.

"The nurses' underground at work," Sara laughed. "Grandma Rose'll be over as soon as she's off shift." She held Baby Craig against her shoulder, patting his back to bring up a burp. "Molly wouldn't let anyone touch her until Grandma wrote her a paper making Mac and me temporary guardians for you two. She had to sign it with her left hand. So they wouldn't put you in a foster home, see."

Chapter Nine

I hated this place when we first moved here. Now I can't think of ever living anywhere else. The house is small, one of two cabins this guy built eighty years ago as part of a beach resort on this headland sticking into the Pacific Ocean, then he died before he built any more. His grand-daughter inherited the place but she's never been here, just rents it out. She's an old lady herself and some day she'll die and it'll all be sold off for some godawful development, but for now there's just us, and Mac and Sara next door, on this whole wild place. I still haven't explored every inch of it, 'cause some of the property's even across the highway in steep woods where our water supply comes from. Last year Howie brought two geologists out to look at the rocks and cliffs and erosion potential as they called it, to make sure the rising sea level wouldn't drown us all. That's just like Howie, to worry about us like that. One of the geologists was a real looker, too. She made me think geology could be a fun trade if there's more like her in it.

—*The Oreo File*

Mac was six inches taller than Grandma Rose, but he never got over the impression that she towered over him. It was the way she stood, he thought, a command of herself that could wither a roomful of generals. A frontier toughness that once quelled macho logging camps now made her the terror of the county hospital, where even almighty doctors feared her wrath. To her patients, though, she was ever an avenging angel of mercy, fierce champion for their needs and comfort.

Typically, Grandma Rose had eyes for no one but the newest patient. News of Molly would have to wait. Mac watched her crouch beside the penguin, inspecting the injured wing and beak. In the sink an ice block full of smelt thawed under the running faucet. Brad pried one of the tiny fish loose and held it in a pan of warm water.

"Looks like it's healing fast," Grandma Rose said. "Can he move that wing, though?"

"Watch," Mac said. He drew a spoon from the dish rack and held it up. The penguin came alert, stretching toward the spoon, wings lifted, beak open. The injured wing rose only halfway.

"No full mobility yet," Grandma Rose said.

"Getting there," Mac insisted. "Last night it just dangled, he couldn't move it at all."

The penguin still stretched toward the spoon. Grandma Rose studied the beak. Only a raw spot on the underside remained from the fish hook puncture.

"No trouble eating?" she asked.

Mac laughed. "Only cleaning up the mess. We're trying him on whole fish now."

He took the thawed fish from Brad and dangled it in front of the bird. No reaction. Its eyes were still on the spoon. Mac brought the spoon closer. The beak gaped wide and he dropped the fish in. The penguin gulped, looked around in surprise, and stretched its beak toward the spoon again. Sal handed Mac another tiny fish. Mac dropped it in the open beak. Another gulp, and the spoon was forgotten. Fish after fish disappeared. After the tenth smelt, the penguin turned away and waddled back to Howie's boot. It preened itself and squirted a stream of whitish shit onto the floor. Brad grabbed paper towels to wipe it up.

"Looks good," Grandma Rose said. "Soon as he can lift that arm all the way, you can turn him loose with his pals."

"But they're gone," Brad said. "We looked this morning."

"They'll be back," Sal said firmly. "They won't go far without the Admiral."

"The Admiral?"

"Well, we have to call him something."

"How do you know it's a him?" Brad asked.

"Doesn't matter, does it?" Sal said. "Admirals can be hims or hers."

Grandma Rose settled in a kitchen chair, taking Baby Craig on her lap. She lifted an eyebrow and Baby Craig smiled. She wiggled both eyebrows, smiling back at him.

"I talked to Marge," she said, speaking as if to Baby Craig alone. "There's a paper in my bag there, Sara. It gives you and Mac power of attorney and names you guardians. Take it to the bank tomorrow and sign it with a notary."

She looked up at Sal and Brad. "No point sugar-coating it, kids. Your mama's in critical condition. Not just broken bones. Her lungs were punctured. She's on a respirator – a breathing machine."

Sal carried the bag of half-thawed smelt to the refrigerator and set it carefully on the bottom shelf. She turned to Grandma Rose, her face deceptively expressionless.

"Will she die?"

"Not yet. But no promises," Grandma Rose said.

Sal stood by the open refrigerator, face pale, blue lines shadowing her mouth and eyes. Sara started toward her, but Mac held her back. Sal's eyes found Brad's, and Mac felt something unseeable flash between them. Sal closed the fridge and faced Grandma Rose.

"Okay," she said. "Now what?"

"She can't talk, mind you, but she made Marge promise to tell you a few things." Grandma Rose pulled a scrap of paper from her pocket. "Molly's orders. School. Music. Baseball. Swimming."

"In other words, keep on keeping on," Sara said. "I'll take you to swimming practice, Sal. But you'll be on your own, Brad."

He nodded. He had his bike. In many ways, he'd been on his own for a long time.

"And one more thing." Grandma Rose consulted the paper again. "You're to look in the third drawer of Molly's desk for a brown envelope."

The envelope was at the bottom of a full drawer, beneath a chronological stack of childhood papers. Brad carefully lifted out plastic sheet protectors covering school photos, recital programs, childish drawings, clippings of Brad's Little League games and Sal's swimming triumphs, team photos, crayoned birthday cards they'd made for Molly. He held up a cover page from the Oregonian with two large color photos at the top: Sal four years ago with an orange stocking cap covering her bald head, and Joe in a similar hat with holes cut out for his ears.

Sal snorted at the headline, "Mystery Horse and Miracle Child Go Home." Brad slid the clipping back into the pile and pulled the brown envelope from the bottom. It was full, but nearly weightless. He carried it to the kitchen, placed it on the table. The envelope was softened with age, a coffee cup stain in one corner. There was nothing written on the front. On the back flap, in Howie's distinctive, small printing, were the words: "When I am dead."

Brad glanced at Sal. She nodded. He pried the metal clasp up and ran his finger under the glued strip, careful not to tear the writing. The flap opened, spilling feathers all over the table. Owl feathers, Brad thought, hundreds of them, some white, some barred with brown and gold with downy edges, buoyant as spider's silk. The slightest breath sent them fluttering around the room; one landed in Grandma Rose's coffee.

A feather for each wind that blows. Where had those words come from? Brad slid some papers from the envelope in another cascade of feathers. Howie's discharge from the Marines. Two laminated, yellowed newspaper clippings, obituaries of his father and mother in Flushing, N.Y. And a note in Howie's writing on Coastal News stationary:

> Molly –
> I will disappear when the dragon wakes. This is the way I want it.
> You and the kids are all the family I have. Everything worth saving is already yours.
>
> Love and all that shit –
> Howie

Beneath the note, yellowed scotch tape held a scrap of newsprint:

> When I am dead, cry for me a little.
> Think of me sometimes, but not too much.
> It is not good for you or your wife or your husband or your children to allow your thoughts to dwell too long on the dead.
> Think of me now and again as I was in life, in some moment which is pleasant to recall, but not for long.
> Leave me in peace, as I shall leave you, too, in peace.
> While you live, let your thoughts be with the living.
>
> —Ishi, the last Yahi-Yana

From the bottom of the envelope, Brad drew a small key, stuck to scotch tape that had peeled from the note paper. That was all.

"What's it for?" Sal asked, taking the key.

"Looks like a safe deposit key," Grandma Rose said. "You know, at the bank."

"But why?" Brad stared at the discharge papers, the obituaries, the strange note in Howie's writing. The key. The poem. The feathers still drifting about the room. "What does it all mean?"

Sal dropped the key into his hand. "It means he's dead."

Silently, Brad stuffed the key and papers back in the envelope and tried to collect the feathers. Sal helped, but it was hopeless. For every handful they managed to collect, an equal number floated away. One drifted into a spider web above the window. A harvester spider darted out, ran its delicate forelegs over the feather, then retreated, jabbing its forelegs in the air like an angry politician. Sal laughed.

Brad glared at her, but she didn't notice. He put the envelope back in Molly's drawer and carefully replaced the stack of papers on top of it. How could she laugh? Howie was dead, for chrissake. Howie. *A feather for each wind that blows.* Had Howie said that? Yes. Probably quoting something. But what? The memory gnawed at him, elusive and irritating.

Sullenly, he followed Sal and the others outside and up the path to the headland, ignoring Joe's friendly nudges.

"Well, goddamn," he heard Mac shout. "They're all back!"

Brad ran to catch up, feathers forgotten. Grandma Rose, her graying hair torn loose from its bun by the wind, stood silently beside him, staring down in wonder.

Below them, four penguins played on a natural water slide. One at a time they rode waves onto the rock ledge and tobogganed back down it, popping back on the next wave for another round.

"Told you!" Sal crowed.

Brad grinned. "The Tempest!" he shouted.

* * *

Molly drifted lazily in and out of consciousness. She dreamed of sleep and seagulls. At one point the gulls spoke in human voices – angry human voices—far overhead.

"Chain her to the friggin' bed? What is this, the Spanish Inquisition?"

"Standard DOC procedure, doctor. Sir."

"DOC – whatever the fuck that is – slaps chains on multiple fractures? Over an open thoracic incision?"

"Department of Corrections regulations, sir."

"Not in my ward, not on my patient."

Molly heard clanking, a man grunting, voices fading. A door closing. The seagulls returned, singing a chorus from Figaro.

Chapter Ten

I was almost five years old when Sal was born and had to have all those surgeries on her heart. Mom and I went to the hospital every day but they wouldn't let little kids up to the surgery so I had to wait in the lobby where the lady at the desk could watch me. One day there was a kid just outside the lobby doors, playing a violin. He was probably about my age now, but he seemed really old to me, a skinny white kid with longish hair, wearing a Hawaiian shirt tucked into blue jeans, just an ordinary kid, except the music he was pouring out. I hung out by that door, watching his fingers on the strings and the way he tilted the bow, moving it so fast. When the desk lady was busy I slipped outside to hear better. It was cold, with an icy wind out there, but I didn't care, just stood and listened and watched. He had his violin case open on the step and people had dropped money in it. He must'a been cold, but he kept playing. And then he played this tune that went right into my brain and heart, I wanted it to go on forever. When it ended he grinned at me.

"Any requests?" he said.

I couldn't speak at first, but finally I said to play it again, that last song. So he did, and it hummed into me all over again, every magic note. Then he asked if I wanted another song and I shook my head, keeping the notes alive inside. He raked the money into his pocket and started to pack his violin away, and I was afraid he'd go away and leave me.

"How do you do it?" I made myself say.

He looked surprised, like no one had ever asked him that before. He looked around and asked where my folks were.

"In there," I told him. "My sister has a hole in her heart."

"Just for a minute, then," he said, and we went inside and sat on the floor by a big fake plant. He took out the violin and showed it to me, naming the strings and plucking them softly. G-D-A-E. He took my left hand and showed me how each finger had a string, a note. The whole universe turned into the magic of making those notes. G-D-A-E. He took out his bow and tightened it, and showed me how to hold it and how to place the violin on my left shoulder. It was too big for me to reach the strings, so he held up the neck and let me play each string with the bow. G-D-A-E.

"You need a half-size," he said. "But here, we can make a melody. What songs do you know?" He named some songs and when he said "Aunt Rhody" I nodded. He pressed each string and named which one to bow, and the notes came staggering out. We did it again, and this time he didn't even have to tell me which string. I was so excited I almost wet my pants.

"You're a natural, kid," he said.

—The Oreo File

Mac woke Brad and Sal before dawn. In the kitchen, he thrust steaming cups of coffee at them.

"Drink up, quick. We gotta get the Admiral outa here."

Sal glanced anxiously at the dark window.

"What for?" Brad asked. "What's the rush?"

"Sooner him and his buddies are on their way, the better," Mac said. He slapped the early edition of The Oregonian on the table. It was folded open to the Northwest News roundup. He pointed to a fuzzy telephoto of birds silhouetted on a rock. The caption read, "Controversy heats up over west coast penguin sightings."

"If that's the Admiral's bunch, they're popping up all along the coast – reports from Cape Perpetua up to Otter Rock."

Sal giggled, reading the story. "The state wants federal funds to protect them, and the feds say it's all a hoax, there are no penguins," she said, laughing.

"It's no joke," Mac said. "Just a matter of time 'til some asshole shoots one or catches 'em for a zoo."

"But the Admiral's wing....?" Sal asked.

"It'll get stronger if he's using it," Mac said. "Move out, now. I already lost a whole day's work yesterday."

"Hey!" Brad shouted. He pulled the discarded main section closer. "Did you see this?"

It was the lead story, headlined, "Maul-murder suspect injured in courtroom escape attempt." The man they had seen in the courtroom, the one Mac said was the district attorney, stared solemnly from a two-column photo.

"I can't believe it! Listen to this," Brad said, reading aloud. "'The arraignment hearing of a suspect in the brutal slaying of FBI agent Howard Borstal erupted in violence and gunfire Tuesday morning. Molly Matthissen, the local videographer accused of killing Borstal in a contested logging unit, was seriously injured in a foiled escape attempt. The suspect was flown by Life-Flight helicopter to University Hospital in Portland for treatment of extensive injuries...'"

Speechless, Mac and Sal crowded over the paper to read along with him.

"How can they say this?" Brad smacked the paper. "The place was full of reporters! They were right there!"

"They were all hiding under the pews," Sal said.

Mac reread the beginning. "No by-line. No reporter's name. And why this asshole's picture?"

"You said he's running for re-election," Brad said. "Prob'ly wrote the story himself."

Mac glanced out at the brightening sky. "You might be right at that. But we gotta get the Admiral moving before the rest of 'em ship out."

The Admiral had other ideas. He stood worshipfully at the sink, waiting for fish, oblivious to their attempts to move him. Mac fed him a couple of smelt. When he turned to shuffle back to Howie's boot, Sal snatched it and walked slowly through the door, dangling the boot. The Admiral followed, hopping down the porch steps and across the yard, his eyes on the boot. Mac and Brad fell in behind them, trailed by Joe with Bertha on his back.

At the cliff edge, the four penguins stood on their ledge, dark shapes in the grey dawn light. Sal hopped slowly down the rocks, the Admiral following. When she reached the penguins' ledge, she stopped. The Admiral forgot his boot and waddled forward to stand with his crew. Sal climbed back up to watch with Mac and Brad.

The waves grew brighter with the dawn. A line of cormorants flew toward the dark western horizon. Bertha flapped heavily from Joe's back and flew north over the bay. The Admiral leaped abruptly off the ledge and swam westward. One by one, the others followed.

"He's swimming!" Sal crowed. "He's okay!"

"One worry down," Mac said. "Back to the grind, guys. I'm late already."

Brad barely heard him. He stared at the ocean long after the birds' heads disappeared in the rippling shadows. A hollow ache of grief spread from his stomach to his throat. Sal, hugging the boot, bounced beside him. He turned on her in rare irritation.

"Hey, we did something right," she said. "He'd be dead by now if we hadn't."

He saw the tell-tale tears in her eyes, though, and suddenly understood her urge to dive in and swim after the birds. Grudgingly, he let her lift his arm in a farewell wave to the Admiral.

* * *

Alone in the smoke hole behind the school, Joey inspected the cache of cigarettes he'd borrowed from teachers' coats in the staff room. He selected a Camel filter from the health teacher's pocket and admired it briefly before lighting up. Half hour until lunch recess, and the rain had stopped, for the moment at least. He settled luxuriously on the cushion of pine needles, sipped from a steaming mug of staff room coffee, and spread out the custodian's Oregonian.

The front page story about Brad's mom puzzled him. In all the talk at Dinkum's yesterday, no one had mentioned an escape. And they were all reporters, they'd been in the courtroom. He finished the continuation on an inside page and turned back to Page One to see if he'd missed something.

Joey looked up, alarmed, all sensors on full alert. He peered into the huckleberry and salal bushes that ringed the clearing, then turned toward the trail that circled the base of the steep ridge behind the school. A sparrow flew across the trail, a spray of berry vines trembled. Joey thought of the cat and stood up, watching the bushes. A small girl stumbled onto the trail. Her shirt was torn, and broken thorns protruded like porcupine quills from her jeans and knitted orange cap. Scratches oozed blood on her arms and cheek. Her pale face had a bluish tinge. Joey recognized her. Brad's little sister, the one who won prizes on the county swim team. He couldn't remember her name. She stared blankly past him, her mouth and throat throbbing like a beached fish. Her eyes rolled up behind the lids, and he caught her as she fell.

Joey sank to his knees, propping her against his arm. With his free hand he pulled the precious Camel from his mouth, spit on the lit end, and stuck it behind his ear. He cocked his head over her mouth, holding his breath to feel hers. In growing panic, he thumped her back. He'd seen an EMT training film one cold night at the fire house, where he'd gone to keep warm. Mouth to mouth something. He shuddered at the thought and thumped her again.

"Hey," he said. "Hey, breathe!"

A short, rasping breath shook her. Her eyes opened. Joey let out his own breath and grinned at her. Another gasping breath. He breathed with her in encouragement, patting her softly on the back. Slowly, the blue faded from her face. He stood and helped her to the smoke hole. Sat her down and held the mug of coffee to her mouth. She swallowed a little; the wheezing subsided into normal breaths. Joey sank back, relieved, but her eyes stared past him, registering nothing. He waited, uncertain, afraid to leave her to get help.

She must have hiked all the way from the grade school, he thought, two miles away up Ridge Road, past the dump. He glanced at the newspaper, its glaring headline, and shoved it quickly behind him with his foot.

He waved a hand in front her face. "Brad?" he said. "You want Brad?" She turned to him, her eyes finding him now. She nodded.

"I'll get him, then."

Joey stood up, still uncertain about leaving her.

"You be okay?"

She nodded again. Tears welled in her eyes, streaking the bloody scratches on her face. He placed the mug of coffee in front of her, found the comic section of the paper and set it by the coffee. The main section he stuffed under his shirt. She didn't notice. He crouched to make sure she was breathing.

"Getting Brad," he announced, louder this time. "Sure you're okay?"

She hiccoughed, nodded. Joey ran.

Brad was just leaving algebra when Joey rounded the hall corner and grabbed his sleeve. Brad shook him off, turning toward the cafeteria.

"Your sister," Joey said.

Brad stopped. Joey had never spoken to him before. He never spoke to anyone, as far as Brad knew. "Sal? Where?"

"Out back. C'mon."

Joey darted back against the lunch break tide, Brad close behind him. Sal sat where Joey had left her, the coffee mug untouched. Soft rain spattered on the comic section. She wobbled to her feet at sight of Brad.

"Sal! What's up? School out early?"

She glared at him, fists clenched, ignoring Joey.

"Never," she said, her voice rasping. "Never. Ever. Going. Back."

The wheezing started again. Brad picked her up. "Okay, okay. Let's go home, then."

He started down the trail toward town. Joey followed. They took turns carrying her along back streets and four miles of Highway 101,

Joey silent, Brad humming scales. The rain grew to a downpour. The last mile, Sal fell asleep in Joey's arms, breathing peacefully, Brad's jacket draped over her. Joey stopped when Brad opened the gate to their driveway to let him through. He handed Sal over and turned back toward town.

"Hey, Joey!" Brad called. Joey kept walking, not looking back. Brad shrugged. "Hey, thanks, man," he called.

* * *

Sara's kitchen was warm and smelled of applesauce. Rain streaked the windows, rattling on the glass in wind gusts. Brad sat at the table, watching the timer.

"Take the cake out and set it on the rack when the timer goes off," Sara had said. She'd taken Sal from him when he carried her in, both drenched, and gotten right in the shower with her. Of course Baby Craig had immediately woken up, wanting his mama. Brad could hear the shower running; steam seeped through the bathroom door and fogged the windows. In his lap, Baby Craig stirred, whimpered a little. How do you get a cake out of the oven with a baby in your arms? He checked the timer again. Ten minutes left.

The baby's whimpering threatened to escalate to full-blown cry. Brad held him to his chest and hummed softly, which had no effect.

Babies like a good, strong beat." Howie, holding a much tinier Baby Craig, bopping vigorously and singing Cajun tunes, his feet flying.

Tentatively, Brad sang "Men of Harlech," rocking in his chair. The crying subsided. He got to his feet, singing, swaying, heel, toe, to "Soldier's Joy," "Mairie's Wedding," danced giant steps to "Walkin' on the Moon." So long as he kept singing, Baby Craig slept; he stirred and whimpered when the singing stopped. Like the girl in the red shoes, Brad thought. Sweating, he started one of Howie's silly songs, a reggae tune. "Oh de papa rana and de granpa rana, de auntie rana and de tadpole rana...." He paused, trying to remember the words, and Baby Craig bellowed. He skipped to another verse. "But de mama rana, Mama

Rana Madonna, wish to be a manatee, tadpoles at her mammary…."

He never heard the timer wailing. Sara bundled Sal into the kitchen wrapped in a huge terry-cloth robe and rescued the cake. She poured a mug of hot chocolate for Sal, laughing at Brad's frantic efforts. He was pounding the floor now, belting it out. "Sing in the spring, sing in the fall, sing when I hear my baby bawl…." Sara relieved him of the baby and sat down to nurse. Brad collapsed in a chair and wiped his forehead.

"Babies are damn hard work." He grinned tentatively at Sal. "You okay now?"

Sal nodded.

"So what happened?" Brad asked.

Sal cringed, pulled herself together. "Kids talking. About Mom and… and…."

"And what?"

Sal choked. "The … the gas chamber."

"Little ghouls," Brad said. "Who? Who said it?"

"Lots of 'em. Mostly Frankie, though. Frankie Caner. He was telling everybody things…."

"Who the hell's Frankie Caner, then?" Brad demanded.

Sal looked stunned. "He's … he thinks he knows everything. His mother's a Fallwell and his dad – his dad's who – you know, the one in the court Mac said was Mom's lawyer."

"Assholes," Brad said. "Don't listen to 'em, Sal."

"And how would they know anything, anyway?" Sara said. She lifted Baby Craig to her shoulder to burp him and frowned at something outside the window. "Oh, no. What are they doing here?"

A cop car pulled up the driveway. Two cops got out. One was Dumb Darryl. He had a plastic shower cap over his hat. Sara handed Baby Craig back to Brad and went out, shutting the door. Brad and Sal stood at the window and watched. Sara planted herself in the front path, her housecoat instantly soaked and clinging to her skin. The two cops spoke to her, their eyes turning to the window when she answered. Dumb Darryl said something else and Sara interrupted him, her back stiffening, the creases in her dress spreading like river deltas. The cops shifted their weight in the mud. They backed up a few steps and nodded. Turning to leave, they tipped their hats at Sara. Darryl's hand snared the plastic shower cap and knocked cap and hat into the mud. He dived to snag the hat before it landed and belly-flopped on top of the hat. Sal giggled.

Sara stood, rigid, while Darryl picked up the flattened, muddy headgear and followed his partner to the car. She didn't move until the car was gone.

"Jerks. Imbeciles!" Sara wrapped a towel around her soaked head. "Don't believe Sal's here. Want to come in and see for themselves. Like I don't know who's in my own house."

The school, she said, had belatedly noticed Sal's absence and called the police. Sara had little good to say about school administrators, either. After warming up a platter of lasagna and garlic bread for their lunch, she packed up Baby Craig and left. Sal was trouncing Brad at Parcheesi when Sara came back.

"Brad, Sal's school books are in the car. So are yours. You're both schooling at home until further notice." She killed Brad's interruption at birth. "Coach'll call you when the field's dried out enough for practice."

Brad shrugged. The way the weather changed, there might be no baseball season at all. Sal's relief was plainly visible. Sara put the sleeping Baby Craig in his perambulator and slapped herself on the forehead.

"Omigosh, Brad, I forgot. Marge called earlier with a message from Molly. Your recital, it's tonight, remember? Mac'll take you."

Brad fled to the silent house next door. Howie's boot lay by the door where Sal had left it after the penguins swam off. Alone in the kitchen, Brad tuned his violin and set up the music stand to catch up on two days' lost practice; it felt like two years since he'd played. Last time he'd picked up his violin, Howie had been alive, adding chords and runs that Boccherini never dreamed of. He took a long breath, exhaled slowly, and lifted his bow. Once it hit the strings the world outside ceased to exist.

He was struggling over a tricky passage, playing it over and over, dissatisfied, when he heard, as soft and natural as ever, Howie's guitar catching the grace note he'd been missing. Without thinking, Brad picked up the grace note and kept going. The guitar stayed with him, faint but sure to the end. Brad lowered his bow. In fear and wild hope, he turned around. It wasn't Howie sitting there, but Sal. Howie's guitar was on her lap, its neck propped against the table. An amazed, proud smile lit her face.

"Jesus H. Roosevelt," Brad said. "When the hell did you learn that?"

"I didn't, really. Howie showed me a few things, you know, but never this. I just got used to hearing him play with you." Sal's fingers danced a run lightly on the strings. "And – I don't know what happened, I came in and you were going over and over those slurs, missing the same note, and I just picked up his guitar and – it's – it's like it played itself."

Brad heard the catch in her voice. "Cool," he said quickly. "Let's do it again."

They worked together on the Boccherini all afternoon until Joe began snorting for his walk. Sal fell asleep halfway through dinner. Mac took Brad to the recital without her. He didn't miss that grace note, or any other.

Chapter Eleven

"You're a natural, kid," he said.

G-D-A-E.

I wanted to play it again, play it forever, but he packed the violin and bow carefully in their case. "I gotta go."

I was just a little kid. I started crying. He crouched down by me. "Tell your ma to get lessons for you. Then you can play every day. All day. All night. Forever."

He patted my back and was gone. I never saw him again or even knew his name. When Mom came down I was still sitting by the fake plant, humming. G-D-A-E. She picked me up and sat on a shiny couch there in the lobby, hugging me, half laughing, half crying.

"Sal's going to be all right, Brad. She's going to make it," she said. I couldn't answer, just held on to her, humming. "Are you okay, hon?" She held me away to look at me.

"G-D-A-E." I sang each note. She must'a thought I was round the bend. I told her about the kid with the violin. "He said they make smaller violins, too, for little kids, and Mom, he said there's lessons, to teach how to play it."

Mom was so happy about Sal's heart she would'a promised me the moon. And she didn't forget, even when my fake dad yelled that violin was for sissies and faggots, whatever they were. I didn't care. I was still holding those notes in my head, just waiting for strings to play them on. By the time Sal came home from the hospital, I had a half-size violin and two lessons a week, and it was all 'cause of Sal being born with a hole in her heart in that hospital where a kid played violin for handouts. Sal looked like a salamander and took a lot of Mom's trouble, but I thought she was the best thing ever happened to me.

—The Oreo File

Molly woke only enough to be grateful for the drugs that put her back to sleep. Marge had warned her about the discomforts of a respirator, but discomfort came nowhere near the terrifying sense of choking to death the machine caused. The drugs that suppressed her gag reflex seemed to seal her eyelids, too. Even in her half-waking spells, she had trouble opening her one good eye. She needed few visual cues to follow the drama taking place around her that evening, though.

After seven hours of surgery and two of post-op tension, Dr. Samuel Kahn had little patience for the minions of law. The two Multnomah cops hired by Branscombe County to guard his patient he just managed to tolerate; they sat outside the ICU doorway, carefully keeping out of everyone's way. Molly only dimly remembered Kahn's earlier run-in with a special deputy trying to chain her to the bed. In fact, she wondered if that had been a dream until the new visitor, a Branscombe detective sergeant, arrived and Kahn lost what little patience he had left.

"A tape recorder! Are you out of your fuckin' mind?"

The same voice, Molly thought. Same profanity. The chains weren't a dream, then. Her surgeon sounded more like a logger or long-haul trucker. For some reason, she found this immensely pleasing. She tried to open her eye and failed.

The detective continued to fiddle with dials on his equipment. "DA's orders, doc," he said.

"The DA's orders?"

On a tray table next to Molly, the tape recorder hummed indifferently. Fuzzily, Molly wondered what it could possibly record, since the respirator prevented her from speaking at all. The only voices being recorded were Dr. Kahn's and the detective's. Kahn lowered his voice, speaking directly toward the mike. "Not in my surgery, buster. Get that thing out of here. Now."

Molly forced her good eye open half-way, in time for the fun part. The detective was standing his ground, stolid and unyielding, bloated with authority. He had seriously misjudged his opponent. Kahn nodded to the nurse who had moved into position. She pulled the plug on the recorder. Kahn picked it up, wires dangling, and thrust it into the detective's hands.

"Out. Now."

The detective opened his mouth to speak. Kahn didn't wait for any words. He picked the man up and carried him to the door, shutting it behind him on a trailing mike cable. The cable snapped. Kahn opened the door again and kicked the cable end out.

"That's county property!" the detective protested.

Kahn raised his voice enough for the entire nurses'station to hear. "Mister, this here is hospital property and you are trespassing. You're also contaminating a sterile environment, jeopardizing a patient's welfare, impeding surgical procedure, violating physician-patient confidentiality, disturbing other patients, seriously pissing off a surgeon, and you can take your county property and stuff it up your a....anatomy."

Kahn closed the door and turned to his patient. Molly's eye closed and she faded out again. He shrugged. "Jesus. What the hell was that about, anyway?"

"He showed up and said it was national security," the nurse said. "Staff didn't know what to do so they called me, and I paged you."

"National security? Taping an unconscious post-op patient? On a friggin' respirator? I never heard of such a thing. Is it even legal?"

"No," the nurse said. "I called administration, the legal department. They said no way, not without a court order. And they'd never heard of any court ordering such a thing."

"Fucking cops." Kahn looked at the nurse appreciatively. Her face, black and impassive under the white cap, was stern, but the eyes held a hint of mischief. She was certainly big enough to throw out any detective that came along. "Margaret," he read from her name tag.

"Marge, doctor," she said. "Just plain Marge."

His eyes met hers, and a fleeting, boyish grin lit up Kahn's face. Then he frowned, studying the monitors, the small, damaged figure on the bed.

"National security?" He shook his head. "What'd she do, blow up a public toilet?"

"Murder," Marge said. "They say she killed that FBI agent. On the coast." She rubbed the tray table with a sterile wipe. "But she didn't," she hissed.

"Oh?" Kahn looked at her, eyebrows raised.

"I know this lady. Her neighbor's my best friend, we took care of her boy." Marge's face glowed with the memory. "That child! I never met a prodigy before."

"Prodigy?" Kahn wondered what connections his addled brain was missing.

"Violin," Marge said, as if that explained everything. She looked at his puzzled face and laughed softly. "Besides, she told me. Tried to tell me, anyways. It's some kind of frame-up."

"Jesus," Kahn said. "They got that on tape?"

"No way. This was before, when the chopper brought her in. She tried to write it down for me, with her left hand."

Kahn's pager buzzed. "Shit," he said. "Okay. Call me if there's any change, any at all, or if that asshole comes back. And no one, not god himself, gets in here. Who's on tonight?"

Marge drew herself up as if to salute. "Marge Taylor, doctor. Twenty-four seven. I'm having a cot brought in."

Kahn nodded. On his way to the door he pulled the plug of the patients' phone from the wall jack. "Just in case," he said.

"Doctor?" Marge asked.

He paused in the doorway.

"She wants Brad. Her son."

"The prodigy?" He smiled. "Good. Get him up here soon as she's stable."

The door closed. Marge pulled a cell phone from her pocket and punched a well-used number.

* * *

Mac sat in the back of the recital hall. He kept his jacket on over the sawdust and grime of his work clothes. The hall was filled with parents and relatives, all dressed as if for church. Mac had never been to a recital. He'd supposed it to be like a night at Dinkum's and was unpleasantly surprised by the tense formality of the affair. He dozed through an interminable hour of small, terrified children dressed in miniature suits and satin dresses, mechanically sawing through Twinkle variations, each punctuated by polite, muted applause. He woke up a little when the older children played more complicated tunes. They stood stiffly in prescribed position, faces intent and determined. Some of them were quite good, he thought, noting the expanded applause.

When Brad ambled up onto the stage, Mac sat up. So did many in the audience, though not for the same reason. Unlike the formal dress of the others, Brad wore a brilliant orange and red Hawaiian shirt and clean, faded khaki pants. He stood center stage for a moment, ignoring the audience, then took a deep breath and lowered his bow. For the next seven and a half minutes, Mac grinned non-stop at an audience being treated to a Dinkum's experience. No formal position for Brad, Mac saw. His feet tapped beats, his body became an instrument, swaying, stretching, flowing, pouring itself into every note from the strings. His eyes focused on some invisible galaxy, and the frowns and smiles that flitted across his face had no target. He finished on an upbow, frozen for a moment in the spotlight, startled by the audience rising to its feet, whistling, stomping, clapping. Nodding briefly in embarrassment, Brad strode off the stage and up the aisle, followed by girls – and a few boys – clamoring to speak to him, touch him.

Oblivious to the uproar and the small crowd surrounding him, Brad crouched beside Mac, carefully placing his violin in its case. He held up his bow, inspecting it; hairs had sprung loose in his performance, and he frowned.

"Have to get it re-haired again," he said to Mac.

"His bow needs re-hairing," a girl echoed reverently, as if he'd made a profound statement.

"Jesus. I'm out of here," Brad said, and was gone. Mac made his way through the adoring crowd and followed him.

* * *

In his truck, Mac turned on the wipers to clear a heavy dew and pulled onto the highway. Beside him, Brad slumped wordlessly in his seat belt, staring at his hands. Mac, still high on the performance, glanced at him.

"You sure knocked their socks off, pal."

"Oh sure," Brad snorted. "I fucked up that first repeat, big time."

"Can't say I noticed," Mac said. "Bet no one else did, either."

"Oh, them." Brad snorted again. "Well, I sure as hell noticed."

Mac glimpsed his tormented face in the flashes of bridge lights. He really hasn't a clue, Mac thought, amazed. Not the slightest clue how his playing affects people. He doesn't even care, somehow. Secretly, Mac felt privileged just to be driving him tonight; he smiled, imagining the kid's snort of incredulity at the very idea.

The turn-off for Dinkum's lay just ahead. "Hungry?" Mac asked. "Wanna stop for a bite?"

"Nah." Brad pulled himself out of his slump. "I mean, no thanks. I just want to be home." He crossed his arms, tucking his hands under his armpits. "God, I hate recitals."

* * *

Sara had waited up for them. Brad looked toward the empty couch.

"Where's Sal?"

Sara grinned at him sleepily and pointed next door, where a soft light glowed in the kitchen window.

"She's home – alone?"

"Go look," Sara said.

Mac followed Brad over the fence, stumbling in the dark. At the back steps they stopped. On the porch, dimly lit from the kitchen window, four penguins stood in a row, heads under wings. Just inside the kitchen door they found the Admiral, asleep on Howie's boot. A block of frozen smelt was thawing in the sink. On a couch cushion next to the stove, Sal was curled up, fast asleep.

Chapter Twelve

After the day Ronald broke his ankle, I stayed as far as I could get from the Smear the Queer crowd. The game was always on, though, and the teachers sure didn't care, even when the mob busted little Joey Wire's arm and nose. Joey was a skinny foster kid in way-too-big clothes, the perfect prey. They ran away and left him in the dirt, and I wanted to hunt them all down and tear their guts out, but Joey was lying there bleeding and unconscious. I carried him into the office and the principal gave me detention for being late for class. Chief Roberts came with the ambulance and wanted to arrest me for assault and attempted murder.

Chief Roberts just plain hates me, see, ever since Mrs. Robinson at the drug store tried to make him arrest me for stealing a candy bar I'd already paid for. This time he thought he had me, but Joey woke up and told what happened. Even then the Chief wouldn't believe him 'til a secretary came in who saw the whole thing. And still no one ever stopped Smear the Queer.

—*The Oreo File*

Mrs. Frederick J. Robinson, sole proprietor, manager, and tyrant of Mallon's Drug Store and Sundries, found no greater pleasure in life than relentless seek and destroy missions against shoplifters. Her definition of the word included small children, non-Caucasians of any color, and anyone in tie-dyed clothing. She had a blind spot, however, which was good manners. Joey took full advantage of that flaw; in his mind, stealing everything possible from Mrs. Robinson was a solemn duty, irrevocably imposed the first time he'd entered the store.

He was nine years old at the time, small for his age, and newly arrived from Portland. Having exhausted all urban foster homes that would take him, Children's Services had sent him to a family on the coast; it might as well have been on Venus or Mercury. His first day in the new home, the foster mother had dragged him by the hand into Mallon's where he immediately gagged on the heavy odors of scented candles, soaps, and perfumes. Slipping away while she waited for a prescription, Joey had stood by the door, where he could breathe. Small, quiet, dressed in the obligatory new clothes provided by the state for every home change, he passed beneath Mrs. Robinson's radar. He watched a young couple with a toddler collect beach toys, paperbacks, sun-screen, towels, postcards, diapers, and other items, which they piled on the counter to Mrs. Robinson's fawning delight. They had gone to the back of the shop for something else when Joey saw Brad for the first time.

He didn't know Brad's name then, wouldn't learn it until school started. He saw a kid not much taller than himself, but pudgier. Brad came through the door, jingling change in his pocket, and carefully inspected the candy bars arranged next to the check-out counter. Joey noted his black skin and features with approval; the only one of countless foster homes that he remembered with fondness was a rowdy, crowded black family in Northeast Portland where he'd stayed almost a year before the socials decided it was racially inappropriate. The Webster's.

Staring at Brad, Joey felt a pang of homesickness. Pop Webster, a stone-deaf, one-legged veteran, kept two milk goats and ran a chop shop in a back shed with his older boys. It was there Joey learned before he was six to unlock and hotwire any vehicle and fix or tweak almost any mechanical problem. He had been dragged from the Webster's in tears; that was the last time he'd ever cried. The familiar appearance of a black kid in this strange new town was somehow comforting.

He watched the kid count his change and select a Hershey bar from the display marked fifty cents. Holding the candy in one hand, he placed a quarter, two dimes, and a nickel on the counter. Mrs. Robinson had picked up the phone when the kid walked in. She hung up and pointed to the Hershey bar in his hand.

"That's a dollar," she said.

Brad looked at the candy bar, backed up to look at the sign saying fifty cents. "But … the sign – I don't have …." He shrugged, moved to put the candy back on the shelf. Mrs. Robinson reached over the counter and grabbed his arm.

"Don't have a dollar? That's stealing, that is. I know your kind, boy. Know what we do with shoplifters here?"

Brad cringed, trying to free his arm. The door opened and the police chief walked in, a large man with a red face, his uniform bulging over his belt. He smelled of peppermint and aftershave. Joey sneezed. He backed against the door frame, watching. Behind Brad in the toy aisle, he saw the young husband, a beach ball in his arms, watching, too.

"Got another one, eh, Inez?" the police chief boomed. He pulled a pair of handcuffs from his belt and towered over Brad, who stood frozen. The chief took his arm and laughed at the candy bar in his hand. "Don't make nigger babies no more, eh, boy?"

"Pickaninnies," Mrs. Robinson said, disgusted.

The shopper and his wife appeared at the counter. They added the beach ball, a camera, a hair dryer, and a beach umbrella to the pile, which filled the counter. The police chief shoved Brad out of the way against the wall. Mrs. Robinson beamed at the young couple and began ringing up their purchases. They smiled back at her. She read out the total.

"Oh, one more thing," the man said. He picked a Hershey bar from the fifty-cent shelf. "How much are these?" he asked.

"Fifty cents," Mrs. Robinson said automatically. She rang it up and read out the new total.

The man looked at the coins Brad had put on the counter, then at Brad in the grip of the chief. "I believe that young man was here first," he said loudly. "This is his fifty cents."

His wife, holding the toddler, smiled sweetly at Mrs. Robinson.

"Yes, it is. I saw him pay for it."

Joey saw Mrs. Robinson's smile petrify. She glared at the police chief, who released Brad's arm. Brad walked hesitantly back to the counter, welcomed by the smiling couple.

"Be sure you get a receipt for that, son," the man said. He and his wife, still smiling, watched Mrs. Robinson bang out a receipt and slap it on the counter. The man put his hand on Brad's shoulder. He turned to his wife. "I think, dear, since prices seem so uncertain here, perhaps we don't want anything after all?"

His wife nodded. From where Joey stood, he saw her wink at Brad. The man bowed slightly to Mrs. Robinson and the chief. "Thank you both for an illuminating experience," he said. He and his wife walked out of the store, his hand still on Brad's shoulder. Joey saw them shake hands with Brad and then drive off in a car with British Columbia plates. Joey didn't think Brad saw him at all that day, never showed a sign of recognition when school started that fall. But Joey never forgot. From that day on, Mrs. Robinson and her store were in play.

He stood patiently now at the counter while an old man struggled through the task of paying. Joey had fished an empty pharmacy bag from the dumpster out back; it bulged now with unchecked merchandise. He set it unobtrusively on the floor. The man leaned heavily on the counter, dropping a cane from his left hand to dig through his pockets. His right arm hung uselessly; withered fingers curled like frozen parsnips from his sleeve. Joey picked up the cane and held it while the man scooped a handful of cash onto the counter, anxiously sorting through it. A quarter and a dime spun to the floor and Joey picked them up, returning them to the counter.

Behind the register, Mrs. Robinson tapped her fingers on the counter, irritation oozing through a forced smile. Her eyes never met the old man's, too busy scanning the aisles for shoplifters or idle clerks. There were fewer clerks every week, Joey knew; even the most desperate found other work as fast as they could. The old man handed over his selection of bills and coins at last, then dropped a twenty trying to stuff the rest back in his pocket. Joey picked it up and held it out to him along with the cane.

"Thank you, son," the old man said. He reached for his two pharmacy bags and dropped the cane again.

"Can I carry those for you, sir?" Joey asked, handing back the cane.

"Kind of you, boy," the man said. He turned to Mrs. Robinson. "Most youngsters these days ..." he began, but she was already swooping around the counter toward a hapless girl shelving sunscreen. Joey picked up his own bag and carried it out along with the old man's purchases. He walked slowly to accommodate the old man's stiff-legged limp. Behind them as the door closed, Mrs. Robinson's shrill invectives drove another clerk to the employment office.

The man's car was a ten-year-old Chrysler. Joey recognized it with a twinge of guilt and a happy memory of Stephen Hawking. He sighed. In the old days – six months ago – a hot-wired car was Joey's ticket to a few weeks of real beds, clean sheets, and cooked meals. The detention center was crowded and grim, but it was warm, and a library lady brought a book cart around twice a week. It was she who had taught Joey to read, unwittingly escalating local car thefts as his literary horizons expanded. For Joey, each stolen car was vehicle to a new title, a new author, a glorious new world.

"Ah, the auld days, the daft days," he thought, words that Geordie crooned in the Scottish burr of someone called Harry Lauder. The old, daft days had ended when Joey moved into the feral cat's domain.

Joey had never met one of his actual victims before. He hid his discomfort in solicitude, holding the cane while the old man fumbled for his car keys. Joey scrambled for the loose change that spun across the sidewalk, and opened the driver's door. In a barely controlled fall, the man slumped onto the seat. With his left hand, he hoisted his right leg into the car. The ignition was on the right side of the steering column. Joey stood helpless, watching the man lurch sideways and twist his body to insert the key with his left hand. He pressed his knuckle against the start button while trying to turn the key. After several excruciating attempts, the car started.

The automatic transmission controls, Joey well remembered, were located between the front seats, to the man's right. The man twisted sideways again to place the cane and pharmacy bags on the passenger seat.

"How do you – um – drive?" Joey blurted.

"Slowly," the old man said. "And seldom. Once I get 'er in drive she stays there 'til we stop."

Joey closed the car door. The man fumbled in his pants pocket. Joey waited, in case more help was needed. He stared in horror at the crumpled bills the old man held out through the open window.

"For you, son," the man said. "And go tell your ma for me, tell her you was worth raising."

Joey shook his head, backing away. A five dollar bill fluttered to the ground from the wad in the man's hand. Joey picked it up, thrust it through the window onto the old man's lap, and ran. Behind the drug store, he snatched up the newspaper and bag of Dinkum's scraps he'd left on top of the dumpster bin earlier. Tucking his own pharmacy bag under his shirt, he ran on past the paint store, the subsidy housing, the ballfield where volunteers were cleaning up muck from last week's flood. He slowed only when the steep woods of the ridge hid the town behind him.

Inside the Dawson's Electric van, the cat waited for him, sitting on a down pillow Joey had retrieved from the dump. Joey's dark thoughts receded in relief. For a while after he had started the tetracycline, the cat had seemed to get worse, lying on Joey's bedroll all day, eating very little, too weak to run away when Joey came in. He had brought the pillow home when the infected eye began oozing pus on his blanket. The cat had been too sick to reject the new bed, and with every foray into the world Joey dreaded returning to find it dead. Now, miraculously, it was sitting up, washing its matted fur. The gory infection had subsided to marble dimensions; between the reddened, puffy lids, Joey could now see the gleam of an intact eye.

Joey separated choice meat scraps from the ox-tail bones in the Dinkum's bag and put a small portion in the cat's Wedgewood bowl. Sitting down cross-legged, he dumped his pharmacy haul on the floor of the van. The two packets of tetracycline would last another nine days. The medical encyclopedia in the library had recommended a ten-day course of antibiotic, but in his uncertainty about dosage, Joey had decided on fourteen days, just to be sure. He shook two capsules onto the cat's food and stirred it well. Before he finished stirring, the cat approached and began to eat. Tentatively, Joey stroked its back, touching the cat for the first time, feeling the bony ribs. The cat licked the bowl clean, but did not move away; it sat, allowing Joey to continue stroking it, then licked the bowl hopefully again. Joey laughed and gave it a second helping.

Giddy with relief at the cat's recovery, Joey sorted out the rest of his drug store haul. The two packs of Marlboroughs and box of condoms he stowed in his jacket pockets; these were for trade only, barter for information or favors from the townies or RIPs. The t-shirt with a whale on it saying "Welcome to the Oregon Coast" he folded and stuffed into his bedroll. He skimmed the blurbs on two fat paperbacks called "Dune" and "Tripwire" and set them carefully, spine out, on the shelf with his magazines.

Housekeeping done, Joey opened the last item from his haul, a ritual Hershey bar, and sat down with the morning paper. A small banner over the masthead proclaimed, "Retailers prepare for Harry Potter release next week, page D-1." Joey flipped to the D section eagerly, never noticing the front page headlines.

* * *

"Oh, shit." Brad spread the morning Oregonian on Sara's kitchen table. Sal leaned over his shoulder to look. The top front page headline read, "Antarctic visitors confirmed." A large color photo showed four penguins standing at attention on the rip-rap of North Jetty.

"Unusual birds sighted on the central Oregon coast have been positively identified as penguins. 'There is no doubt whatsoever. They are Emperor Penguins,' Dr. Saul M. Ellsworth, avian specialist at the Portland Zoo, told the Oregonian. 'This is unprecedented,' he said. 'No penguin species has ever been observed north of the equator.'"

An entire inside page displayed more photos of the birds in different locations, and of tourists with cameras crowding turnouts, bridges, and highway guard rails, stopping traffic. A boxed story reported the U.S. Coast Guard's dramatic sea rescue of a Terre Haute, Indiana, bank manager who was swept off a Seal Rock promontory while filming the birds; his three hundred dollar Nikon and accessories were not recovered, the article noted. A small photo at the bottom of the page, of a BBC-TV satellite van, accompanied a paragraph listing major networks en route to film the penguins. The last paragraph was a warning from Greenpeace and World Wildlife Fund that the birds might be protected under international Antarctic treaties.

"Shit," Brad said again. "This Cornell institute wants to capture them. So does Waterworld in California. The Admiral's all healed up, why the hell don't they head out and keep going?"

Wherever the birds went during the day – and they seemed to roam widely – they returned every evening, following the Admiral to the Matthissens' porch; the Admiral filled up on smelt and slept on Howie's boot by the door. In the morning after a smelt breakfast he led his troops back to the cliff and out to sea.

"It's the Admiral," Sal said. "He looks okay, but I don't think he swims fast enough to catch his own food yet."

Sara laughed. "Or he's discovered the free lunch."

Sal pulled the front page closer and pointed to a headline near the bottom. "Maul murder autopsy reports HIV."

"This says Howie had HIV. That's AIDS – – what gay people get, isn't it?"

Brad read the brief article. Blood tests had found Howie positive for HIV, and the three loggers "exposed while trying to save him" would be tested for the virus. An unnamed FBI spokesman had no comment.

Brad skimmed the article again.

"You think it's true?" Sal asked. "I mean, they say he's an FBI agent and I know that's a lie."

"I don't know," Brad said. "I mean, there's other ways, transfusions and stuff, to get AIDS...."

Sara glanced at the article, then at Brad. "But Howie is – was – gay, you know," she said.

Brad stared at her. "Howie? No way!"

"It was no secret," Sara said gently. "But he was afraid of your reaction. Afraid you'd think less of him."

Brad looked away, avoiding her eyes. Howie had been right, he knew, which made him think less of himself.

"Well, he could wear dresses, I wouldn't care," Sal announced, "or feather boas even, that still doesn't make him an FBI agent."

Brad gaped at her a moment, then laughed.

* * *

Marge stood beside the hospital bed, holding the newspaper up between traction bars and IV tubes so Molly could see the penguin photos while Marge read aloud. Around the bandages covering her damaged eye, Molly squinted at the pictures, then went rigid. Monitors beeped alarms. Marge dropped the paper on the floor and buzzed for Dr. Kahn.

The next few minutes were a flurry of re-inserting tubes, adjusting air flow, calculating dosages. Fighting the medication Kahn had added to her IV, Molly made writing motions with her left hand. Marge handed her a pen and held a clipboard up for her. "Paper," Molly scrawled shakily. "Pics."

"The penguin story?" Marge asked. Molly nodded. Marge picked up the paper and held it up again. Molly jabbed the pen at one of the photos.

"Save," she wrote.

"We'll save the whole damn thing," Marge said.

Molly tried to smile. Marge slipped the newspaper into an x-ray envelope and placed it in the bedside cabinet. Molly was trying to write again, her hand slipping down the page. "Brad."

"Soon as that tube's out," Dr. Kahn reassured her. "A couple more days. We'll get him here."

Molly's hand dropped, the pen falling to the floor. Kahn picked it up, checked the monitors. "Get hold of her son," he told Marge. "You know him, right? Tell him next week. Wednesday, maybe."

Marge grinned. After he left, she stared at her sleeping patient, then pulled out her cell phone.

Chapter Thirteen

If you really wanna get Howie going sometime, ask about subways. The trains, not the sandwich. Besides birds the only other thing he tells about growing up is the New York subway system. How for a nickel you could go crosstown, uptown, places as far and different as another country, and if you were a kid you could duck under the turnstile without a token. He never drove a car 'til the Marines taught him. He says you could live your whole life in Brooklyn or Manhattan without ever driving a car.

Out here, you're just fucked if you don't have a car. There's a bus runs twice a day, once each direction, between a few towns on the coast, but between times or if you live inland you're shit out'a luck. I used to hitch home from practice sometimes, but hitchin's a high risk thing in this county if you're black or Mexican. Like most times, forget it. Most folks who stop are actually okay, even nice, but then there's the big-wheel rednecks or assholes lookin' for someone disposable to get their rocks off on, disposable meaning black or Hispanic or female, which are all fair game for raping and beating and leaving dead in a ditch. It happens. One time I didn't even have my thumb out and these guys stop in a big SUV askin' do I want a ride. I can smell the booze and I guess I could smell something else, if hate has a smell, and their smiles aren't from kindness. I tell them no thanks, which they take like it's a major insult. They jump out of the rig – there's four of 'em, mean and laughing how they'll give me a ride I won't forget, and I don't like to think what would'a happened if there hadn't been a bunch of sirens go off. The drunks were back in the car and gone by the time a couple fire trucks raced past.

Mom bought me a bike last year. It's an old three-speed but I can go about anywhere on it. In tourist season, which is almost all the time now, there's so many cars you have to ride backwards practically to keep safe. I wish we had subways here.

—The Oreo File

"'When' without an H is a big, puss-filled boil."

"Brad, that's totally gross."

"Only if you leave out the H."

Sal grabbed a much-smeared paper from Brad and attacked it with her eraser. Brad continued repairs on a polynomial that had degenerated into chord progressions. His feet bounced to Cape Breton fiddle tunes coming from Molly's flour-crusted kitchen CD player. In the laundry basket by the table, Baby Craig slept between a plush zebra and bear.

"Watch out for 'where,' too," Brad said. "Without an H it's half a werewolf."

In the doorway, Sara hid a smile. "Chow time, guys." She shoveled books aside to set a pot of soup on the table. "Marge called again, Brad. Molly'll be off the respirator in the morning. So you're on for tomorrow night. Mac'll drive you up." She glanced out the window. "Speak of the devil – just in time for lunch. Baby Craig give you any trouble?"

"Nope." Brad piled books and papers on a cookie sheet and set them on the counter. "Long as we kept the music going."

"He likes Dolly Parton," Sal said.

"Chip off the old block, that boy." Mac filled the doorway, shedding sawdust. He stood one-legged, taking off his boots and tossing them onto the porch. "Looks like a guano factory out here."

Sal wrinkled her face at Brad.

"Okay, okay. It was my turn," he said. "I'll do it after lunch."

"Don't put it off," Sara warned. "Practice at three-thirty, remember, rain or shine."

Sal ladled a bowl of soup for Mac. "How come you're home? It's only one-thirty."

"Movin' to a unit on Table Mountain." Mac crumbled three biscuits into his soup and turned to Brad, his mouth full. "Throw your bike in the truck, I'll drop you at the field on my way."

"Good," said Sara. The CD had ended. She picked up Baby Craig and changed his diaper on the cutting board. "Sal's got swimming practice, we're going the other way."

Mac ate three bowls of soup and finished off the biscuits. Sal set a plate of oatmeal cookies on the table.

"Me and Brad made 'em," she said.

"Brad and I," Sara corrected.

"No, me and Brad. You weren't here."

Sara laughed. Outside, Joe snorted, then whinnied. Sara glanced out. "Oh, no. Not again."

Through the window, they saw the cop car pull up. Dumb Darryl and his partner got out and headed toward the front door, Darryl holding a clipboard. Joe stood in their way, snorting. He pawed the mud with his forelegs and reared, his ears laid back.

"Sweet Jesus. Call Joe," Mac said. "I'll see what they want."

Sal whistled out the back door for Joe. Mac swallowed his fourth cookie and wrestled open the seldom-used front door. Darryl stood outside, his clipboard spattered with mud from Joe's guard duty. The plastic bag over his hat this time had "HOMESTEAD 100% WHOLE WHEAT" printed among red and yellow balloons.

Sal, on the back porch reassuring Joe, looked panicked. Brad moved to her side, wondering how they could ever explain the blobs of penguin shit on the porch floor. They watched the figures in the opposite doorway, Sal poised to run. Mac was reading something on the mud-smeared clipboard.

"A search warrant?" Mac said. "What the hell you searching for?"

Sal patted Joe's head, relieved. "Oh, is that all. I thought he was coming to take me back to school."

Darryl explained something at length, inaudibly. Mac scratched his head, adding sawdust to the muddy clipboard.

With a thump, Bertha landed on the porch beside Sal and waddled toward the kitchen, her beak and throat pouch bulging with fish. Brad and Sal watched her, amazed. Bertha had never before brought her catch home, and certainly not into the house. At the doorway, the pelican flapped her wings and launched herself toward the sink. Sara ducked, shielding Baby Craig. Precariously airborne, Bertha overshot her mark, her frantic wings knocking dishes off the table. She veered toward the open front door and collided heavily with Dumb Darryl.

Joe whinnied. Sal giggled. "Uh-oh. Think he has a mud complex?"

Framed in the front doorway, Darryl lay sprawled in the mud, Bertha's outstretched wings shrouding his face, her cargo spilled around his head. His hat and the bread bag lay nearby in a muddy collage of fish. Darryl's partner turned aside, choking with laughter.

Mac scooped the indignant pelican off Darryl and held out a hand to pull him up. "Sorry about that." He handed Darryl a diaper to wipe mud and fish gurry off his face and uniform. Brad and Sal collected the fish and dumped them in the sink. Bertha followed. She hopped up to the drainboard and fussed anxiously over her catch, arranging the fish in tidy rows, head to tail.

"Wow," Sal said. "What's she doing?"

"You can ask her later," Sara said. "I think we'd better wait next door while they look for whatever it is they want."

* * *

"Video tapes," Mac told them an hour later. He showed them a three-page list of tapes taken for evidence. "And Molly's camera. They turned over the whole house looking for that camera. You know how many socks you had buried in your room, Brad?"

Brad ignored the socks question. "But how could her camera be here? She had it with her that day."

"Dunno. The camera's missing, we know that. Darryl says someone came back to the unit that night, hunting for something."

"He thinks we went there and found it?" Sal asked.

"He don't think nothing," Mac said. "Just jumps to the DA's whistle. The DA says either Molly had an accomplice that day, or someone came back and got the camera."

Brad shook his head. "Well, we sure as hell didn't. So where is it?"

Mac lifted Brad's bike into the pickup bed. "We're still set for Portland tomorrow, right? Your mom'll know. Least I hope to god she does."

* * *

Coach called off practice early, after the second ball was lost in the mud. Brad wiped off his mitt and stowed it in the gym bag on his bike. The pitcher, George Lawson, clapped him on the shoulder.

"Hey, man, me and Larry're going for a soda. Coming?"

Brad looked up in surprise. Like most of the team, George, and Larry, the shortstop, were jocks; they had little to say to him off the field, and barely acknowledged him in school. That was okay, he'd always told himself. He didn't play ball to make friends, he played because he liked being good at something. But for George at least, the invitation obviously had a broader meaning.

"Uh … yeah. Sure," Brad said.

Walking his bike next to the others, he felt the stares from shop doorways and street corners. It wasn't their muddy clothes that attracted so much attention, it was Brad himself. He was used to that in other coastal towns, but not here, where he was known. Inside the convenience store, three women gossiping with the clerk went abruptly silent when the boys entered. At the cooler against the back wall, Brad jostled good-naturedly with George over the last root beer and took an orange drink instead. The women up front were talking again, their voices lowered, occasional words reaching to the back of the store.

"That's her boy? … kicked out of school … FBI, split his head like a melon …"

The women clammed up when Brad followed George and Larry to the register. He set the orange soda on the counter, holding his money.

The clerk rang up his teammates' sodas, then turned away and busied herself arranging cigarette cartons behind the counter.

"Excuse me," Brad said. The clerk ignored him, her back turned.

"Excuse me," Brad said again. "I'd like to pay for this."

The clerk stabbed a pencil into her hairdo and walked to the far end of the cigarette display, refusing to look at him. Brad shrugged. He left the soda on the counter and walked out, avoiding his teammates' eyes. He picked up his bike, his skin burning with shame. George charged out of the store and thrust the orange soda at him.

"They're assholes, don't listen to 'em." He punched Brad lightly on the arm. "See ya Thursday, eh, dude?"

In the convenience store, the largest of the women, her knees bulging like pillows from size eighteen shorts, stacked two sixpacks of Bud and a diet Coke on the counter. "How d'ya stand it, Lonnie, all them blacks, greens, jews, just come in like they own the place."

"Gets to me, it does." The clerk rang up the sale and reached for a paper sack, her sleeve pulling back to reveal a livid, yellowing bruise on her arm. "Got no choice, do I? My Harry been out of work since Johnson's mill closed."

The sight of the bruise fueled the women's anger. "That's eleven mills closed here since them tree-huggers showed up," the short, blond woman snorted.

"Send 'em back to Africa where they belong," the largest woman said.

Unnoticed, four cans of Iams cat food quietly slipped out the door in Joey's pocket.

* * *

Brad took back streets to the bridge, avoiding shop fronts and hostile looks. He rode slowly, carrying his unopened soda. At Bay Street he turned onto the highway bridge approach and stopped. Traffic was backed up in both directions, the bridge a motionless sea of empty vehicles. People crowded the west side pedestrian lane, climbing on the rail and holding children up, pointing to the mouth of the bay, a mile westward, where a small fleet of boats was converging on the sandbar. People poured out of shops, running to the bridge. Brad hung onto his bike, swept along in the crowd. He heard the word "Penguins!" and felt sick.

At the bridge abutment he shoved his bike behind a concrete tower and climbed its base to see what was happening. A small boat was beached midway along the distant sandbar; near the tip where the tide poured through, tiny figures were silhouetted against the water. Were they penguins? If so, there were an awful lot of them. Brad squinted into the glare, trying to see. A man climbed down from the tower above him, binoculars tucked into his shirt.

"A bunch of seals," he said disgustedly. He offered the binoculars to Brad, who took them. One look was enough to distinguish two large groups of seals sunning themselves where the sun had broken through a cloud bank. People were pushing the small boat into the water, and other boats were turning back. Brad handed the man his binoculars.

"Wow. Thank you! Thanks a lot!" Brad jumped down and onto his bike.

The man, a vacationing Safeway manager from Iowa, picked up Brad's unopened orange soda and called out to him. But the strange, excessively grateful boy was gone.

There was no point trying to cross the bridge until traffic was moving again. Brad pedaled along back streets, blessing all seals, the nastiness at the convenience store forgotten. He rode aimlessly past the Catholic church, the auto shop, Stormy's tavern, and the sport-fishing docks, the sounds of horns and shouts from the bridge still audible over the water. At Dane Street, he turned, thinking to swing by the funeral home in case some RIPs were there, and spotted the town police cruiser turning behind him.

The town had only one cruiser, Chief Roberts' pride and joy; he allowed no one else to drive it. Brad's relief over the seals flashed into terror. After passing tourists had thwarted his arrest in the drug store years ago, Brad had become the chief's primary suspect in every crime in his jurisdiction, regardless of wild improbability. Until now, a succession of county prosecutors had ignored Roberts's wild accusations, but with the DA now proclaiming his mother a murderess, Brad could not count on Chief Roberts being ignored again. Glancing back, he saw the cruiser speed up behind him. Around the next corner was the funeral home. Brad knew this neighborhood well. He veered suddenly through a gap in the hedge bordering the yard behind the funeral home and raced over the weedy lawn to the alley on the other side.

On the porch of the old lady's house, Joey looked up, startled, from the cans of Iams he was stacking. A bicycle raced across the lawn, Brad and his gym bag bouncing wildly. Joey saw Brad's terrified, unseeing face, and through the bushes at the back fence the police cruiser slowing to enter the alley. Joey tore across the yard after Brad. Among the huge, untended rhododendrons bordering the alley a small fishing boat had been rotting away for years. Joey grabbed whatever would pull loose – a broken tiller, a small kedge anchor, a length of chain – and heaved them into the alley. He was gone by the time the police cruiser screeched to a stop at his impromptu barricade.

* * *

Looking over his shoulder every few seconds, Brad headed for the hills. He rode hard up the switchbacks of Ridge Road toward a place to hide where he could watch for the bridge to clear. Near the top was an overgrown track with a faded, tilting sign marked "Hospital Street." A century ago, before the bridge was built, there had been the equivalent of a field hospital here, treating loggers and townspeople until they could be ferried north across the bay. He would have a clear view of the bridge from the old foundations.

Brad turned onto the track just as the police cruiser rounded the curve behind him. He ducked behind the rusted hulk of a donkey engine that had powered the hospital and waited, breathless, his legs aching. The squeal of brakes told him he'd been spotted. He didn't wait to be cornered in the old hospital's cliffside pocket. The cruiser was backing toward him when he pushed his bike out on the road and plunged headlong back down toward town. At the second switchback, the cruiser caught up with him. Its siren and lights were going now, a grim measure of Chief Roberts's rage. A FedEx truck rounded the curve below, heading uphill. Brad veered in front of it and turned onto a hiking trail that by-passed the last switchbacks, a precipitous drop down to the long straightaway past the lumberyard into town.

The straightaway, bordered by the lumberyard's cyclone fence on one side and a wetland on the other, offered no concealment. The only turn-off was the overgrown driveway to an old swamp-built house that had been covered with scaffolding for months. Brad scanned the road ahead frantically for the driveway opening. Behind him he heard the siren change pitch. He glanced back. Flashing lights showed through the trees, the cruiser leaving rubber on the last steep curve but not yet in sight.

Chapter Fourteen

Howie was as excited about Sal getting over leukemia as if she was his own kid, even though he'd never even met her. The day she came home he brought his guitar over and made her laugh with silly songs. I got my violin and played along, and almost every night since we play together for Sal. I had already outgrown a three-quarter size violin and my new teacher rented us a full size. The first Christmas after Sal came home, Howie gave me a violin of my own. We found him asleep under the tree Christmas morning, hugging that package. It's a good violin, my teacher says it's priceless, but Howie put it in a ratty old case, I think he didn't want us to know how valuable it is.

By then I knew a lot of songs, but never again heard the tune that kid played outside the hospital where Sal was born. One night Howie was sitting out on the porch with a penny whistle, playing in the dark after we went to bed, and just when I was falling asleep I heard it out there, the same tune, as lonely and magic as I remembered. First I thought I was dreaming, then I knew I wasn't. I tore out there, and Howie told me what it was. "Ashokan Farewell." Funny thing is, Sal heard it, too, and came out, half asleep, to hear it again. She said it was her favorite song, and when I asked where she heard before she couldn't remember. She'd just always known it, she said. Did she remember it from me humming it all the time when she was so tiny? Can people remember tunes they only heard when they were just born? I wonder. It's still the tune she likes me to play when she can't get to sleep.

—The Oreo File

A hand-painted sign on the open gate said, "Opening Soon." Brad swerved at full speed through the gate and plowed his bike into a wall of blackberries flanking the driveway. Heedless of thorns, he forced the bike as far as possible into the jungle. The cruiser, siren blaring, slowed to a stop at the driveway entrance. Brad held his breath until it moved on, speeding toward town, the siren's wail dwindling to silence.

Extricating the bike from its nest of thorns was a battle. Scratched and sweating, swearing vigorously, Brad dragged it out, pulling with it a train of blackberry vines twined through the wheel spokes.

"That's a glove job if ever there was one," a voice called from the old house.

A woman stood on the porch, wearing a long dress covered with lace and ribbons, her face hidden in the kind of bonnet he'd seen only in wagon train movies.

"Be right with you," she said, and vanished into the house. She reappeared carrying a machete and a pair of oven mitts. She tottered down the steps and across the lawn, each step a precarious adventure, but close up, Brad saw she was no older than his mom or Howie. It was the boots that hobbled her, tiny boots of wrinkled, stretched leather, fastened by long rows of small buttons instead of laces. But for the machete and the oven mitts, she might be a ghost from the Oregon Trail.

"Just pull some of them branches out straight," she said, handing him the mitts. He wrapped them around a stout blackberry trunk and pulled it taut through the bicycle spokes. Without warning, she swung the machete between his hands and the spokes, neatly shearing the vine. He jumped back and she laughed. One branch at a time, she slashed her way expertly around the bike. Buttons popped off the back of her dress with each swing of the blade. She whacked the last vine and leaned on her machete, watching Brad kick the branches off the driveway.

"You're not Ted Colby sent from the lodge, then," she said.

"Uh, no. I'm …"

"Didn't think so. Damn. He's supposed to put our sign up today."

Leaning against the front porch was a large signboard, big enough to fit between the center posts. Its gothic lettering read, "South Coast Historical Society."

"Hey," Brad said. "That's where we – where I …"

She stopped him with a glance toward the road, tilting her head to listen. "'Spect you better get that bike out of sight before the Klan comes back."

Brad shivered. "Chief Roberts, you mean?"

"That fat bigot, shoots crows over to the dump, don't even like birds the wrong color."

She hobbled round the back of the house, using the machete as a walking stick. Brad followed and leaned his bike against the back step.

"If Ted Whats-it's coming from the north, he might be real late," he told her. "There's a big traffic jam at the bridge."

"Come in and pour some lemonade while I get out of these things." She limped up the steps and opened the door to a small kitchen. Brad ducked his head at the low doorway, and she smiled. "If Ted don't show we can do it ourselves, eh?"

Brad poured two glasses of lemonade from a frosty pitcher, listening to the tap of her boots upstairs. She reappeared barefoot, dressed in jeans and a sweatshirt. Brad stood up awkwardly; she was scarcely taller than Sal. Released from the bonnet, her hair bounced about her face in a tawny, unruly halo. She swigged lemonade and stretched buoyantly, standing on tiptoe.

"Thought I could get away without wearing stays under that dress," she said. "But I'm running clean out of buttons."

"Stays …?" Brad asked.

"Stays. They're like a whalebone girdle, pull in your waist so tight you can't breathe. Those old dresses were made to fit over 'em. I'm supposed to model all these things at the opening next month, thought if I lost a few pounds I could do it, but no way. And you don't lose weight in your feet. Look at 'em!"

Her bare feet were latticed with red creases, a line of crimson welts marking the tracks of buttons halfway to the knees. Brad thought she was already tiny enough to slip under a door and wondered how whale bones could make her any thinner.

"Would you believe some of those women crossed the plains and great divide in those things – whalebone, button shoes and all?" she said. "'Cause a proper lady wouldn't dream of appearing without 'em. Don't know how they breathed, much less walked."

Hanging the sign was no trouble. Brad measured between the chains fastened to its top edge. Standing on a chair, he drilled holes in the porch framing and screwed in eyebolts. He lifted the sign to join chains and eyebolts with S-hooks, and slowly let the sign swing free.

"Is it level?" he called.

"Oh, it looks grand," the woman said. "Come and see."

Brad walked to the driveway to admire it with her. "I heard," he said hesitantly, "I heard you – the society, that is – have information about Nig – uh – Lew Southworth. The guy Darkey Creek's named for?"

"Nigger Lew? It's okay, that's what he called himself. And yes, we do, if I can find it. We've been moving in for two months, not sure yet where everything is." She held out her hand. "I'm Tess Campbell, by the way."

"Umm. Brad. Brad Matthissen," Brad said.

"Brad! Of course!" She clapped both hands over his. "Dinkum's! Should've known you right away. I know your mom. She's supposed to film the opening, but … oh, damn. I knew Howie, too."

"He was gonna bring me here, to look for Nigger Lew," Brad said.

Tess Campbell wiped her brimming eyes. "Howie. He helped us rebuild this place. Fixed the wiring and built our new display cabinets. I don't believe for a minute she killed him. What happened? Do you know?"

Brad shook his head. "We're trying to find out."

"Do that. You need help, call me. Now, you look around while I find Nigger Lew."

Inside the front door, two big rooms opened into each other

through an unfinished archway. Smells of paint and new wood mingled with the unmistakable scent of old papers and books. Ms. Campbell rummaged in filing cabinets and boxes stacked against a far wall, while Brad examined exhibits of old fishing and logging gear, two-man saws, plows and harness. Stained, glass-fronted cabinets held old photographs, maps, letters written in fading brown script, yellowed newspapers, a sextant, a pair of wire-framed spectacles. Tall glass cases displayed worn-out work clothes, embroidered waistcoats, jackets, bow ties, shawls, dresses, more high-button shoes. In a long case against the end wall, model ships sailed a paper maché sea; beside each ship a card told where its real counterpart had sailed, what cargoes it carried, which ports it frequented.

Brad looked at every exhibit, awed as much by the cabinetry as by the contents. He ran a finger over invisible joins and butter-smooth, hand-wrought moldings and drawer-pulls. The wood was all local timber – cedar, maple, alder, fir, spruce, hemlock. Howie had shown him and Sal how to recognize their distinctive grains, and what each was suited for. Howie. So this was where he disappeared to, for days at a time, over the past year. Brad had never thought to ask.

"Got it!" Ms. Campbell called.

Brad lingered a moment over Howie's cabinet work, pulling himself together. Ms. Campbell set an inch-thick file folder on an antique trestle table, along with a pad of post-it stickers. The tab on the folder was marked in felt pen, "Darkey Creek – Lew Southworth."

Brad thanked her with a vague grin and sat down. His thoughts still on Howie and beveled edges, he flipped open the folder and gasped. The top page was a photograph of the ancestor Howie had chosen for him.

The picture was a photocopy, probably enlarged, of a faded, water-stained original. An elderly black man, graying or white hair cut short, leaned slightly forward and smiled back at Brad, a glint of mischievous joy in his eyes. Behind him was the blurred outline of a doorway. His left hand, thrust forward toward the camera, curled around the neck of a violin; his right held the bow poised above the strings. The picture had the posed, rigid quality of early photography, but the pose itself proclaimed the man's exultant pride – not in himself, but in a beloved instrument.

"Handsome devil, wasn't he," Ms. Campbell said, looking over Brad's shoulder.

Brad tore his eyes from the photograph and looked at her in wonder. "But … the violin. Did Howie know? Did he see this?"

Ms. Campbell thought a moment. "Don't think so. He saw the file name when we packed up the old store room on Front Street. Yeah, he asked if that was the guy in the paper when they renamed the creek, but we were shoveling everything into boxes – had to wear dust masks, it was so bad in there. So no, he didn't open the file, just asked about the name."

Brad set the photograph reverently aside, where he could keep looking at it. For an hour, a lifetime, he pored over the remainder of the file, reading the collection of old letters, articles from long-defunct newspapers, white-on-black photostats of land deeds, plat maps, recent articles about changing the name of Darkey Creek, and a single additional photograph. These patchwork fragments were the only record of a man's life.

In the 1870s, Lew Southworth was the only black person living on the central Oregon coast. Southworth, Brad read, was born a slave in Georgia. From birth he was owned like a bucket or shovel by another man. Even his name, Southworth, was not his own, but his master's. Brad tried to imagine growing up as a piece of property – hands, feet, life, and breath owned by someone else. The idea gave him heartburn. How did Lew Southworth endure? He read further. In 1851, Lew's master moved to Oregon, taking his slave with him. Lew was twenty-one years old then, eight years older than Brad. And over the next eight years, Lew the slave had saved up a thousand dollars to buy himself from his master. He earned the money playing his fiddle at white folks' dances and gold miners' camps in Jacksonville.

Brad reread every article, frustrated by the huge gaps in Nigger Lew's story. Where and how had a slave managed to get a fiddle? Did Master Southworth know his piece of property was moonlighting, earning his own money to buy his freedom? How did he set the price for another man's life? Brad found no answers, only further questions. With Ms. Campbell's help, he copied the entire file, making several copies of the photographs at different exposures.

Ms. Campbell found a large manila envelope for his precious copies and led him to a trail through the swamp back of the museum. "Our own Underground Railway," she said. "In case the Gestapo's still looking for you. It's the old logging railbed, it'll take you round back of Grant Slough to just east of the bridge."

The bridge was clear when Brad reached it. Far below, the darkening water rippled gently at slack tide. Against the fog bank blotting the horizon, riding lights of distant fishing boats winked, and he smelled the salt flats lining the bay shore, the same tides and salt flats Lew Southworth would have known. Nigger Lew. Brad felt the manila envelope crinkle against his skin under his shirt, and pedaled to the beat of songs named in the Southworth articles. "Arkansas Traveler," "Swanee River," "Soldier's Joy" – tunes he'd played a thousand times with Howie, never knowing the same tunes had bought his borrowed ancestor's freedom.

Four penguins stood on the porch when he got home. He barely looked at them, his fingers itching for violin strings. In the kitchen doorway, Sara stopped him, her finger to her lips. Behind her a camera flashed, blinding him. Sara pointed toward the sink. Bertha was perched on the drainboard over her cache of fish. On the floor stood the Admiral, wings outstretched, beak open. Bertha picked up a fish and dropped it into his beak. He swallowed it and opened his beak for another. Sal laughed and snapped another picture. She held up Sara's Polaroid camera and pointed to a stack of photos curing on the table beside her.

"For Mom," Sal said, shoving the photos toward him. "You can give them to her tomorrow."

"Not even Molly would believe this without a picture," said Sara.

* * *

Few tourists ever found their way to the Sinkhole, and never for long. Located in a former machine shed adjacent to the sewage treatment plant on Grant Slough, the tavern inspired – and possibly deserved – crude jokes about the source of its beverages. The odor pervading its muddy, unlit parking area did nothing to dispel rumor. A cyclone-fenced enclosure at one end of the lot housed a crane truck, parked rent-free by a local construction outfit to haul vehicles and their inebriated drivers out of the slough.

By day, the Sinkhole was indistinguishable from other industrial buildings at that side of town; it still looked like a machine shed, even to the remnants of a sign, "...er's Repairs," in faded paint across the front. At night, the only clue to its function was the neon Oregon Lottery sign in the single grimy window, casting a wan, red light on the pickups, SUVs, and vans parked nearby. Joey didn't know if the Sinkhole was even its official name, but he'd never known it to be called anything else. The reason for its existence was simply to get customers as drunk as a pay or unemployment check would allow.

Joey had no interest in getting drunk; he'd never been inside the place, but its parking lot was a handy emporium for moonlight requisitions. People, especially drunks, left all manner of things in their vehicles, and locks were no barrier to Joey. He never took more than could be attributed to drunken forgetfulness, and the Sinkhole offered frequent opportunities to improve his knowledge of human frailty. Tonight he worked the west side of the lot, waiting for the men in the extended cab pickup on the far side to leave or go back into the bar. Joey suspected they were in no shape to do either.

Pickings had been good that night. His pockets bulged with loose change, three packs of cigarettes, one unopened, two Bic lighters, a small bag of popcorn, and a ball-point pen with a naked lady inside that floated up and down when you tilted it. Curiosity rather than larceny drew him toward the pickup still parked in the far side of the lot. Its dome light was on, and the ground beneath Joey's feet throbbed with the heavy bass amplifier. The passenger door was open. In the light spilling from the cab he recognized the pickup. It was the one he had seen plastered with mud in Dinkum's yard, most of the mud now ineptly washed off. Joey eased between stacks of crab traps for a clear view of the cab. The same three men were in it, arguing incoherently.

"Already told the cops. Why we gotta hang around for this grand jury?"

"....fuckin' rewind ... There, see them pelicans? Sell 'em to CBS, ABC...."

"Penguins. Them's penguins."

"'S what I said, pelicans."

"Put that thing away, man. Fuckin' cops keep askin' if she had it."

One of the men tumbled out of the open door and staggered off to take a leak, tossing a beer can into the shadows where Joey lurked. Joey abandoned the impulse to toss it back and quietly slipped away.

* * *

Mac woke when Sara got up to nurse Baby Craig. She sat in the old rocker by the open window, a blanket over the baby, and hummed softly to the music from next door. Mac looked at the digital numbers on his alarm clock.

"Those kids still up? It's almost two a.m."

"Putting a long day behind them," Sara said. "And nervous, maybe, about tomorrow."

Mac sat up and yawned. "What—seeing Molly, you mean?"

"They're scared, Mac. Of finding out what happened."

"Shit, they don't think she killed him!"

"Of course not." Sara stared at the lit window next door, the dark shapes of penguins on the porch. "But the rest of the world does. They're just kids, they get the flak."

"All the more reason to find out for sure."

Mac yawned again and fell back on his pillow. The familiar opening bars of "Swanee River" stopped abruptly, followed by halting guitar chords. Then Sal's delighted laugh. "I got it now – start again!"

"Sounds like a Civil War revival over there," Mac murmured.

He didn't wake when Sara came back to bed, Baby Craig nestled in her arms, or hear Brad's solo finale, the aching lilt of "Ashokan Farewell" that lulled Sal to sleep.

Chapter Fifteen

Me and Mom moved here when Sal got leukemia, to get away from my fake dad and the poison that made her sick. That was the year we lived on roadkill and oatmeal all winter. It wasn't really oatmeal, it was a couple sacks of COB, which is corn, oats, and barley with molasses, that got busted in shipment and the feed store threw them out. It's better than oatmeal when you cook it up, kind of nuttier and sweeter, and in winter when it's cold and no vultures to fight off, the venison is prime, better than any store meat. If you luck out it's a doe. The bucks taste sort of sour but they're okay for chili or spaghetti. I got so I could gut one out in minutes, they're not so heavy to lug home that way. If you hit the main highway when it's just getting light – especially on weekends when all the drunks are out – you can get 'em fresh, and once the truckers, the log truck drivers, once they saw me out there guttin' a few times, they'd stop and tell me if they saw a good kill that morning. They're okay, those drivers, I just hope there's other kinds of trucks they can drive when all the trees are gone.

It was Mac showed me how to gut and cut up a deer. Him and Sara live next door, it's the only other house on this spit of land. I sure didn't like the people here at first – bein' black was like having a disease. At school the principal read me a gangsta from day one, and store people pegged me for shoplifter the second I walked in. But Mac and Sara weren't like that. Sara worked in the county hospital and she liked to cook. After school if Mom wasn't back from seeing Sal I stayed with Sara. She'd bake something and let me lick the bowl and tell stories about other nurses. Mac was big and shed sawdust all over and I never saw anyone eat as much as he could. He never made fun of the violin, and taught me how to play baseball. That year Sal was dyin' would'a been nothin' but bad if it wasn't for Mac and Sara.

—*The Oreo File*

Old Dan and I with throats burned dry and souls that cry for water ...

Water. Molly couldn't get enough of it.

All day I pace the barren waste without the taste of water ...

Water!

Brad's voice cracks on the high note, Sal's dissolves into giggles....

Drops of water and bits of flaked ice slid over Molly's tongue, leaving her parched, swollen throat craving more. Groggily, she willed the icy liquids to clear morphine-fogged brain cells. She needed her wits and couldn't find them. Needed her eyes and couldn't open them.

"Molly? Molly, wake up!" Marge's voice over a symphony of water – trickling, splashing, gurgling.

Don't you listen to him, Dan, he's a devil not a man and he spreads the burning sand with water....

Thirst. Pain. Molly explored the pain – head, eye, arm, ribs, ankle – a fractured geology of pain, crushing the memory of what had caused it.

"D, A7, G, D, A7, D – a repeating chord pattern, Sal." Howie....

* * *

"Good golly, Miss Molly, wake up and drink!"

Molly opened her left eye. "What day is it?"

"Wednesday," Marge said. She'd answered the same question at least five times today. "Still Wednesday." She filled Molly's glass and handed her a cup of chipped ice. "Sure you don't want something for pain?"

"Just water. Water and ice." Molly tipped ice chips into her mouth, soothing her swollen tongue. She closed her eye against the light, counting on pain to keep her awake. Wednesday. Wednesday was important, so important she had refused pain-killers all day. She fought to remember why. "Brad! Where's Brad?"

"On their way," Marge said. "Doc's meeting them at nine-thirty."

Molly forced her good eye open, tried to focus on Marge. There was something else. "The picture? The newspaper …?"

Marge opened the bedside cabinet. "Right where I put it. You want it now?"

"No, no. Brad. Need to tell him …. God, I sound like a sick frog, don't I!"

"Better'n a squashed one." Marge laughed. "Believe me, Brad don't care how you sound. He still playin' that fiddle?"

"Never stops." Molly took a long drink through the bent straw. "Marge, he's so good it scares me sometimes …. Not just virtuoso good …." She drank again, searching for words. "Some mathematician said infinity was an adventure in endless possibilities. That's what music is for Brad…." She laughed, wincing at the pain. "Hey, listen to me – my voice! It's back."

"Never shut you up now, girl," Marge said. "So tell me, who's this Dan? Got you a new man?"

"Dan? I don't know any Dan."

"You say. And you callin' to him 'fore I woke you up."

"Uh-uh. Must've got signals crossed, someone else's dream. What time is it?"

* * *

"Will ya look at that!"

Mac stood with Brad, waiting to pay for gas, chips, and juice before heading inland to the interstate. The station counter overflowed with penguin merchandise – matchbooks, lighters, penguin-shaped chocolates, plush penguin key rings, plastic penguin wind-up toys, penguin Frisbees, penguin bumper stickers. A row of t-shirts hanging over the counter sported truly bad penguin art, each stamped "I saw them on the Oregon Coast."

Brad grimaced. Every motel they'd passed was full. Enterprising sign artists had obviously been busy; neon penguins beamed from restaurant, motel, and curio shop signs up and down the coast. The highway department had added penguin silhouettes to every roadside turnout and coastal park. News vehicles traveled the coast highway in packs, poised to descend on the next penguin sighting or boat wreck. Molly should be leading the pack, Brad thought. He bought a penguin mug for her as a joke.

Coming out of the shop, Mac ducked reflexively at a crackling sound overhead. Straining at its wire tethers, a thirty-foot high helium-filled penguin bobbed in the wind above the Chevron sign. Lit from within, letters on both sides warned "LAST CHANCE!!"

"Last chance for gas – or for the penguins?" Mac snorted.

"It's like Keiko all over again," Brad said.

Keiko, the killer whale movie star of "Free Willy" fame, had created a phenomenal economic bubble on the Oregon coast. Brought to the local aquarium to recover from malnutrition and disease, the whale had drawn tourists from all over the globe. Motels, campgrounds, restaurants, land developers, and retail shops had surpassed all profit records in a frenzied, unprecedented boom; a mini-mall had even sprung up overnight in a storage park adjoining the aquarium, to siphon money from the millions of visitors pouring through. When Keiko recovered and was shipped out to Iceland, the coastal economy had crashed ignominiously and never recovered.

"Keiko. Poor bugger died anyway," Mac said, starting the pickup. "Aquarium's already gearing up for penguins now. Paper printed plans to turn Keiko's tank into a model of McMurdo Sound. But some casino in Vegas wants 'em, too."

"Why?" Brad demanded. "Why can't they just leave 'em alone?"

Mac slowed to a crawl behind a motor home with Nebraska plates. "Money is why. If the end of the world was comin' tomorrow, people'd be lining up to make a buck off it. Like Howie said – about Keiko, remember? – 'Don't kill the messenger, just turn him into a tourist attraction.'"

Howie. Brad was silent, gripping Sal's small packet of Polaroids and four notebook pages titled "The Admural – TOP Seecrit." Until today, some stubborn hope had lingered that all the news stories, his mom's arrest, the insanity in the courtroom, the police with their search warrant, had been a horrible mistake; that Howie would walk in some dinner time or turn up on the couch one morning. Now, taking Sal's grubby package to a hospital one hundred fifty miles away, hope and Howie were as dead as old Winston.

Playing an old Civil War song a few weeks earlier, Brad had set his violin down when Howie sang, "We shall meet but we shall miss him – there will be one vacant chair." Overwhelmed suddenly by longing for Winston, he had told Howie how even after four years he still missed his shaggy friend, and how the day of his death still haunted him. "It's not fair!" he'd said, tearful and angry.

"Who says life is fair?" Howie had asked. "Is life fair to the newt squashed on the road? The baby deformed by Agent Orange? The child blown to bits by landmines?"

Brad stared angrily through the windshield. Another goddamned empty chair. No, it wasn't fair, but that didn't mean he had to like it.

Mac glanced at his glowering passenger and thought better of saying any more. The Nebraska motor home in front of them turned off at an RV park, and Mac sped up, leaving town. The road skirted a broad bay fringed with docks, moored boats, small homes on stilts. In silence they passed fishing camps, trailer parks, the water treatment plant. Neither Mac nor Brad noticed the dirty pickup mired in a ditch at the Sinkhole, or the three men arguing at its side.

Past the last fishing camp, just before the road climbed into national forest overlooking the upper bay, Brad broke the silence, pointing at a side road just ahead. "Look! There it is!"

Mac slowed abruptly. "There what is? Where?"

"The sign! The one that used to say 'Darkey Creek.' I didn't know it was right here!"

It was a regulation state highway sign, white on green, "Southworth Creek."

"Well, whaddya know. I never noticed they changed it," Mac said, glad for a topic that snapped Brad out of his funk. "Last time I saw, some kids had turned the A into an O, made it Dorkey Creek. That why they changed the name?"

"No. People said it was racist, calling it Darkey."

Just past the sign and bridge over a small creek, a side road bore the sign "Darkey Creek Road."

"Funny they changed the creek name, but not the road sign," Mac said. "Why'd they call it Darkey in the first place?"

"It was a slave who named it that. Lew Southworth. This was all his land right here. He called himself Nigger Lew."

"A slave? In Oregon?"

"'Til he bought himself for a thousand bucks," Brad said.

"A thousand bucks? You're shittin' me. Where'd you hear that?"

"I needed ancestors for this autobiography project, and Howie said I could have Nigger Lew. He was gonna take me to the historical society to find out about him. So yesterday I was there and looked him up – and hey, you know what?"

"No, what?" Mac pulled over past the sign for Darkey Creek Road. They sat looking at the swampy grassland and forest that once were Lew Southworth's homestead.

"Nigger Lew – honest, that's what he called himself – you know how he earned the money to buy himself? Playing violin! He played fiddle for white people's dances – some of his favorite songs were ones we play, like that one Mom likes? 'Oh, hard times come again no more,'" Brad sang. "That one? And the one Sara sings to Baby Craig, 'Slumber my darling.' And Arkansas Traveler, Soldier's Joy – Howie picked him for my ancestor and didn't even know!"

"Gives me chills," Mac said. "Howie really didn't know – even about the fiddle?"

"He never had time to look in the file," Brad said. "And after Lew was free he bought this land and voted and everything. He was the only black man on the whole coast."

Mac shook his head. "Man, I never knew that. Drove past that sign a zillion times and never knew a single thing about him."

Brad looked at the bleak landscape, broken on the bay side of the road by two mobile homes and concrete pads for three more. At water's edge, rotten pilings extended into the bay in broken rows. He wondered if they could be the remains of Lew's dock.

"One time there was this huge storm on voting day – this was back in the eighteen seventies, before any bridges. No one could get across the bay to vote, the waves were so high. Except Lew. He tied a bunch of empty oil cans to his boat and rowed all the way across, the only person who made it over there to vote."

"Huh," Mac said. "Even with cars and bridges, folks around here don't bother voting."

"Well, they were never slaves. Lew said Abe Lincoln's on trial every time there's an election. Abe Lincoln was his hero, because of freeing the slaves, see. There's a photo of him – Nigger Lew, that is – sitting by his fireplace when he was old, and over the fireplace is this big picture of Lincoln. I made a copy – I'll show you when we get home."

Mac watched the light fading from the bay for a long moment, then put the truck in gear. Back on the highway, he said, "Must'a been hard."

"Rowing through a storm like that? 'Course it was. No one else even tried it."

Mac glanced at Brad, then back at the road. "Yeah, that. And living here, in white territory…."

"The articles were all written way after he died," Brad said. "So it's confusing. He was respected, I think. He gave some of his land to build the first schoolhouse here. And he was chairman of the first school board. But at the same time the church wouldn't let him play his violin, said it was a tool of the devil."

"No!" Mac said. "No, no. That ain't right. They made him give up his music?"

"Not exactly. He couldn't, see. He said his music was the only company he had, so he gave up church."

"All right!" Mac punched the steering wheel, grinning. "That's all right, then."

There was little to say after that. The narrow switchbacks over the coast range demanded all Mac's concentration. Brad hummed fiddle tunes and kept watch for deer. It was dark before they reached the interstate. Mac finally broke the comfortable silence.

"Darkey Creek, huh? Almost like you're wearing his shoes."

* * *

The visitors' section of the hospital parking lot was nearly empty; visiting hours were long over. Mac drove through the lot to a door marked "Staff Only" and checked the time.

"Nine thirty-five. Marge'll be waiting to let us in."

Brad climbed out of the truck. His stomach lurched and he fought the impulse to run away. Giving him no time to hesitate, Mac walked to the door and rapped smartly on it. The door opened instantly, but instead of Marge, a stranger stood in the floodlit doorway. He wore surgical scrubs, a green plastic cap, and rubber-soled slippers over his shoes; a stethoscope hung around his neck. A classic TV doctor, except for the shoulders and arms of a linebacker and the jagged, par-boiled ribbon of scar tissue that snaked across his chin, pulling one corner of his mouth downward when he smiled. He held his hand out to Brad.

"Samuel Morse Kahn," he said. "Your mom's surgeon. Marge asked me to meet you. You must be Bradford. And …?" He looked questioningly at Mac.

"James Stuart MacCrae," Mac said, standing at attention. "Pleased to meet you, Doc, or can we stow the horse pucky and call you Bullhead?"

Dr. Kahn stared hard at Mac, then punched him on the shoulder, grinning. "Mac! Holy shit, what the …. Mac! This is fucking unbelievable…."

Mac slapped Dr. Kahn's back and tapped his name badge. "Damn straight it's unbelievable." He turned to Brad. "Meet my old drinkin' buddy, Bullhead. Last I saw him was settin' choker in the Siskiyous."

"That was back in the last century! Oh man, were we wild and crazy, or what? Remember Peters?"

Mac laughed. "Still can't believe we got away with that. But come off it, Bullhead. What kind'a con are you running here?"

"No con at all, Mac. Not this time. Remember we used to wonder what we'd do when all the trees were gone? Well, after I busted my collar bone the second time – and got this," he traced the scar with his finger, "I figured it was time to look for another trade. Doctoring seemed a good bet – when the logging jobs dried up there'd always be people having car wrecks and sports injuries – and getting stomped by cops." He grinned at Brad. "And we could stand here jawing all night but that won't get Brad into heaven – or ICU."

Between them, Mac and Bullhead draped Brad in a white lab coat and helped him slip static-protection booties over his Reeboks. Bullhead clipped a name card on the coat pocket reading "Michael D. Landauer," and handed Brad a green plastic shower cap. Brad held it gingerly between two fingers, frowning.

"Oh man, I can't go around with that thing on my head. This is crazy, we'll never get away with it."

"Of course it's crazy, dude. It's crazy because we *will* get away with it," Dr. Kahn laughed. "Nobody looks past the uniform, see. And this outfit says who you are – Dr. Samuel Morse Kahn's assistant, right out of surgery, too big a shit to fuck with." He grabbed the plastic cap and arranged it on Brad's head. "Put this on and presto, you're Affirmative Action Man! You could walk into the fuckin' White House."

Mac headed outside to his truck, laughing. Bullhead handed Brad a tray of bottles and test tubes and led him to an elevator. "Just remember, you're Mike for tonight. You're a resident learning at the feet of world famous surgeon Samuel Morse Kahn. And for chrissake, don't call me Bullhead."

They left the elevator at the fourth floor. Bullhead strode purposefully down a long hallway, Brad trying to keep up and look professional. They stopped at a heavy steel door marked "Staff Only." Bullhead placed a clipboard on top of the bottles on Brad's tray.

"Okay. Shit or go blind time. Anyone talks to us, you're too busy reading charts to look up, okay?"

The Intensive Care Unit had a nurses' station in the center, with patients' rooms arranged in a circle around it. Beside one door, two cops sat, one reading Business Week, the other playing a Game Boy with the sound turned off. Nobody challenged Brad, and the cops didn't look up when Bullhead opened the door. He closed it quickly behind them. Brad forgot all about being Affirmative Action Man at the sight of his mother.

Chapter Sixteen

The best way my dad made a difference in my life was by getting out of it. I don't remember much about him, good or bad, until after Sal was born, when he got so mad at my violin lessons and wouldn't go to the hospital with us to see her. He was hardly ever around after that. I thought it was 'cause he hated the violin. After Sal got sick and Mom found out how many other kids had died from leukemia in that neighborhood, he went ballistic 'cause it was his company that poisoned the dirt there. Then his secretary wrote some kind of complaint about him screwing her twelve-year-old daughter and his company sent him to D.C. Mom got the divorce without him and we never saw him again, which was fine by me.

He was an asshole, but he was only my fake dad, 'cause Mom adopted me herself before she ever met him. But he's Sal's real dad, so I don't say anything about him to her. She never brings it up, but I think she knows more than she lets on. Once we were reading about the female praying mantis eating the male's head off after they mate, and she said maybe they have the right idea.

—*The Oreo File*

"Mom?"

The single syllable struck every nerve ending at once. Like a whale battling heavy seas to reach her child, Molly fought through waves of pain to reach her son. Marge had turned off the overhead lights, leaving on only a shaded lamp by the bed. Molly lay in semi-darkness, her right eye heavily bandaged, her left eye closed.

"Mom? You okay, Mom?"

She groped with her left hand, felt the calloused tips of his fingers close softly around it.

"Fiddle Fingers," she said, her voice raspy, barely above a whisper. "G-D-A-E." Her good eye opened and filled with tears. Brad leaned awkwardly over the bed, his brown face anxious. "Shit," Molly said. "Getting maudlin's hazardous to your health. It's not as bad as it looks, honest."

To Brad it seemed worse than it looked. Molly's dark hair, usually an unruly, shining mass of curls, spread lifelessly on the pillow. A massive bandage covered one eye and part of her forehead; purple and yellow bruising spread beneath her other eye. Her right arm, in a cast to the shoulder, was strapped to a traction bar; her right leg, encased in metal and fabric bracing, was strung up to another set of rigging. IV tubes snaked between the traction cables, and ranks of green-lit monitors silently charted heart beats, blood pressure, and other mysterious rhythms.

"Damn, Mom, you look like an erector set."

"Don't make her move her eyes," Marge warned Brad. "Moving the good eye hurts the other. You gotta sit right in front so's her eye don't move." She pressed a lever on the bed to raise Molly's head slightly. Brad perched carefully among IV tubes and traction rigging.

"Sal sent these," he said, holding up Sal's packet. He opened it, showing her the pictures of Bertha feeding the Admiral. "Sara said you wouldn't believe it without a picture. And Sal wrote you a penguin diary – only she calls it a dairy—I didn't have time to fix the spelling. Want me to read it?"

Bullhead interrupted. "Later, Brad. We don't have much time."

"Hey, Mom, you know this dude says he's your doctor is really Bullhead? Mac's old choker-setter from way back?"

"Save that for later, too," Bullhead laughed. He opened a cooler marked "Biological Samples KEEP FROZEN" and took out a box of popsicles. He unwrapped one for Molly and passed another to Brad, then glanced at Marge. "We can leave you and Brad for a few minutes...."

"No. Stay, please," Molly croaked. "I don't have enough voice to say it more than once."

Not sure she had the heart to tell it at all, she bit off a chunk of popsicle to cool her throat. "Telling the truth is like throwing up," Howie once told Brad, "the sooner you get it over with, the better." She swallowed hard and forced the words out in choppy fragments.

"Okay. I was supposed to meet Howie at Fisher Creek. Before seven. I was only a few minutes late. He wasn't there. A strange pickup was parked on the landing. Heard chainsaws, thought Fallwell had sent a crew to cut the nest tree before the court found out. Couldn't wait for Howie. Grabbed my camera. Hiked in. To film them cutting before the court deadline."

Molly paused. The popsicle slipped from her hand, and Marge caught it in a metal bowl. "I didn't know Howie was up the tree they were cutting. It wasn't the nest tree, it was the one across from it. He must've been up there rigging a place for me to film from." She reached for her glass of water, gulped it feverishly. "Three guys were setting wedges, taking turns sawing. Acted drunk, laughing, gunning their saws."

Bullhead wiped tears from Molly's cheek with a gauze pad. She drank again and went on, her eye fixed on Brad.

"Brad, I don't know if they really meant to fell the tree. I had the camera rolling. Then the tree exploded, like a – like a huge spring uncoiling – and it split up the middle. It crashed against other trees and then ... and then – Howie hit the ground. Don't know if he was still alive....Before I could move those goons made sure he wasn't...."

Her voice choked up. Monitor dials were swinging, and a buzzer sounded. Bullhead picked up a syringe.

"Brad, it's all on the tape. Get the tape!" Molly croaked.

"But where is it?" Brad said. "The cops didn't even find your camera."

Molly waved Bullhead off. "They got the camera. The three men. I – I wasn't thinking. They didn't know I was there 'til they hit Howie and I ran out to stop them. They came after me. With mauls, and an ax.

Yelling about the camera. I – oh, god, Brad, I left him. Left Howie. I ran away."

"Jesus, Mom, you'd be dead too if you hadn't!"

Molly gripped Brad's hand silently. She breathed as deeply as her broken ribs would allow, willing herself to relax, keep Dr. Kahn and his hypodermic at bay.

"They would've caught me, but one guy tripped. The others fell over him. I kept running. They were after the camera. I swapped the tape with a blank one. Dropped the camera down a gully. They all jumped down after it. I ran out to their truck. Called nine-one-one on their radio.

"I could hear them, heading to their truck. So scared. Had to hide the tape. Stuffed it under the driver's seat of their rig. In a McDonald's bag behind their trash. Lots of trash. Then I – I worked my way back to Howie. He was dead. But I couldn't leave him – leave him again."

Molly breathed in ragged gasps. "Wait. Please," she told Bullhead. "He made me promise, if anything happened to him. If he was bleeding. Not to touch him even to save his life. Every climb we did, he reminded me." She grabbed the metal bowl and poured the remains of her popsicle down her burning throat. "I hid near him. Waiting for the ambulance. Never occurred to me they'd say I killed him."

"So we find the pickup and get the tape, right?" Brad said.

"There's a picture." Molly waved her hand, unable to turn her head. "Marge, that picture…."

Marge handed Brad the Sunday photo section on the penguins.

"Yeah, we saw this," Brad said.

"That one, there." Molly pointed to a photo of a man peering into the viewer of a video camera. He wore a brown bomber jacket and a Raiders cap; the caption said he was Robert Marley, from Seattle, filming the penguins at Heceta Head. "My camera," Molly said. "See the chip? Where you dropped the hatchet on it?"

"Damn," Brad said. "We all laughed at that picture – the dude's name, I mean – we never even noticed your camera. But Mom, that means...."

"He's one of them, yes."

Voices approached the door, answered by the police guards. Brad slid off Molly's bed and picked up his Affirmative Action Man tray. Bullhead jabbed the hypodermic into a junction of the IV tubing.

"Ford pickup. New," Molly whispered. "Teal blue. Extended cab. Oregon plates. AVP 190."

Bullhead pressed the plunger. He was writing on a prescription pad when a night nurse came in with blood pressure cuffs and thermometers. Molly's good eye closed on the sight of Brad silently mouthing, "I love you."

* * *

Sal couldn't sleep. Brad had known she wouldn't. "Find me more songs for Nigger Lew," he'd said. "They only named a few in the articles – Swanee River, Arkansas Traveler, Soldier's Joy – so there must be lots more. He played for dances and parties, so see what was popular then – around the Civil War and afterward. And slave songs, too."

Sal was surprised at how many there were, and how many were songs Howie and Brad often played. She had filled three notebook pages already with song titles. Songbooks and CD liner notes covered the table, Howie's guitar perched on top of them. In Molly's room, the computer screen glowed next to the still-flashing alarm clock.

"Ooooh, I know this one, too, Admiral." Sal lifted the guitar onto her lap and picked out a melody. "Remember this? The Jenny Lynd Polka, it was really popular during the Civil War. You know, they didn't even have radios then?"

Her audience stood on Howie's boot by the door, his head under his wing.

"But who was Jenny Lynd?"

The Admiral didn't answer. Sal put the guitar down and went back to the computer. Brad's e-mail program was still up on the screen. Sal checked for new messages, hoping for a reply to the e-mail she'd sent earlier. She was disappointed but not surprised. Antarctica was a long way even for e-mail, and she had no idea what time it was there. She clicked back to the search engine, carefully typed in "Jenny Lynd" and waited.

Brad's quick lesson in search protocols had opened an exciting new world, a world forgiving even of Sal's spelling. Songs, her searches revealed, told stories far more real than the history books at school. She heard Brad's voice in chain-gang songs, in the escape code of "The Drinking Gourd." Every battleground lament mourned Howie, and one lyric after another sent her to the internet for its story.

"Sal, it's nearly midnight!" Sara stood in the doorway, Baby Craig asleep in her arms.

"Hey, the book spelled Jenny's name wrong," Sal said. "It's L-i-n-d, not L-y." She grinned happily at the computer screen. "I'm not the only one who's spelling impaired!"

"Who's Jenny?" Sara looked at the crowded table. "What's all this?"

"Jenny Lind. She was an opera singer. Had fans all over the world. So famous, P.T. Barnum, the big circus guy, put her in his show and someone wrote a polka about her and everybody danced." She hummed a few bars. "That one, remember?"

Sal trotted to the table to add a note to her list. "It's for Brad, see. He needs songs for his ancestor."

"His what?"

"His ancestor. For his autobiography." Sal giggled. "He's making the whole thing up, but Nigger Lew's for real. I mean, he was a real person, but not Brad's ancestor."

Sara laughed. "Okay, sorry I asked!"

"It's cool finding out. There's a story behind almost every song. Remember this one?" Sal picked up the guitar, her fingers rippling over the strings. "The theme for Popeye – it's really the Sailor's Hornpipe, from four hundred years ago. Lew must've played it, it was real popular for dances."

Sara yawned. "I can't wait up much longer. They should be back soon. You'll be okay?"

Sal looked up from the guitar. "Okay? Sure." She frowned, remembering Brad's mission. "I really wanted 'Handsome Molly' for Lew, but I can't find it before 1909. You think that's too late?"

"Oh lord, Sal, don't ask me. You call if you need me, okay?"

Sal didn't answer. Her fingers launched confidently on the first chord pattern Howie had taught her. Sara shut the door softly and tiptoed past the four sentinels on the porch. Sal's voice followed her home.

> "Sailing around the ocean, sailing around the sea
> I think of Handsome Molly, wherever she may be..."

* * *

Brad held the page from Bullhead's prescription pad tightly in his fist, the plate number written on it sounding in his head. AVP 190. He checked the license plates of every rig on the interstate, just for practice.

Beside him, Mac drove in grim silence, his large hands clenched on the wheel. He had said nothing since Brad told him Molly's story, more than an hour ago. Headlights and neon freeway signs burned Brad's eyes, but he couldn't close them against Mac's silent fury. When they turned off the garish interstate onto the unlit state highway to the coast, the darkness soothed his eyes. He tucked the memorized paper in his pocket.

"You okay, Mac?"

"Huh?" Mac grunted. "Oh. Yeah, right as rain."

The bitter tone startled Brad, but at least Mac was talking. "Bullhead said to make you tell about Peters. So who was he?"

Surprisingly, Mac laughed. "Oh, man, don't think I've even told Sara about that. Peters was on our crew – this is back in the eighties, mind you, we were all pretty wild then. We were working a unit up Cougar Creek. A log upended, killed him, right in front of us. They had to bring a life flight chopper in to get him, and we went on a two-day drunk that weekend, partyin' for Peters, see. And I mean really drunk."

Mac slowed down through the last sleeping town before the road twisted up into coast range mountains. "Peters didn't have no real family, his body was stuck in a damn funeral home until some cousin or something back in Pennsylvania coughed up for a burial. Peters himself didn't have any money, everything he didn't spend on booze he'd put into a little piece of land and the cabin he built. Drunk as lords, we convinced ourselves what he wanted was to be laid to rest in his own ground."

Mac laughed again. "So five of us crammed into Bullhead's cab with a sack of quart bottles and drove to the funeral home. It was storming so bad – hundred plus mile an hour winds almost blew the pickup off the highway, rain no wipers could handle – no one noticed us busting a window to get in. We found Peters in one of their charity coffins and loaded him, coffin and all, into the back of Bullhead's pickup. Oh man, were we sloshed! The coast highway was flooded in every low spot, and Bullhead plowed into water hub deep at Marion Slough. Stopped the rig dead and Peters' coffin fell out the back. Should'a seen it, the coffin floating on the tide and five drunks splashing after it in the dark.

"That sobered us up some, but not enough. We loaded him back aboard and I don't know how we made it all the way to Peters' place, but we did. Soaking wet, digging six feet into mud, I tell you, it was nuts."

Brad laughed, wondering at the rowdy past of his serious, responsible neighbor. "Did you get in trouble?"

"Hell no. 'Cause of the storm. The funeral people thought the wind broke their window, didn't even notice Peters was gone 'til a week later when the cousin's check showed up."

"But what about the grave? Didn't anyone ever find it?" Brad said.

"Far as I know, Peters is still where we laid him. We all split up a few months later – I came north to work, that was the last I saw Bullhead. 'Til tonight, I mean. I heard somewhere Peters' property got sold for taxes a while back. Trees woulda' grown over it by then, no one would know."

"Mac," Brad asked a while later. "What about Howie? Where will he get buried?"

"Oh, man, I dunno," Mac said. "If the feds really think he's FBI, they'll give him a hero's grave, I guess. Or the VA. He was a 'Nam vet, after all."

They were out of the mountains and passed Darkey Creek before Mac spoke again. "But if you're thinkin' what I think you're thinkin', forget it. My body-snatching days are over, pal."

* * *

They found Sal asleep in a kitchen chair, her head pillowed on open music books, one arm flung over Howie's guitar. She didn't wake when Mac carried her to her room. Brad covered her with a quilt and set the guitar carefully beside her. Going to Molly's room to turn off the computer, he saw a new, unread message notice on the screen from *Liza@gpantarct.com.* He opened it, puzzled.

> Dear Sal – Thank you for your message about the penguins. We have been reading about them on line. The Admural, I presume, is a penguin? A greenpeace research vessel left the San Juan Islands yesterday to investigate, and Greenpeace lawyers are preparing court actions to protect them. I am forwarding your message to my colleague, Seb Ainsworth, aboard the vessel Orca. He may contact you when they are in your area. Best wishes – Liza

Below this was Sal's initial message, with a link to an Oregonian story about the penguins:

> Dear Greenpece Antartica – I found your juronal of ice melting and the penguin picterers their just like the emporers in this Oregonian story. Their sleeping on our

> porch until the Admural is better he was hert bad and evryon is trieing to cach thm. Please help we cant hid them to long.

Shaking his head at Sal's spelling, Brad printed out the message for Sal to read in the morning.

Chapter Seventeen

When Sal gets too tired or really freaked, she gets these dark shadows under her eyes and blue lines around her mouth like when she was in the hospital. It always scares the shit out of me. For a long time after she came home I had night fears of her dying, of the cancer coming back, of her being cold and dead like Winston and burying her forever. Funny thing is I didn't have those fears when she really was dying, I don't know why. But after she was better I would wake up in the night sweating all over like I was digging her grave.

I woke up like that one night when Howie was sleeping on the couch and I woke him up, too freaked to be alone. He made hot chocolate and popcorn and we played checkers here on the table. Fear is the engine of survival, he said, the instinct to avoid immediate threats like predators or fire, but humans are the only animals that fear things that only might happen and consciously prepare for them. That's a real survival advantage, he said, unless you stretch it too far. Fear of what might happen can blind you to real dangers.

"Sure, that bridge up ahead might be mined," he said, 'but focus on that worry and a sniper takes you out before you get there."

So I think of snipers now when I go to sleep. Always makes me laugh, 'cause how many snipers run around on the Oregon coast, but I don't wake up with those sweat fears any more.

—The Oreo File

The first game of the season was delayed an hour by road repairs. A flood-damaged bridge had sent the Monroe team bus on a fifty-mile detour.

Joey sat on the tarmac of the school bus lot behind the ball field, fixing new trucks to a battered skateboard. A small boy sat beside him, hands cupped over precious bearings. Joey knew him as Pete, had never bothered to ask his last name. Brad, in his baseball uniform, drifted over and crouched to watch Joey's deft handling of a wrench.

"Yo, Mystery Man," Joey said. He grinned at the flush that darkened Brad's brown face.

"Who?" asked Pete.

"Joke," Brad said quickly. "He means me. Brad. First base."

"This here's Pete," Joey said.

Pete eyed Brad's uniform. "The game's late. Monroe bus is stuck in road work. I found a skateboard but it had no wheels."

"Oh. Uh – cool," Brad said. "The skateboard, I mean."

"Joey found me some trucks, he's gonna show me how to ride. You ever hit a homer?"

"Not often enough," Brad laughed.

"I start t-ball next week, but it's dumb," Pete said. "My dad won't let me have a skateboard."

Brad wasn't sure how to respond. This kid seemed to talk on two tracks at once.

"He says it's too dangerous," Pete went on. "Next year I can play real ball."

"T-ball's too dangerous?"

Pete giggled. "Nah. Skating."

Joey fastened the last screw and spun the wheels with his hand. Pete stood up, grinning, and reached for the board. Joey held it aside. "Get those pads on," he said, nodding toward a moldy field pack. "Your dad's right."

Pete opened the pack and ripped the shrink wrap off pairs of knee and elbow pads. Brad knew better than to ask how Joey acquired them or to look for a receipt. He helped fasten the Velcro around Pete's skinny limbs. Beaming, Pete set the skateboard on the pavement and hopped onto it. A second later he was sitting on the ground, the skateboard rolling across the lot by itself. Joey trotted after it.

"Start slow," Joey said, demonstrating. "Keep one foot off for balance 'til you get the hang of it, see? Tomorrow we find a helmet for you."

Pete wobbled away, his face intense. He got off the board to turn it around and returned, careening into Brad. Joey pulled a sawed-off Marlboro from behind his ear and lit it. He wondered what Brad wanted.

"You know Howie?" Brad began.

"Yeah. He's dead," Joey said.

"Well, here's the thing." Brad scuffed the tarmac with his cleats. "They busted my mom, said she killed him. But she didn't. The three dudes who said she did it, they're the ones who killed him."

Joey stared at Brad and grinned. Brad told him about Molly hiding the tape under the seat of the killers' pickup.

"She stuck it behind all their trash," Brad said. "Now we – I – gotta find it before they do. It's a Ford, extended cab, teal blue, she says."

"Like darkish blue, a little green? Yeah. Seen it at Dinkum's once. Three jerks. Had a video camera. That your mom's?"

"You saw it? The camera, too?"

"Yup. Seen 'em again at the Sinkhole t'other night. Asshole hit me with a beer can."

"Jesus, they're still around, then," Brad said.

"Trying to film penguins." Joey laughed. "With the lens cap on. Callin' 'em pelicans." He darted out to retrieve the skateboard again for Pete, missing what Brad said next.

"So, can you show me?" Brad finished.

"Show you what?"

Brad re-fastened Pete's knee pads and helped him aboard again. "How to hot-wire a rig. I need wheels, gotta find that pickup, man."

"No way, José," Joey said.

Brad stared at him, not sure he was serious. "Why the hell not?"

"Dude, Chief Gut-For-Brains'll make Rodney King of you in two miles."

"So what?" Brad's voice was shrill. He forced it lower. "My mom's looking at the death penalty. That tape's all there is to stop 'em. I gotta get it!"

"All you'll get's a cell up at county." Joey grabbed Pete's arm when he toppled. "Eddyville's far as I ever got myself. Fell asleep by the mill waitin' for a cop."

Brad's fury withered in confusion. He hadn't considered being locked up himself. "Waiting? Why?"

Joey shrugged, letting Pete go again. "Beds. Sheets. Books. TV. Hot food. Books. Shower…."

Brad gaped at him. "Books?"

"Cool books, dude. A library lady brings 'em. Anything you want, or you can take 'em from her cart. Got me every Hardy Boys in the state for a Toyota Corolla. All the old Three Investigators – you know, the ones Albert Hitchcock's really in 'em – that was for the Sentra.

Brad stared at him. "Alfred Hitchcock, you mean?"

"Yeah, him."

A school bus marked Monroe School District swung into the lot. Joey ran to pull Pete out of the way. Brad watched. Books? Alfred Hitchcock? Shaking his head, he picked up his gym bag and headed to the dugout.

* * *

Sara expected the game to be nearly over by the time Sal's swimming practice ended. She tucked Baby Craig into a sling carrier and handed Sal an umbrella in case of rain. They climbed the rickety stands to sit with Mac. The Monroe team was just coming off the field.

"Zero – zero, top of the fourth," Mac said. "They started late."

"How's Brad doing?" Sal asked.

"Struck out once," Mac said. "Caught a pop fly, tagged Monroe's catcher out."

"He misses Howie," Sal said.

Howie had never missed a game. With a can of beer in his pocket, waving a bag of popcorn for Sal, he would shout himself hoarse, bellowing cheers and outrageous insults at Brad and his team. He never called their right names, hurling advice to Pee Wee or Carl or some other long-dead Brooklyn hero. Brad, Sal thought, had been secretly embarrassed by Howie's blasts from the stands; now, watching him trot out to first base, Sal felt the lonely regret in every step. He glanced back and caught her eye, nodding imperceptibly before concentrating on the play.

Both teams scored two runs in the fourth. The score stayed at two and two right up to the ninth inning. The sun sank into a fog bank and the field lights came on. Sara took Baby Craig home when the tie held through the ninth, missing Brad's spectacularly casual double play in the tenth. Mac wrapped his jacket around Sal.

The stands had become more crowded as word went out about the tied game. Monroe failed to score in the eleventh inning, but Sal suddenly felt the crowd's tension shift. The score was still tied when Brad came to bat, with two out and a man on second, but suddenly the stands were emptying. Sal caught the word "penguins" from an excited mob and grabbed Joey as he darted past.

"Yeah," he said. "Penguins. Fishing boat caught 'em, bringin' 'em in to Foster's Landing."

Joey ran on. Sal stood up. The word had reached Brad, too. He stood at the plate, distracted, facing the pitch like a deer in the headlights. Strike two. He met Sal's eye with a pleading, furious look, then turned as the next pitch came, swinging blindly. The crack of the ball connecting jarred him. Dumbly, he watched the ball soar out of the park. Shouts from the dugout sent him round the bases at top speed. He crossed the plate and kept on running out of the park, following the crowd.

In the stands, Mac cheered the winning run alone. He turned to find Sal gone, his jacket abandoned on the bench.

Five blocks from the boat landing, the street was blocked by cars, trucks, motor homes, campers, news vans, and a Trailways bus, massed on roadway and sidewalk. Brad charged frantically through the crowd toward the boat ramp, looking for Sal. Over the ocean beyond the bay, clouds broke on a gory streak of sunset, blinding all eyes watching for a boat.

The boat ramp was blocked by Chief Roberts's empty cruiser, its lights flashing. Behind it was a large white satellite TV van. Brad saw no sign of Sal. It was almost low water. Up on the dock, two cops tried to keep the mob from shoving camera crews overboard. Someone grabbed Brad's baseball cap.

"Brad? Up here!"

Sal sat on top of the satellite van, wearing a headset that coiled from the open window. Beside her sat Joey, holding a hotdog, a cigarette in his mouth. Two RIPs crouched behind them, passing a joint. Street lights lit the crowded parking lot, blotting out the dark water of the bay. Kids clung to light poles like monkeys, and people swarmed on top of vehicles, up shade trees, on roofs of bait shops and bayside houses. In the garish mercury vapor light, Sal's face was a silvery blue, dark veins webbing her mouth. Brad looked questioningly at Joey, wondering about the teal-blue pickup.

"Ain't seen it," Joey said. "Hard to spot in this mob."

Sal held up her hand, listening to the headphones. "They're just north of the breakwater. Maybe. They sound drunk or retarded or something." She bit her lip. "They only got one. Probably the Admiral."

She was silent, listening to fragmented squawks on the headset, her eyes battling tears. Brad stared blindly into the darkness, wonder what the boat was doing out there. The small harbor here handled only bay and river boats, not ocean-going vessels. The river mouth shifted with every tide, its shallow channel too unpredictable for navigation; not even the Coast Guard would risk a boat through. Only a drunk or a lunatic would try it.

The RIPs laughed at something. Brad shushed them when Sal stiffened. "They're over the bar....don't have any lights, or don't know how to work them....they found the channel buoy...."

Halogen camera lights flared on the dock. Chief Roberts marched importantly down the ramp and turned on the headlights of his cruiser, lighting up a swath of dark water. He rigged a rooftop spotlight and aimed it, too, in the general direction of the ocean. Brad saw Dumb Darryl on the dock, urging the crowd back from the camera crews. The crowd was almost silent now, all staring west into the darkness beyond the highway bridge. A thin streak of daylight faded on the horizon. Bridge lights flickered on tide ripples in the black water.

Beyond the bridge, where the bay narrowed at its shifting mouth, a light winked briefly, vanished, winked again. The crowd burst into renewed shouting. Sal grabbed Brad's arm. The light bobbed and weaved, vanished and reappeared. It cleared the distant breakwater and swooped into a straight run toward the shouting crowd. Dimming rapidly, the light shot under the bridge. The spotlights picked up a boat streaking out of the blackness, churning up a swollen bow wave. The crowd surged onto the dock and boat ramp.

A halogen light on the dock toppled. Brad saw Dumb Darryl vainly trying to right it. The boat roared toward the dock at full throttle, missing the end piers by inches. Four men stood in it, waving beer cans. The man in the bow held a dying flashlight. They swept into a wide turn and slowed up in the floodlights fifty feet off the dock. The two in the middle mugged for the cameras and tried to hoist a large, wrapped bundle over their heads. The boat lurched in its own wake, knocking them off balance. They dropped the bundle and fell overboard as the man at the wheel revved up again. The boat veered into another sharp turn, the bow man waving his flashlight at the two thrashing figures in the water. The boat stalled abruptly in mid-turn and stopped on the edge of the floodlights.

The crowd screamed. Brad saw the men's heads go under in the glare, the boat rocking in shadow, the TV cameras rolling. Dumb Darryl leaped off the dock and swam toward the drowning men. The crowd followed, splashing like lemmings into the water, churning loudly after

Darryl. Brad looked for the boat, which had now drifted seaward out of the light. Sal was gone, the headset left dangling from the van window. He knew instantly where she'd gone.

The RIPs stomped on the van roof, laughing at the chaos. Brad yelled at Joey, "Where's Sal? Where's Sal?"

Joey didn't answer, his eyes fixed on something at the edge of the crowd. Brad grabbed his arm, hopping on one foot to pull off his cleats. Joey turned but said nothing. "A diversion – quick!" Brad yelled. "DO something! Hear me?"

Brad didn't wait for an answer. He jumped down and stumbled through the crowd, heading for the western edge of the floodlit water where the boat had vanished. He tossed his uniform pants onto the rip-rap and waded into the bay. The water was icy cold; he felt his balls shrinking. Behind him, the rescue operation sounded more like a mass drowning. He glanced back in time to see Chief Roberts's cruiser roll in slow motion down the boat ramp. It slid into the water, headlights and spotlight spreading a submerged glow. Brad paused to watch. An extra crescendo of yells accompanied the satellite van rolling into the water behind the cruiser. Brad choked on a laugh. When it came to diversions, Joey had no equal.

Outside the halo of floodlights, the blackness was frightening. Brad tried not to think about sting rays and eels or Nessie lurking beneath him. Over the roar of the mob he located the boat by the swearing and thumps of someone yanking a starter. He swam toward it, trying not to splash. Sal was out here somewhere, but he dared not call out. The boat loomed up suddenly, bigger than it had looked from shore. He swam quietly to the seaward side to see it against the shore lights, listening hard for any sound from Sal. Two men stood in the boat, facing the receding shoreline, yelling. No one on shore could possibly have heard them.

Sal bobbed up beside Brad, her hand icy on his shoulder. He grabbed it in relief. The men were shouting at each other now, each blaming the other for running out of gas. The bow man swung his flashlight at the other and missed, dropping the flashlight into the cockpit. The second man swung back wildly. Treading water, Brad and Sal watched the snarling silhouettes thrash each other, hearing fists hit wood, fiberglass, and flesh. One of them broke free and scrambled onto the foredeck. The other lunged after him, and both disappeared in a single splash, sending the boat broadside into Brad.

* * *

Sal was over the gunwale by the time he caught his breath. He heaved himself after her. In the faint light of the dying flashlight, a bundle lay on the cockpit floor, a mass of fishnet wound around it. Together, they lifted it over the side, Sal slipping into the water with it. Brad jumped after her, kicking the boat toward the two men thrashing off the starboard side. Numb to the cold now, he joined Sal. They towed the bundle toward the dark edge of town behind the middle school, helped by the tide sweeping them away from the boat landing.

They brought the bird ashore at a small picnic ground adjacent to the school. There were no lights, only the glow from house windows across the road. Frantically, they tugged at the net. The bird didn't move. Brad said nothing. He thought it was dead. Sal unwound part of the net, her hands shaking from cold. Brad felt goosebumps on his bare legs and stood up.

"Need a knife. Stay here, I'll find Mac."

He ran hard along the beach, found his uniform pants on the rocks where he'd left them and put them on. The crowd was milling around in disappointment and aftershock, parting sullenly for three ambulances. The police cruiser's lights still gleamed under water, the hind end of the satellite van sticking up behind it at the bottom of the boat ramp. Joey stood with a small crowd, admiring his handiwork. He handed Brad his shoes with a puzzled look, then faded into the crowd.

All eyes were now on a small skiff moving slowly toward the beach, towing the disabled motorboat, its wet, drunk passengers still yelling at each other. One of the two men rowing the skiff was Mac; they beached it and hauled the motorboat on shore. Ignoring the drunks, Mac pushed off the skiff and his partner rowed away.

"Mac!" Brad yelled.

Mac turned. Brad ran to him in his stocking feet, carrying his cleats. His baseball shirt dripped onto his pants.

"Where is she?" Mac asked.

Brad nodded westward. "At the park. With the Admiral. I think it's the Admiral."

Mac didn't wait for details. He ran for his truck.

Chapter Eighteen

My mom calls the RIPs gang wannabes, which is kinda true and kinda pathetic 'cause they're really just bored stiff dropouts and crackheads. They call me their bro, think I'm big and black and cool. It's kinda weird, when you think about it, white dudes wanting only the black part of me, so there's a whole side they never see. "Hybrid vigor," my mom says, "you got the best of both worlds." Sounds good. I like the words. Maybe someday I'll have me a band, call it Hybrid Vigor. But if there's even one best thing in me it's not black or white and it's sure as shit not what the RIPs see.

It's funny how when geese or sparrows get together in a flock and all move together it's for reasons that protect them from predators or help them migrate to warm places, but when a bunch of people get together it's usually for something absolutely dumb like racism or blowing each other up. Howie says he doesn't know why this is, either. When I think about those puppies I don't miss the RIPs anyway.

—*The Oreo File*

Joey clung halfway up a light pole on the fishing dock. Bewildered, he watched Brad race into the darkness with someone from the skiff. Whatever Brad was after, it didn't seem to be the teal-blue pickup.

From the roof of the satellite van, Joey had seen the three goons charging the dock, one carrying the video camera. He'd assumed Brad's frantic call for a diversion to be cover for finding their truck and the all-important videotape. But Brad had returned without the tape. Dripping wet and terrified, he'd just grabbed his shoes and torn off again. Joey scanned the milling crowd on the dock. The three goons were still there, aiming the camera at the submerged police car. Joey slid down the pole. No point wasting a good diversion.

The disappointed mob was dispersing to the streets, where knots of angry drivers surrounded trapped vehicles. Brake lights shattered in their attempts to get away. Joey avoided the pavement, darting through yards and hedges, climbing porches to scan the sea of rigs. On a side street he spotted the teal-blue pickup easily, parked crookedly across the mouth of a driveway. It was backlit by the headlights of a car trapped in the drive. Ahead of the car were the red tail lights of another, facing a closed garage door. Joey watched it jerk forward into the door and swerve backwards across the small lawn. A man charged out of the house yelling at the car, which flattened a hedge of rose bushes, smashed a garden gnome, and veered into the street, one headlight broken. The other car backed up and followed, narrowly missing the furious homeowner.

From a neighboring porch, Joey watched the man inspect his dented garage door and flattened hedge, snapping angrily at a couple walking past with a stroller. With a last look at the damage, the man picked up shards of garden gnome and disappeared into the house, slamming the door. Joey waited until the couple with the stroller had turned the corner. He climbed over the porch railing and froze. From the shadows across the street, a figure approached the teal blue pickup, walking purposefully around it, testing the doors. A cop. Puzzled, Joey watched him run his fingers along the tops of the closed windows. Glancing up and down the street, the cop pulled something from his pocket and bent to the lock of the driver's door. Headlights loomed from a vehicle turning into the street, and the cop vanished into the rose hedge.

Joey waited, alarmed and frustrated. Why was a cop trying to break into that particular rig? More cars turned into the street and groups of people fanned across it, talking, getting into vehicles. Joey dared not move. The cop was out of sight, but he could be watching from the shadows just as Joey was. Curiosity kept him at his post until the three goons came back, beer cans in their hands. Not even a bent cop, Joey thought, would ignore such provocation, but the men got into the truck and peeled out with no interference from the law. Joey trotted back to the fishing dock to watch a crane lift the satellite van and police cruiser out of the water.

* * *

The Admiral lay across Sal's lap, limp and wet. In the glare of Mac's headlights, blood shone black on his wing, where the barely healed scar had ripped open again. One of his feet was twisted backward, obviously broken. Shivering and dripping, Sal cradled him, humming softly. Brad recognized the song, a Jacobite lament for the massacre at Glencoe. Mac pressed a hand against the sodden feathers.

"Still kicking," he said.

Sal sobbed. Gently, Mac lifted the Admiral. Brad carried Sal to the truck and squeezed into the cab with her, the Admiral across their laps. Sara had hot soup ready for them at home. The Admiral showed some signs of life when Mac set him down in his old spot on Howie's boot. He struggled frantically, flapping his one good wing, trying to balance on one foot, then fell over and lay still. Sal, in dry pajamas with a blanket wrapped around her, sat with him. When Brad came back to the kitchen after changing into dry clothes, Mac was on the phone giving directions to someone.

"Bullhead," he said, hanging up. "Lucked out, he's just going off duty. He's on his way."

"Doc Kahn?" Brad asked. "But he's not…."

"A vet? 'Course not, but who else we gonna call? By law a vet has to report wildlife injuries, but not a people doctor. That wing's buggered, looks like the tendon's snapped, and his leg's broken – way beyond me fixin' him." Mac glanced anxiously at Sal. "Jerks must've rolled him in that net any old way."

"They dropped him, too," Brad said. "Then stomped all over him fighting in the boat."

Sal drank a little soup, still huddled with the Admiral, stroking his back and head. Brad saw her eyes close, her head nodding. He grabbed her soup mug just in time, then brought a chair cushion from Molly's room and draped a quilt over her and the penguin. Sara fell asleep with Baby Craig on the couch, while Brad and Mac washed dishes and scrubbed the table.

Bullhead found them there an hour later, half asleep over a cribbage board. He sent Brad to his car for a suitcase and satchel of tools. Brad helped him spread a mat and sterile paper over the table, placing trays of instruments on chairs and counter. Sara, fortified with Mac's fresh pot of coffee, rigged up extra trouble lights. She and Bullhead put on masks, gowns, and surgical gloves. Mac lifted the Admiral onto the table. He raised his head but didn't struggle. Sal perched on the counter, watching every move.

Bullhead inspected the damage, then injected novocain around the Admiral's wing and leg. "Don't dare use a general," he said. "Nothing in the books about dose for a penguin."

Quietly, with few words, he and Sara went to work, Sara slipping into her old job easily, handing him tools before he had to ask. He worked on the wing first, probing for the ends of tendons that had snapped back inside like broken rubber bands. Sara held them together while he sewed. They stitched rows of tiny sutures patching the ugly gash and ripped skin, then wrapped the wing against the bird's body to immobilize it.

The broken leg troubled him. "Need a fuckin' x-ray, dammit," he said. He closed his eyes and explored the bones with his fingertips, explaining its structure to himself as much as to the others.

"This isn't really his leg, see. On us it'd be the long part of your foot, heel up here, so he's really walking on his toes." With his eyes still closed, Bullhead moved the bones, a tiny fraction at a time. He opened his eyes finally, holding both hands over the leg, and nodded. Sara slipped an L-shaped splint between his hand and the leg, binding it in place with fluffy gauze. She soaked a roll of prepared bandage in warm water, and together they wrapped the leg quickly before the plasticized bandage hardened. When they finished, the cast bent in a right angle at the bottom, with the clawed tips of the bird's toes poking out. Bullhead drew antibiotic into a syringe.

"He weighs – what, about sixty pounds, you said?" He took the needle off the syringe and squirted the contents into the Admiral's beak. "Three times a day," he ordered. "And keep that wing and leg immobilized at least ten days."

Mac lifted the Admiral to the floor. He wobbled, flailing with his good wing, and fell over. Sal propped him against her cushion and sat with him, humming. They fell asleep leaning on each other like two drunks. Sara filled Bullhead's coffee thermos and put brownies in a sack for the road.

Bullhead stood at the sink, rubbing disinfectant soap on his hands and arms. "That was a first. A penguin. Who'd a' thought?" He took the towel Sara handed him and grinned. "You ever move to Portland, the job's open – surgical nurses are in short supply." He turned to Mac. "Speaking of Portland, I almost forgot. You know they want to move Molly next week?"

"Move her! Where?" Sara demanded.

"Coast hospital."

"Who said they can do that?"

"Hey, I told 'em she couldn't be moved, but your DA sent some quack – shit, the guy's an osteopath or something – sent him to 'examine' her. He just looked in the door, didn't even read the chart. Went back and signed a statement for the judge."

Brad rolled up the paper from the table and stuffed it in the firebox. "When?"

"End of next week. What's their goddamn hurry, anyway?"

"Dunno," Mac said, thinking. "The DA's in some kind'a bind. Fallwell's his biggest campaign money. He's up for re-election, and the company's on his case, I bet – first they couldn't log 'cause of the murrelets, and now the whole unit's a crime scene."

“He sure wants Molly back in jail,” Bullhead said. “At least their tame quack stopped short of that.”

“She’ll be in county hospital, then?” Sara asked, thinking of Grandma Rose.

Bullhead nodded. “Me, too. I’m taking leave to come down with her.” He inspected the Admiral quickly. “Keep tabs on this patient, too.”

Brad helped Bullhead pack up and carry his equipment to the car. He patted Joe a goodnight on his way back to the house and was in bed, nearly asleep, when it struck him. There were no penguins on the porch. The Admiral’s crew had not come home.

Chapter Nineteen

Howie keeps his guitar and books at our house where it's dry. He lives in an old sawdust cone, a sheet-metal teepee that they used to burn sawdust in, part of the abandoned mill next to the big Rock Creek wilderness area. You can't get to it by road any more since the old bridge washed out. You go across the creek on the old bridge timbers on foot and hike the last mile. If I ever want to get away from the world – the world of people, that is – I'll find me a place like Howie's. You can't hear a single sound of civilization there, just the river and wind singing, and birds everywhere. Little trees grow through the old mill buildings, and blackberries make huge mounds over old sheds and machinery, covering ugliness with green life. Howie keeps paths cleared through the brush and sets benches from the old cookhouse in the clearings so he can sit outside and carve things. Any old hunk of wood he finds, he chips and whittles away at until it's a bear or a chipmunk or elk. You never know what you'll find along those paths he's cleared. Over by the old cookhouse there's a carved fawn and Snow White and the seven dwarves, and on top of pilings in the old mill pond are four heads of Richard Nixon staring down at a new beaver dam. Once Mom asked him why all the Richard Nixons, and he said no one else had a nose to fit the grain of burl wood.

My favorite carving is this huge frog made from a cedar stump. Howie calls her Rana Madonna *and wrote a song about her, a frog who wants to be a mammal. She's holding two pollywogs and smiling that same smile Sara gets when she nurses Baby Craig. He carved it after we all went out there for a picnic last Fourth of July, and Mac stood up on the huge slab cookhouse table between the potato salad and deviled eggs and gave his big announcement about the baby coming. For Christmas, Howie carved a set of manger figures for Mac and Sara. They're made out of maple and alder and some dark red madrone from over in the valley. His shepherds have faces of me and Sal and Mom, and the Three Kings are loggers carrying chainsaws and axes, and Mary and Joseph of course are Mac and Sara, with Joe and Bertha hanging around the manger with some sheep. The manger was empty until Baby Craig was born. Then he added a perfect little Baby Craig made of hazel wood. But I still like the Rana Madonna Best.*

—*The Oreo File*

Seventy feet off the ground, Molly pauses in her climb, blinded by sunlight flashing off the water below. The tree sways gently in the cool breeze off the river. Downstream, a heron belches out its ghastly croak and takes off, flapping ponderously over the trees. Two kingfishers dart past, calling to each other in rasping squawks. Molly sways with the tree, her climbing spikes firmly wedged in the moss and lichen matted trunk. Savoring the soft, candy-flavored scent of licorice ferns growing on the branches, she wonders fleetingly how a big-leaf maple has grown so tall, why she's wearing a pirate hat, and why it doesn't matter.

A trout leaps in a backwater, sending ripples onto the bank. A woodpecker hammers a tree nearby. Molly breathes the river-soaked breeze and sings, "I have a song to sing – oh." She holds the "Oh," waiting for Howie's response. It never comes. Instead, the high, excited voice of her son:

"Mom, look!"

In horror, she looks down. Brad, his pudgy four-year-old body stark naked, sways easily on a branch ten feet below her, one hand waving cheerfully, the other on his penis, peeing into the depths.

"Look, Mom! It goes all the way down!"

* * *

The pain of laughing and cold sweat of fear woke her. A dream or a memory? Molly wasn't sure. The overhead light blinded her good eye, the smells of disinfectant and flowers mingled unpleasantly. Her sore throat reminded her where she was, and she suppressed a new laugh.

Strangely, she was alone in the room. At Molly's urging, Marge had finally gone home to sleep; her replacement, Molly vaguely remembered, had been called suddenly to ER. Some kind of big accident. Yes, she remembered that, now. She looked at the small pot of chrysanthemums on the bedside cart, the garish arrangement of flowers on the window-sill. Both from Mort, her boss. Next to the chrysanthemums was the penguin mug Brad had brought, a flexible straw draped over its rim. Proud of herself, she itemized each gift. Groping for the button that raised the head of her bed, she pressed it until she was sitting as near to upright as her ribs would allow. She reached for the penguin mug and drank.

The ice had melted, the water was nearly warm. She must have slept a long time. The clock over the door said ten twenty, and it was dark outside the windows. Except for the background hum of pumps and monitors, the room was quiet. She could hear the faint murmur of voices and intercom commands far off, the muffled sounds of urgency, but the curtain was drawn over the window to the nurses' station; she was cut off, isolated. The small CD player Marge had brought her was silent, Marge's Gilbert and Sullivan CD no longer spinning. For the moment, Molly didn't mind. In hospitals, solitude was a precious commodity. Her head clearing finally of pain-killers, she had some serious remembering to do.

The problem, she realized, was too many memories. The smells and sounds of the hospital replayed a year of days in a children's cancer ward. The small, pinched faces and bald heads crowding eagerly around her in a heartbreaking playroom, hanging on every word of Freddy the Pig. All twenty-six books. The faces that vanished, never to hear the end. Their simple joy in seeing what hat she'd be wearing each day; the boxes of absurd headgear sent weekly, with no rental charge, by a stranger named Leon at Willamette Prop and Costume after her hesitant phone call. The bizarre arrival of a homeless horse on the hospital lawn, and her icy dread when Sal announced that his name was Joe and he'd come to take her home.

Before the cancer ward, there was the infant ICU where a baby named Salamander fought for life while a panhandling fiddler handed her brother the keys to a musical kingdom. G-D-A-E. And the marriage meant to give her son a family fell apart. Molly cringed inside at the word husband and refused to think his name. Was she really the person whose dreams of family had blinded her to a monster's true colors? With Sal's birth, an over-ambitious husband and stepfather became overnight a brutal tyrant, inexplicably blaming her and Brad for his daughter's three-chambered heart.

She hadn't understood, until Sal was diagnosed with leukemia, the eleventh child in their suburban neighborhood to come down with the disease. Going door to door, talking to grieving mothers, she learned the grim history of their pleasantly landscaped haven. In its previous incarnation, the land had belonged to Fallwell Wood Products. For forty years, the company had treated lumber, railroad ties, and power poles on the once-secluded site, saturating the soil and water table with deadly preservatives and solvents. Cashing in on urban growth and soaring real estate values, Fallwell had covered the dead land with topsoil and sold it to developers, neglecting to mention the toxic stew brewing beneath the turf and seeping into every home.

Fallwell happened to be her husband's employer. He filed for divorce when Molly and ten other mothers chained themselves to the Fallwell main office gate, with signs calling the company baby killers. She and the other women had spent a night in the local jail, writing press releases and eating pizza brought in by a sympathetic female sheriff. Fallwell eventually dropped the charges against them, and after a sordid episode with her husband and the CEO's daughter, the marriage was gone for good, relegated to the memorable mistakes file of Molly's life.

Her thoughts drifted even further back, to a rural clinic where a mixed-race Baby Boy Doe languished, unclaimed and unwanted, until a harried nurse thrust him into the arms of a visiting freelance videographer. Being struck by lightning couldn't be more shocking, Molly thought, remembering the searing joy of that moment. She'd come to the clinic to film a documentary for a nonprofit adoption group, who gladly made arrangements for her unplanned motherhood. Unplanned, indeed. She smiled, remembering her frantic call to Planned Parenthood for help changing a diaper.

Get a grip, Mom, Brad would say. Molly sipped warm water from the penguin mug. Okay. Start with penguins. She'd never seen the birds that now filled headlines. Why had they come here? Were they another harbinger of climate change, like the storms that had wiped out coastal towns last year, the islands now submerged in rising oceans, the new diseases threatening the globe? What kind of world would her children face when she was gone? With both polar icecaps melting, where on earth could wayward penguins survive?

Wayward penguins. Wayward thoughts. Get a grip, Molly. She hadn't seen the penguins because she'd been arrested. Because Howie was dead. Murdered. On tape. Yes, she'd managed to remember that for Brad, made sure her children knew what really happened. Sal. Brad. She tried to picture them – Sal the survivor, Brad the big, so ungainly until he picked up a violin bow – but oh god, picturing them was a mistake. In every picture was Howie. Howie with a book. A hoof pick. A guitar. A wounded fawn. Howie….

"Howie!"

The scream she'd silenced in the clearing ten days ago escaped at last. The penguin mug dropped from her hand. She heard it hit the floor, heard the crack of breaking porcelain. Fumbling for the call button, her left hand knocked the pot of chrysanthemums off the bedside tray. Another crash. She heard sobbing. Her ribs hurt. Tears burned under the bandage over her eye.

"Uh, ma'am?"

The door opened a crack. She couldn't see the speaker.

"Ma'am? You okay?" A male voice, young, hesitant.

Molly pulled herself together. "Yes. I mean, no. No."

"You need something? I'm not supposed to come in."

"A nurse, please." Molly's convulsive grief had jerked the IV stand into the rigging holding her right arm rigid; it tilted over the bed, wobbling.

"Um..." The door opened. A young black cop stood in the doorway, his face anxious, his voice hesitating on unfamiliar jargon. "They all got called to ER, ma'am, except two with post-op patients...."

He saw the teetering IV stand, its tubes snarled in traction cables, and came in, grabbing the stand before it fell. Standing in a puddle of chrysanthemums, he untangled the tubing.

"Thank you," Molly said, simple courtesy arresting her plunge into despair. Tell-tale callouses on his fingertips caught her attention. "What do you play?" she asked.

He followed her glance. "Bass. Double bass sometimes." He grinned. "Well, anything with strings."

"What happened? Where are the nurses?"

"Big fire down at the river. A chemical plant. They're evacuating the area. Hospital's flooded with casualties – firemen, cops, kids." He glanced anxiously toward the door, lowering his voice. "It's bad. Real bad. My partner's off hunting up decontamination suits."

"And you're stuck here? Why?" Molly asked.

He looked uncomfortable. "Guard detail."

"Guarding me? Against what?"

"Um – escape. Orders from Branscombe DA." He looked at her casts, the oxygen apparatus, the rigging he'd just untangled, and laughed softly. "About as much chance as a tree escaping, but it pays overtime. Anyway, everyone's down in ER. I'll find a mop."

Mopping under the bed, he raked out the remains of the penguin mug.

"Oh, man, that's too bad." He looked at it sorrowfully, then brightened. "Hey, it's not really broken – no cracks, even."

He groped under the bed and found the handle. "A little glue's all she needs. I can bring it back tomorrow. If you want, that is."

Molly nodded. A spark in his eager, changeable eyes drew her further from the spiraling black hole of loss. "The world is full of breakers," Howie had told Brad, "and too few fixers – healers, musicians, saints, rescuers of birds and newts – fellow travelers in a world of hurt." She smiled.

He wrapped the mug and its severed handle in paper towels. "Those penguins – you seen 'em? Me, neither. Was going to take my kid brother down this weekend, try to spot 'em."

"How old's your brother?" Molly asked.

"Just fifteen. I'm all he's got since the folks died last year."

"Oh, I'm sorry," Molly said. "An accident?"

He shook his head. "Dad of cancer. Mom's heart went a few months later. All real sudden. Gaspar – my brother – was one fu—messed up kid. I wasn't much better, going to police academy, playin' gigs at night, I didn't see where he was going 'til it was too late, almost – into drugs and gang stuff, thievin', you name it."

"Oh, no." Molly thought of Brad, the RIP's, the times she and Howie had sat up wondering where he was. "What did you do? Is he still …?"

"Didn't know what to do. I'm eight years older, it's not like we were ever close, see. But when he was little he used to hang around when I practiced. He'd try to play my old guitar, it was bigger'n he was. That was our only real connection. So I offered him a deal. We went and bought him a guitar. The deal was I'd teach him to play and he'd practice two hours a day, no exceptions. All I thought was, keep him off the streets two hours a day. Next thing, he's practicing four, five, six hours a day, keeping me up all hours playin' together, he's getting' so far ahead now, I'll never catch up!"

Molly smiled at the familiar story. "Kept him out of trouble, did it?"

"Funny thing," he said. "More like inviting trouble – and turning it around. His friends'd come by and he'd show 'em what he was doing.

One at a time, they come back, wanting more, wanting to learn, too. Neighbors start complaining about all the gangsta kids hanging around, so I go to the bank – in my uniform, see, which could probably get me fired, but it works. I tell 'em what we need, and they let us use this vacant storefront down on MLK, was a pawn shop 'til the owner died and the bank took over."

"A pawn shop?" Molly laughed, in spite of the pain.

"Fairly Honest Eddie's. The name's still over the door." He smiled, shaking his head in wonder. "It was scary, really, all these toughs expecting me to make 'em into rap or rock stars overnight. But Gaspar took over, told 'em it was about music, not stars, worked 'em so hard they'd forget to eat. I come in and teach 'em stuff but he's the driver, keepin' 'em at it. He's so good, see, they all look up to him."

He took the mop out and came back with a fresh jug of ice water and a plastic cup. "You won't tell anybody, will you?"

"About what?"

"The kids, teachin' 'em. Some of 'em have bad records, warrants out even. I need this job, see. Like being an undercover musician, you understand?"

Molly nodded. He smiled proudly. "Gaspar found a computer geek who's got the equipment to record. They're putting together a CD. And it all makes me wonder…"

"About what?"

"Well, I'm showing these kids music theory, chord progressions, showing 'em riffs in songs they know and where they come from – blues, Cajun, classical, bluegrass. And I think music changes their brain cells around somehow. They start thinking, and not just about music, either. Making connections, curiosity, wanting to learn. You think that's possible?"

"Absolutely," Molly said. "My friend How…."

He started guiltily at a rush of activity outside the open door. "I better – uh – "

Molly took his hand, smiling. "Absolutely," she said again. "And –

thanks."

He turned in the doorway, holding the wrapped penguin mug. "They call themselves the Fairly Honest Eddies."

The door closed behind him. He hadn't even told her his name. A fellow traveler passing through like a gravity wave, shifting reality. Molly sipped the ice water and closed her eye.

Passing through. A packed evening at Dinkum's, the entire place joining Howie, Mex, and Sal in chorus: "Passing through – passing through, Sometimes happy, sometimes blue, Glad that I ran into you…."

Bullhead, bleary from a long drive and kitchen-table penguin surgery, swung by the hospital to check on his patient before heading home to sleep. At Molly's door, he nodded absently at the young black cop leafing through pages of sheet music propped on a paper towel bundle in his lap. Inside the room, Bullhead stared in puzzlement at a bedpan full of potting soil and chrysanthemums on the bedside tray. Beside it, Molly smiled peacefully, sound asleep.

Chapter Twenty

Sal can't spell worth a shit, but she's the smartest person I know. Way smarter than me. It's not so much what she knows, it's how she puts things together and figures out what they mean before I've even collected all the pieces. Even when she was real little you could see it, she never stopped watching and noticing every little thing. She'd watch me doin' something like tune my violin or put a glider together and you could see her mind work, and she'd make a big happy smile like she'd figured it all out. Reading stories to her was a trip. She made you read every single word, even the copyright stuff, watching so you didn't skip any. It's not like she could read, she just watched the page and knew how many words you should be saying or something. And she never stops wanting to know what everything is and how it works.

Just when she was supposed to start school she got leukemia and was in the hospital a whole year, but she learned more that one year than a whole twelve years of school. By the time she'd been there a few weeks she was jabbering away in Russian and Spanish to these other kids in the ward, translating for them to the nurses. And she learned to read, not from kids' books but from newspapers that people left behind, just asking and asking nurses or visitors what the words were. I asked her once why she liked newspapers and she said 'cause she was going to die and needed to find out everything first. I didn't want her to die so I told her there's lots of things the newspapers don't write about. She just shrugged and said newspapers were all she had, so me and Mom had to go to Powell's and thrift shops and find books about turtles and stars and how to grow peanuts or build rockets or sail a schooner. Her favorites were the field guides to everything, everywhere. She can still tell you every animal and bird in Madagascar.

The day the doctors said she was gonna live was the best day of my life.

—*The Oreo File*

Brad drilled a hole for the last screw of a latch for the gate he'd built across the porch steps. Fine curls of wood sprouted from the tip of Molly's hand drill. Sara had said he could use Mac's cordless, but he refused, remembering one of Howie's casual commandments, "A worker's tools are like his hands – you don't touch 'em unless they're offered." Hand tools were more gratifying, anyway, he thought, like acoustic instruments. He tightened the screw and swung the gate shut; the latch caught with a satisfying click. He swept up the sawdust and collected the drill, cross-cut saw, and screwdriver, admiring his work for a moment before opening the door.

"All done," he said. "Come and see."

Sal jumped up from a disarray of math papers. Home schooling certainly agreed with her, Brad thought. He wished her teacher could see her now, the teacher who'd wanted Sal put on Ritalin because she couldn't spell. Freed from such ignorant censure, Sal had flown through her third-grade math book in a single afternoon, and was already halfway through Brad's seventh-year algebra text. Her idea of quiet recreation was an afternoon with one of Howie's calculus books. How could a kid who amused herself calculating rocket trajectories and stock market odds possibly go back to the inanities of third grade, Brad wondered.

"Welcome to Little Antarctica," he said.

Sal looked at his rearrangement of the porch and laughed. Early that morning, Mac had delivered two barrels of ice from the fish plant and a derelict but functional refrigerator for the Admiral. "He can't stay in the kitchen, it's too warm," he'd said. "And he can't swim 'til he's healed, so fix up some cooler quarters for him." Brad had taken the door off the fridge and set the machine in the corner of the porch, running the plug through the window. A tarp made a kind of glacial cave over the fridge and a glittering mountain of ice in front of it. Brad showed Sal how well the gate opened and clicked shut.

"Think he'll like it?" he asked.

"Let's ask him," Sal said. She nudged the Admiral off Howie's boot and picked it up. Clumping awkwardly on his cast, the Admiral followed her and the boot onto the porch. Sal set the boot down next to the ice heap, but the Admiral hobbled past it to stand, beak upright, at the gate. The bandaged, lopsided figure, gazing through the slats at the path to the sea, silently rebuked all Brad's construction efforts.

"His friends are out there. He doesn't understand," Sal said.

"Shit!" Brad turned angrily into the kitchen. Sal followed him.

"Brad, it's not his fault."

"Of course it's not his fault!" Brad dropped his tools into an oyster crate toolbox and slumped into a chair. "None of it's his fault!"

"Not yours, either," Sal said. "And he's healing. We saved him, didn't we?"

Brad turned on her. "Oh yeah, and for what? So he can swim off into the sunset with his friends?"

"Yes," Sal said simply. "We can't keep them…."

"That's not what I mean!" Brad struggled for words, glaring out at the Admiral. "So they swim off – what then? Even if they don't end up in a tourist trap, where can they go? The North Pole's melting, Antarctica's being planted to winter wheat – what's left for them? What's the point of saving 'em if they just swim off and die?"

Sal rarely got angry. Brad had never seen her in a rage. She stood before his chair, hands balled into fists, a four-foot dynamo of crackling fury.

"How can you *say* that? Even *think* it? Everything dies, even Howie …." She stamped her foot, spitting words. "Even the sun'll die in a billion years – so there's no point saving Mom? Or the Admiral? Why bother living at all, then?"

Brad stared bleakly at the paper-strewn table, avoiding her eyes. "I'm sorry, Sal. I didn't mean – oh, shit, I don't know what I meant, but it wasn't that."

Sal said nothing, her fists still clenched.

"What's that?" Brad pointed to a paper parcel half buried under math papers. Sal pulled it out and grinned, all anger forgotten.

"Yesterday's mail. Mac brought it in this morning."

The flimsy brown paper bore air mail foreign postage and a customs stamp. They both knew what it was. The new Harry Potter book, ordered for them by Howie a year ago. He'd ordered all of the series from England. "Read it like the lady wrote it," he'd said, "not some dumbed-down Yankee version." Sal handed it to Brad.

"Your turn. I opened the last one, remember?"

They turned at the sound of a cast thumping on the porch. The Admiral had abandoned his vigil at the gate and stood again on Howie's boot. Head cocked, he peered at the pile of ice, then bent and rummaged with his beak, tossing ice cubes over the floor. Abruptly, he belly-flopped into the crater he'd made, wagging his free flipper and wriggling in what could only be pleasure. Sal laughed. Brad felt his own grin spread down his backbone.

Brad never heard the Lexus pull up in Mac's driveway an hour later. "When nothing makes sense and there's no point to it all, pick the most impossible thing imaginable and work like hell on it," Howie had said. Fingers, ears, brain and feet were immersed in the impossible first part of The Devil's Trill. He might never master its baroque position changes, but the challenge of those fiendish bowing and rhythm shifts was irresistible. Even in his total concentration, he was aware of Sal on the porch, reading Harry Potter to the Admiral. Neither heard the approach of Molly's boss, Mort, followed by Sara and Baby Craig, or knew how long Mort stood outside the handmade gate, gaping at the Admiral. Brad was turning back pages to repeat the first part when Mort interrupted.

"Pardon the intrusion. May I come in?"

Sal dropped Harry Potter in horror. Brad came to the doorway with his violin and looked accusingly at Sara.

"It's okay, guys," she said. "He's sworn to secrecy. He has some news, and it's time we gave him our own."

Her words sailed past Brad without registering. Mort owned the local TV outlet, he was a newsman; his presence could only be followed by mobs of reporters, microphones, cameras – and inevitably, a parade of officials to take the Admiral away.

Sal pulled herself together first. She picked up Harry Potter and marched to the gate, staring hard at Mort. "You absolutely, honest to god, cross-your-heart-and-hope-to-die promise not to tell anyone?"

Mort placed his hands solemnly on the thick Harry Potter tome. "I absolutely, honest to god, cross-my-heart-and-hope-to-die promise not to tell anyone what I see and hear in this place today. So help me, Walter Cronkite, amen. Will that do?"

Sal nodded, and Mort sat down, placing a thick file folder on the kitchen table. Molly had said Mort sat on a special stool for his evening news show, and now Brad saw why. The man was all legs. Standing on the porch, he was as tall as Brad, but when he sat in a kitchen chair, his head barely cleared the table top. He wore a tan sports jacket over a nondescript sweater the color of parched moss, and his pockmarked, asymmetrical face was too homely to distrust. The man was a good listener, too. He chortled with conspiratorial delight at their rescue of the Admiral.

"We had a cameraman front and center on the dock, and he never saw what really happened!"

Brad's hostility wavered. At Sal's urging, he hesitantly related Molly's account of Howie's murder in Fisher's Grove. Mort took no notes, except to write on the file cover the make and license number of the loggers' pickup.

"I thought it must be something like that," he said. "But now I need your permission to amend my oath of silence – if necessary, that is. I've been talking to some criminal attorneys – heavy hitters nationally, you understand – about Molly's situation. Assuming one is interested, may I reveal this information, in confidence?"

Sal glanced at Brad and nodded. Mort opened the file and handed Sara an envelope. "I came for three reasons. First, I understand you are handling Molly's affairs in her absence. I've arranged that her paychecks be assigned to you."

Spreading papers from the open file on the table, he continued, "Second, you'll be interested in these, I believe. They are responses from trusted former colleagues – my somewhat lurid past paying off, you might say."

Seeing the headers and insignia of FBI, CIA, and NSA on the collection of faxes and printouts, Brad remembered the rumors of Mort's intelligence background. Sal picked up one page after another, frowning in disappointment.

"But we knew this already. Of course Howie wasn't FBI!"

"You knew it, and I knew it, my dear," Mort said. "But could we prove it in court? These letters are a roadmap for a competent defense lawyer to obtain that proof. The prosecutor's case is that Molly killed Howie because he was a special agent investigating timber sabotage – and that he was working with those three loggers. Proof that the FBI angle is a lie seriously unravels his case."

Brad dropped an e-mail from a liaison officer at MI6. "But you broadcast the DA's press conferences, fed them to the networks – even that stupid story about an escape attempt!"

"But of course. It's news, and news is my business." Mort's eyes twinkled merrily through thick-lensed glasses, his British origins invading a cultivated American accent. "A public official digging himself into a hole is always news, wouldn't you say?"

"So you knew all along it was all a lie?"

Mort swept nicotine-stained fingers through his thinning hair. "Knew? Not precisely. Incredulous, yes, when they arrested Molly. But I was in that courtroom, too. When the prosecutor called that Keystone Cops fiasco an escape attempt, that's when I knew for certain and began to make inquiries."

Sara, nursing Baby Craig in a chair by the stove, spoke for the first time. "How could they think they'd get away with it? Such an easy lie to disprove?"

"Money," Mort said. "Fallwell owns this county, lock, stock, and mostly barrel. The feds own eighty percent of county land area as national forest, and Fallwell controls timber contracts on almost all of it. Their money buys county elections, judges, prosecutors, planning and zoning commissions, the county newspaper, and half the local businesses. If it weren't for small potatoes like me, they would get away with it."

He tucked the papers neatly back into his folder and checked his watch, then turned to Brad. "My third reason for coming was to communicate a request from the tenants of one of my business establishments."

"Tenants?" Brad stared at him, mystified.

"I believe you're acquainted with the place. Dinkum Donuts, it's called."

"Oh yeah. Dinkum's!" Brad laughed. "You – you own Dinkum's?"

"I do," Mort said. "They wished me to ask if you would provide musical accompaniment to a celebration of Howie. Not a memorial, they took pains to say." Seeing the instant rejection on Brad's face, Mort added, "No date set, they just ask if you'll think about it."

Brad didn't want to think about it. To play at Dinkum's without Howie was unthinkable. Later, riding his bike to practice, he thought instead about Mort. Brad had known Molly's boss only as a face on the local news. A rich dude, heir to a British industrial fortune playing at small-time media mogul, who drove a Lexus and lived in a big custom-built house somewhere upriver. In a county where unemployment and alcoholism were double national rates, personal wealth on such a scale was beyond Brad's comprehension. Mort's casual hiring of high-power lawyers for Molly and his obvious delight in protecting the Admiral were almost as surprising as his secret ownership of Dinkum's. Brad struggled to reconcile his instinctive mistrust with the hope that Mort offered.

The wind on the bridge tore his thoughts from Mort's contradictions. The gym bag on his shoulder lifted in a gust, nearly pulling him off the bike despite the weight of the gear inside it. Shifting the awkward bag back in position, he passed the giant inflatable penguin floating over the gas station and pedaled nervously through town. Vehicles bore "jobs not birds" bumper stickers, and penguin posters filled shop fronts. In the window of Mrs. Robinson's pharmacy, display racks crammed with penguin merchandize competed with magnetic hate signs and yellow ribbons urging death to tree-huggers. Outside the convenience store, the clerk who had refused to sell him a soda stood next to a big-wheeled silver SUV, smoking a cigarette and laughing with its occupants. She gave Brad the finger as he rode past.

It was a relief to turn off onto the gravel road to the ball field. Here the tacky allure of Main Street vanished abruptly. The pot-holed road ran along a flood ditch where foul-smelling green scum coated trash from the subsidy apartments on the opposite bank. Brad always held his breath along this stretch. Behind him, he heard the crunch of tires on gravel and the sudden blare of a horn. He glanced back. The big-wheeled SUV veered onto the shoulder directly at him. He caught only a glimpse of silver paint and chrome before it struck, tossing boy, bike, and gym bag into the ditch like so many empty beer cans.

Brad sprawled in the muck of the ditch and tried to lift his head, hearing still the cacophony of impact – horn, motor, spitting tires, country music, jeering voices calling "tree hugger," "nigger brat." He pulled himself to his knees and vomited green slime. His head throbbed, gripped in a vise. The bike, its frame twisted and split, was wrapped around a rusty shopping cart, trapping his leg between them. Ripping at gear cables and twisted metal, he freed his leg and stood up, dizzy and shaken. Cautiously, he felt his head and dislodged from his scalp the split torso of an armless, legless plastic doll.

Knee-deep in muck, Brad looked for his gym bag. He spotted it snagged on a rusty bed spring blocking the mouth of a culvert, but his legs trembled too violently to take a step. Warm blood trickled from his head where the broken doll had been embedded. He felt eyes staring from windows of the subsidy apartments, and across the road a woman stood at the back door of a flower shop, watching him. The doll's vacuous smile stared at him, too. He was about to toss it when he saw the bread bag wrapped around his handlebar.

It was a Homestead Bread wrapper, like the one Dumb Darryl wore over his hat, but in Brad's addled state it wasn't Darryl he thought of, but Nigger Lew. Nigger Lew, the old homesteader, black and alone. His pious Christian neighbors kicking him out of church, staring at him with eyes as cold as the subsidy apartment windows. Nigger Lew, building a school for those neighbors on the homestead he'd worked so hard to own.

Brad stared at the smiling face of the limbless doll in his hand. What child had once cherished it? What thoughtless hand had tossed it into the ditch? With his free hand, he disentangled the Homestead Bread bag from the handlebars. It hardly qualified as swaddling clothes, but he wrapped the bag around the broken doll with all the care of a midwife and gently placed it in the warped shopping cart. From the swill of algae and used condoms, he fished out his smashed bicycle light, a broken Tonka truck, empty toothpaste tubes, part of a potty seat, a mess of beer cans. These he placed reverently around the doll. He studied the arrangement, looked at his filthy but undamaged hands. He needed his violin to complete the ceremony.

Ceremony. He stood upright abruptly, his legs no longer weak. Dinkum's celebration of Howie was suddenly not unthinkable but necessary. Howie would hate any ceremony glorifying him – but a tribute to the ancestor Howie had given him – yes, Lew's tunes, with Sal on Howie's guitar – Howie would love it. Brad never looked back at his totaled bike or the doll in the shopping cart. Wading through the muck he fetched his gym bag from the culvert and strode tall to the ball field, arranging tunes in his head.

* * *

Joey trotted up the ridge trail, a bag of Dinkum's meat scraps swinging from one arm. His other hand clutched a parcel against his chest. Where the trail emerged at the old hospital site, he stopped to get his breath. Perched on a lichen-crusted foundation stone, he allowed himself to admire his parcel.

The cream-colored paper bag bore the logo of Gorman's Books, a cartoon of Groucho Marx, captioned, "Outside of a dog, a book is man's best friend. Inside of a dog, it's too dark to read."

Proudly, Joey smoothed a tiny wrinkle in the paper. For the hundredth time, he peeked into the bag at the gloriously fat Harry Potter hardcover in its crisp dust jacket. Even more miraculous was the receipt tucked between its pages.

"Oh, duck poop!" Mex had said when they presented it to him. "I forgot to take that out." She had reached for the receipt, but Joey backed away, shaking his head, too stunned to speak, unable in any case to explain the receipt's importance.

He had meant to slip away from Dinkum's unnoticed after the noon rush subsided, too shaken by a decaf incident to endure any sympathy or kindness. The lunch crowd had been larger than usual. A swarm of suits – lawyers or judges, or both, Joey thought – had commandeered one of the two big tables for almost three hours. Customers gathered around the fireplace waiting for tables, and the Dinkum's crew were in their element. Mex took orders and served, resplendent in what Joey called her Little Prince outfit, billowing satin pantaloons, a silk top with trailing sleeves, and a wide, fringed sash. Joey navigated the crowd, bussing dishes and setting up tables as fast as they were vacated. He had been setting up for an approaching couple when something jabbed him in the back. He spun round into the florid, oily face of one of the suits at the big table. The man was tilted back in his chair, fork in hand, his lips flapping in Joey's face.

"You deaf, boy? I said more decaf!"

Joey froze, cringing, one arm raised to ward off a blow. The silverware in his hand dropped to the floor. The man's face loomed closer, its features closing in like schoolyard bullies. Every pore in the bloated skin sneered in concert with the cruel mouth opening, pursing. "I said decaf. What, cat got your tongue?"

A swirl of gaudy silk swept mercifully between them. Mex refilled the man's cup, set a platter of Harpo's Florentines on the table with a flourish, and restored order to Dinkum's suspended universe. Joey had finished the hour on automatic pilot, avoiding all eyes, desperate to escape. He had loaded the last of the mugs in the dishwasher and hung up his apron, when Geordie snagged him at the kitchen door.

"What's the hurry, mate?"

Joey tried to pull away, but Geordie spun him back and steered him toward the empty dining room. "Don't blow it now, pal," he said. "Mex stood in line a whole hour after midnight for this."

Mex and Harpo had placed the parcel on a glass platter, next to Joey's abandoned mug of cocoa. They hovered while he opened the Gorman's bag, expectant grins facing to concern when Joey's face went white. Mex hugged him, lifting him off his feet, and lowered him into a chair. He stared blankly at the book in his hands.

Once long ago, at Pop Webster's, they'd given him a birthday party – a Safeway cake, icecream, a gift-wrapped toolbox full of allen wrenches, socket sets, spark plug wrench, all the tools of their trade. It was the first and only gift he'd ever received. The socials wouldn't let him bring it when they took him away, and he no longer remembered the date of his birthday. He glanced at the Dinkum's crew, hesitant, speechless.

"It's for you, Angel," Mex said. "For keeps. Today's the big day. They weren't allowed to sell them 'til after midnight – the line went around the whole block!"

The horror of the decaf incident had faded by the time he left them. He was able to laugh when Geordie handed him a sack of marinated beef tongue for the cat, saying, "The next asshole asks if the cat got your tongue, tell him too right it did."

Perched on the hospital ruins above the town, Joey smiled. He pulled the receipt from the book, reading again the date, the time, the title and ISBN, the price, the change due. No Harvard diploma or Purple Heart ever commanded such reverence. Carefully, he tucked it back into the book and folded the ends of the bag closed. He stood up, ready for the steep trail home, eager to feed the cat and immerse himself in those crisp new pages.

Below him, the town looked like a toy train layout. He saw the team gathering on the ball field and recognized Brad turning his bike onto the access road. Helplessly, he watched the silver SUV follow him, speed up, toss him into the ditch, and race away. He saw Brad sprawl in the mud, then stand up and pull something off his head. One eye on Brad, making sure he was okay, Joey tracked the SUV, charting its course out to the highway and into a driveway in the new development south of town.

Late that night, when his batteries faded in the middle of chapter six, Joey left the cat to keep his bed warm and went for a hike. His pockets bulged with BB pellets and a small collection of borrowed tools. He returned an hour later with a satisfied smile and no BB pellets. Joey didn't see – or need to see – the silver SUV trucked out of town next day on a flatbed trailer. Mysteriously, every moving part in its engine and transmission had simultaneously committed suicide when its owner turned on the ignition that morning.

Chapter Twenty-One

Sal hardly ever talks about school. She said once it's like chemotherapy, something you just have to do and get over it. The only good grades she gets are in math and the only friend she ever had was a girl named Jody who was autistic and got sent away somewhere. Jody never talked but they sang and swam together and laughed a lot. The teachers treat Sal like she's autistic, too, but secretly I think they know deep down she's a whole lot smarter than they are. Howie calls her Pythagoras sometimes. We had to look him up and Sal thought it was funny 'cause he was a math whizz but kind of a nutball, too.

Sal can really sing. She picks up harmonies and counterpoints automatically and is always in tune. She says a doctor at the hospital who was in a choir had this theory that singing could strengthen your lungs and when Sal started getting better they sang together a lot. But when Howie tries to show her how harmony works on the guitar she gets totally sidetracked by the ratios and progressions and things get pretty silly. "Okay," Howie says, "F has one flat, B-flat has two flats, F-flat has eight, so what has seventeen flats?" Sat stares at the strings, getting frustrated, and he says, "An eighteen-wheeler with only one good tire."

—The Oreo File

Sal waved to the vulture every morning. It sat on a wind-sculpted spruce snag at the edge of the trees, on sunny mornings hanging its wings out to dry like sodden laundry. This morning it was still asleep, a dark blister against the lesser darkness of dawn. Sal waved at it anyway.

Until a few years ago, Mac said, you never saw a vulture over the beach; their turf was the inland hills, where they rode thermals effortlessly and converged on roadkill along the highways. Now vultures flew regular patrols over the beach, some, like this one, settling along the shore permanently through the spring and summer. Vultures lived on carrion, Howie had explained, and an ocean too warm and acidic to support its food chains deposited thousands of dead fish, cormorants, auklets, murres, and seal babies on the beaches, a fast-food paradise for vultures.

Sal walked slowly out to the headland, Joe close behind her, uneasy in the uncertain light. The ocean looked flat and tired after thunderstorms the night before, the waves slopping half-heartedly on the rocks. Sal thought sadly of seabirds starving to death in the waves that had always fed them, of vultures flocking to the beach like a company picnic. She liked vultures. It wasn't their fault the sea was dying. When she died, she'd told Brad once, she'd rather it be here, as a vulture's dinner, than in a steely smelling hospital. Brad had thought about it and nodded.

"Me, too," he'd said. "But it's prob'ly illegal or something."

At least there were still enough fish for the Admiral, she thought. Despite her anger at Brad's pessimism, she was afraid for the penguins. Their whole world was melting away, but could it be that ice was not so important to them as food? Maybe instead of slowly starving like the cormorants and murres, they were moving on, like the vultures, to where food still grew. In all the vast ocean, there must still be some cooler pockets, like hidden valleys, where plankton and other creatures survived. The Admiral and his crew, having come so far, had at least a chance of finding such a place, if only people would leave them alone.

Sal scanned the horizon for a glimpse of the Greenpeace ship. She wore her bright yellow rain slicker, for visibility more than dryness; the irritating removable hood was stuffed in her pocket. Behind her, Joe plucked at clumps of shore grass that thrust through rubble and between rocks, a new treat for him. Grass had never grown among these stones before.

It had been a strange spring. February and March, usually the coldest, stormiest season, had been sunny and dry. Flowers and fruit trees had bloomed weeks earlier than usual. Then the storms swept in, one after another, all through April and most of May. The Oregonian had reported that apple and cherry crops were failing throughout the region, with newborn fruits rotting on their stems. Now grasses grew through the rocks of the headland, vultures roamed the beach, and penguins had arrived in Oregon. In Sal's short lifetime, the world had changed in ways unimaginable only a few years before.

Visibility was better than she had expected. A southwest wind drove boiling cloud masses overhead, but through the fine drizzle she could see a good mile out to the dark line where day met night and sea and sky merged. The e-mail from Seb aboard the Orca had said to look for them an hour or so past dawn. "Look for me, to," Sal had written back, sending a link to the coastal chart Brad had located. The Orca was too big to sail close to shore. Sal wore Molly's binoculars around her neck, but there was no need for them yet.

Greenpeace would have no difficulty locating the penguins. The Admiral's crew had lingered almost a week in the area of Heceta Head, where the Admiral had been captured by the drunks. Now they were on the move, showing up a little farther north each day. A growing army of news teams and tourists followed, creating daily traffic jams on the two-lane coast highway. On the water, an armada of party boats and news vessels defied all navigation rules; news broadcasts showed more footage of wrecks than of penguins. The Coast Guard had called in boats and crews from Washington and California to keep up with patrol and rescue operations.

Weary of scanning an empty horizon, Sal turned to watch Bertha plunge for fish in the bay. The Admiral would be waiting for his breakfast, and by now Brad would be hosing off the porch and dumping two more barrels of fresh ice for him. Tomorrow, she thought. Tomorrow Molly was to be moved back to the coast hospital. Bullhead would ride in the ambulance with her, and tomorrow night the Admiral's cast and bandage would come off. And then what, she wondered. How would he find his crew?

When she turned her eyes back to the horizon, it was no longer empty. Far to the north, the running lights of a ship glowed against the dark western sky, winking out behind storm swells and reappearing. She held the binoculars to her eyes, but they were little help at such a distance, and the swells interfered. Sal climbed on a boulder next to Joe and scrabbled onto his back. On tiptoes, balanced on Joe's shoulders, she tracked the ship through the binoculars as it slowly moved south and eased shoreward a few degrees. It never came close enough to identify, but Sal pulled her yellow hood from her pocket and waved it anyway. A blinding burst of light from the ship dazzled her, flashing on and off in a repeated pattern. She recognized the shorts and longs of her name from Howie's Morse code games. Slowly, on the third repetition, she spelled out, "AHOY, SAL."

Not sure how well they could see her, Sal stretched her arms wide, then crossed them in front, again and again. Joe, catching her excitement, arched his neck and tail and pranced in place. When the ship flashed a message acknowledged and steamed on south, Sal stood on Joe's back all the way home. Brad, heading out to meet her, heard her before she came in sight, singing the Skye Boat Song.

* * *

Mac pulled off the highway after leaving work and puzzled over the tiny cell phone Mort had insisted on loaning him. Its buttons were too small for his large, calloused fingers, caked with sawdust and machine oil. He kept it in a sandwich bag and pushed buttons through the plastic with a carpenter's pencil.

"You don't need to answer," Mort had said. "Just push here for messages. I'll keep updating the penguins' location for you. If Brad's pal Joey is right, those goons'll be wherever the birds are, and there's just a chance of – um – retrieving Molly's tape."

Mort's strategy was sound, up to a point. Following his recorded tips, Mac had twice spotted the crucial teal-blue pickup, both times late in the day. Both times it had been on the move, heading up the coast highway from the daily penguin circus. Mac listened to Mort's current message and checked his watch. A yarder breakdown had ended work early today, giving him several hours before Brad's game.

After Brad's encounter with the silver SUV, Coach had retrieved the totaled bike from the storm ditch and spoken to the flower shop clerk and subsidy apartment witnesses. That night he had called Mac. For the remainder of the season, Coach would drive Brad to the ball field, and Mac would pick him up after work.

Today's game with Oakdale wouldn't start for another hour. Mac drove south and west through a network of old logging roads and power line rights-of-way. He left his rig at an abandoned quarry where he and his brother had once played. From here, he hiked up the low ridge above the coast highway for a clear view over the campground at Little Bear Cove. Below him, vehicles were backed up two miles from the park. The penguins were nowhere in sight, but the crowds swarming into the surf and the boats converging on the hump-backed rock known as Little Bear were obvious indicators. Two zodiacs bearing Greenpeace insignias fended other boats off the rock.

Mac was not looking for the penguins. Quickly, he scanned the hundreds of vehicles along the highway and in the campground. The teal blue pickup was parked alongside a school bus in the crowded, day-use parking area. Mac ran down a fire trail and crossed the highway between stalled vehicles. Approaching the pickup through the picnic ground, concealed by its trees, he could see no one in the cab. He pulled a heavy lug wrench from his belt; if the truck was locked, he had no compunctions about smashing a window. Seeing no one in the parking lot, he started forward. The sound of nearby voices sent him back into the trees. Slipping the lug wrench back into his belt, he worked his way toward the school bus.

Large black lettering under the bus windows identified it. "Eugene Consolidated School District." A long way from home, Mac thought. Its door was open, and the driver stood between the bus and the teal blue pickup, smoking. The other speaker faced away from Mac, but the hat and voice were unmistakable. It was Dumb Darryl.

Mac waited, hoping they would follow the mob out to the beach. Wind, waves, and the mob's yells and roars of motorboats drowned out most of the conversation, but Darryl's polite impatience showed in his small shufflings and questioning glances. During a momentary lull in the wind, Mac heard the bus driver's voice clearly.

"Nah. Seen 'em twice already this week. Just birds like you can see any day at the zoo, but it's overtime, I ain't complaining."

The driver sat on the bus steps and poured coffee from a thermos into two cups. Frustrated, Mac gave up and headed back to his truck. He missed only the first inning of Brad's game. Brad knocked in the winning run with a double in the eighth inning, and Coach took the team for pizza to celebrate. Mac ordered an extra pizza to take home.

"Sara took Sal up to Beaverton for their last meet, they'll be home late and hungry."

It was almost full dark when Mac's pickup pulled into the driveway. Brad swung his door open to get out and open the gate, but there was no need. The gate stood wide open. Before he could shut his door again, high beam headlights burst upon them, hurtling down the driveway.

"Fuck!" Mac threw his gears into reverse, backing blindly onto the highway. The headlights flashed past, the teal-blue pickup clipping Brad's open door. Behind it, eyes flaring red in Mac's headlights, Joe galloped full tilt. Brad leaped from the cab to head him off and threw his arms around the horse's neck to bring him to a stop. Joe's ear was bleeding, and blood welled from a ragged gash across his shoulders. His body gleamed with sweat, sticky to the touch. Still holding Joe's neck, Brad could feel the muscles twitching. Mac pulled his rig back into the driveway and jumped out.

"Fuck!" Mac said again. Mac, who almost never swore. "How bad is he?"

Joe snorted, nostrils puffing steam. Brad turned him for inspection in the headlights.

"Just his ear and withers," Mac said. "Walk him home ahead of me. I'll get the gate."

Slowly, one hand stroking Joe's neck, Brad led him through the pine belt. Coming from the dark trees into the twilit yard, he saw the black outlines of the two houses. Mac's headlights shone past him onto their open front door and the mud churned up before it. Bertha indignantly rummaged for her spilled fish in the doorway.

"Oh Jesus, the Admiral!" Brad ran for the back porch, Joe trotting behind. Mac grabbed a flashlight and followed. Sobbing, Brad fumbled at the porch gate, desperately peering into the vacant shadows of ice pile and humming fridge.

"Oh god, Mac, they got him!"

Mac's big halogen flashlight beamed over his shoulder, lighting the whole porch. In the corner by the railing, the Admiral stood, unharmed and patient, staring hopefully at the rail. Brad choked back sobs of relief. Mac pushed past him and switched on porch and kitchen lights. Into the swath of light, Bertha waddled importantly and hopped onto the railing to disgorge the Admiral's somewhat muddy dinner.

After swabbing Joe's wounds with warm water and gentian violet solution, Brad and Mac surveyed the yard with flashlights, piecing together a likely scenario. Apparently the goons had shown up at dusk and opened the front door.

"Why?" Brad asked. "Why the hell would they come here?"

"The tape," Mac said. "If the cops figured it might be here, so could those assholes – maybe even thought you or Sal was out there with Molly that day."

The mud told a chilling tale. No tracks came farther than the doorway, where fish gurry and feathers clung to the frame. Bertha, confused again by the open front door, must have tried to fly her cargo to the sink and collided with one or more of the goons. Brad laughed, thinking about it. They wouldn't have seen her coming, just suddenly been slammed by a fully loaded fish bomb. Then Joe must have trotted up to check out the disturbance. From the mud near the door, Mac picked up a chainsaw wrench, a steel bar flattened at one end for adjusting chain screws. Wisps of Joe's mane were twisted around it.

"To jimmy the door, which wasn't locked, anyway," Mac said. "They freaked and hit Joe with it, looks like."

Deep hoofprints and skidmarks of caulk boots told clearly Joe's response. Brad kicked gouges of turf back into the ruts where the truck had spun out. He picked up empty Marlboro wrappers, a McDonald's container, a beer can, and a flimsy sheet of paper left behind from the invaders' rig. In the kitchen after their yard inspection, he dropped the rubbish into the trash.

"Hey, what's that?" Mac lifted the muddy scrap of paper from the trash bucket and laughed. "No wonder those boys are getting edgy."

"What is it?" Brad tried to read through the muddy smudges, bewildered.

"A goddamn subpoena – they're called before a grand jury next week. Well, at least we know one thing – they haven't found that tape yet."

* * *

Bullhead met the lawyer from Philadelphia at the hospital staff door, carrying Michael Landauer's surgical gown for another camouflage mission. Mort had told him only the lawyer's last name and profession, and Bullhead had promptly forgotten the name. He had expected the tailored suit and Rolex, but not the elegant female body or the disconcertingly black face. The lawyer stretched the surgical cap over her shining black hair and grinned back at Bullhead's angry, suspicious glare.

"I've seen you on TV." Bullhead's voice was accusatory.

"A good many people have," the lawyer from Philadelphia said.

"Good god," Bullhead exploded. "This woman – my patient – is charged with murder. For real. She needs a real lawyer, not a TV actor!"

The lawyer looked puzzled, then bemused. "Wrong show. You probably saw the press conference after the Olmstead acquittal."

Bullhead slapped himself on the head. "Oh, man, the only TV I see is in patients' rooms. Can't tell drama from news any more." He held out his hand. "I forget the name, but I know who you are now. You took on that Oregon prison, too – the one that treated a ruptured appendix with Maalox. Proud to meet you, ma'am."

The lawyer from Philadelphia shook hands, grinning. "Eleanor Thomas. Absolutely no relation to the Supreme Court's Uncle Tom."

Bullhead laughed. He opened a locker and handed Thomas a clipboard. "Put what you need on this. That briefcase is a dead giveaway."

Leading the way to a section of hospital still under construction, Bullhead reviewed Molly's status. "The last surgery on her wrist was yesterday. She's out of intensive care now. Refuses any more pain-killers. They're moving her to Branscombe General tomorrow – over my strong objections."

Workmen installing electronic controls on the massive doors of an entrance chamber stood aside for them. Passing through a second doorway, Bullhead gestured mockingly at the draped painters' cloths, stacks of fluorescent tubes, and construction debris piled in the large circular room. He shouted over a cacophony of hammers, drills, nail guns, power saws.

"Welcome to Guantánamo West, the latest in high security wards. Federal requirement, paid for out of state education funds – in case bin Laden turns up in Pioneer Square."

Eleanor Thomas surveyed the room in amazement. The unfinished concrete subfloor was a minefield of pipes, cables, wires, and conduit snaking over it haphazardly. The doorways to patients' rooms had no doors yet, and a crude chalk outline marked the future site of a central nurses' or guard station. Workmen's droplights provided the only illumination. The place reeked of wet concrete and PVC fumes. Thomas turned to Bullhead, appalled.

"Court order," Bullhead shouted. "That idiot prosecutor claimed national security."

They stepped carefully over pipes and cables to a doorway draped with plastic construction sheeting. A chair stood outside the doorway, piled with books and sheet music. Over the construction din, Thomas heard what sounded like "Blue Train" on harmonica. Bullhead grinned and lifted aside the plastic sheeting.

Eleanor Thomas's new client lay in a wheeled hospital bed perched on shipping pallets over the unfinished floor. Fat power cables snaked through the doorway and under the bed, powering drop lights, monitors, and oxygen apparatus. From a vacant IV stand a bedpan filled with chrysanthemums dangled next to traction cables elevating Molly's right arm and leg. Blocking a clear view of her face, a police officer sat cross-legged on a gurney, his back to the doorway. Beside him on the gurney, just within reach of the bed, stood a jug of ice water and a mug decorated with penguins. Unaware of visitors, cop and patient spun a playful improvisation, ending on a grating harmonic.

"Not enough range, let's try it in F," came Molly's voice. The cop shifted his weight. Over his shoulder, she saw their audience. "Oops. Company."

The cop turned, grinned at Bullhead, and slid to the floor, careful not to rock the gurney. He glanced guiltily at Thomas and placed the harmonica in a crowded pocket.

"Eleanor Thomas, meet your new client," Bullhead said. "And her – uh – music advisor."

"Mel Liston," the cop said. "Multnomah County security detail." He shook hands with Thomas. "I know who you are, ma'am. Honored to meet you."

Liston filled the penguin mug with ice water and placed a harmonica case within Molly's reach. "End-of-tour blues. I'm off duty in ten minutes," he said.

"No goodbyes," Molly said, "but thanks for all the fish." They both laughed. Molly reached for his hand and held it a long moment. "Dinkum's. The Fairly Honest Eddies?"

"Whenever you're free." Liston grinned at his own word play and nodded toward the bemused lawyer. "And you will be, soon enough. You're in good hands, Miss Molly."

Chapter Twenty-Two

What I like about baseball is its infinite possibilities for screwing up. And ditto for absolute miracles. Football and basketball and soccer, they're basically a team of guys racing back and forth to get a ball into a goal, but baseball's different, it's a solo sport and team sport all at the same time. You're up at bat or pitching, man, you're flying solo, not a damn thing your team can do to help—you can strike out, pop out, not make it to first, throw an easy or wild pitch, and it's all on your own watch. But once you're on base or out in the field, every move you make is a team move—throw to first or home, tag or pass, steal second or fake it, you're all moving in tune or you're all a disaster."

—*The Oreo File*

Joey kept his new backpack on even to bus tables. The backpack wasn't exactly new, but it looked as pristine as anything on Walmart shelves. He'd found it in the laundromat's Unclaimed Items bin. Never mind that it was pink, with Barbie posing on both sides. What mattered was that it was clean inside, no candy or greasy chip residues to contaminate his book and its precious receipt.

He had only three chapters left to read before Harry Potter went on loan to the Dinkum's crew, who would take turns reading it aloud before bedding down each night. The receipt, enshrined in a discarded American Express envelope with a clear plastic window, he would keep forever, Joey thought. Or at least until the ink faded.

Only two tables remained occupied after a hectic lunch hour. At a four-top near the window, Mex served éclairs and sacher torte to three skinny women and a boyish, long–limbed man, dancers with a visiting

Canadian step-dancing troupe. Clearing and wiping vacant tables throughout the room, Joey kept a wary eye on some latecomers, two customers waiting their order at a table near the fireplace. One was Dinkum's landlord. Mort Somebody. Joey had seen him in Dinkum's only twice since he'd shared their fireplace soup and made his astonishing offer to bankroll three ragbag squatters.

The landlord had been a hero in Joey's book. Now he was bewildered. Mort's companion was a tall black woman in a power suit and maroon scarf. Joey had seen her picture that morning on the front page of a customer's Oregonian, alongside a larger photo of the Decaf Monster who still haunted Joey's nightmares. The headline running over both photos was, "DA to seek death penalty in ecoterror murder." Joey had been too disgusted by the photo to read the article.

That the Decaf Monster was the district attorney was no surprise. But if the black chick was the Decaf Monster's sidekick, why was she meeting with Dinkum's landlord? They had the same Oregonian spread on their table. The black woman was facing away from Joey, and the fragments of Mort's conversation that Joey could decipher offered little enlightenment.

"Outrageous…." Mort slapped the newspaper angrily. "…would spin his own hemorrhoids into a federal case…."

Joey's literal mind reeled at the image. Other phrases were simply baffling: "Grand Jury indictment…dueling harmonicas… gag order…." The two stopped talking when Mex brought their order. Mort winked at Mex, beaming proudly at the laden table, and launched into a history of Dinkum Donuts. Joey's attention drifted. The dancers had left and he had nearly finished sweeping before he glanced at the landlord's table again. The word "videotape" stopped him in his tracks.

"…under the driver's seat," Mort said.

Joey bent to the dust pan to hide his face. He swept his way to the kitchen, head down, afraid to look at Mort again, and ran for the door. That the landlord knew about the videotape was bad enough, but telling the DA's flunky about it? Confused and frightened, Joey forgot the scrap bag for the cat and pedaled madly toward town to find Brad.

The ball field was empty. A schedule posted on the dugout listed today's game at Eden Valley, forty miles inland. Joey shrugged. Brad wouldn't be back for hours. Heading for the high school to return today's bike, he stopped at the sight of traffic backed up through town. West of the highway, a Coast Guard helicopter raced low over the shoreline, heading south.

"Cook's Point," a man in a snack van told him. "Party boat wrecked. Fishing for penguins."

Penguins. Cook's Point was only a mile south of town. Joey turned the bike and headed south, riding on the shoulder, checking every vehicle he passed. Just in time, he dodged into the stalled traffic when an ambulance loomed up behind him on the narrow shoulder, lights flashing, and raced past. At Cook's Point, a Life Flight helicopter hovered over the state park while cops tried to move enough vehicles for it to land. Joey scanned the lot, looking for a teal blue pickup. He pedaled on to check the northbound vehicles south of the park. No luck.

Joey hid the bike in a bank of salal bushes and climbed a shore pine. Perched in its wind-sculpted branches, he watched two Greenpeace zodiacs and the Coast Guard helicopter pluck thrashing people from sea and rocks. He kept an eye on all traffic, but the teal blue pickup never appeared.

* * *

Eden Valley, once a dying railroad town of crumbling grain elevators and abandoned canneries, had transformed itself into a picture perfect bedroom community for the international offices of Fallwell Timber Products. At the south end of the town, the company's glass and California redwood complex sprawled over what had been the railroad station and surrounding, once-prime farmland. To Brad, Eden Valley's white picket fences, shining church spires, even its buzz-cut ball field, had the computer-generated look of a time-travel fantasy.

Eden Valley's baseball team fit the mold of the town. Uniformly tall, white, and blessed with the best coaches and equipment money could buy, they had swept the league title, unbeaten and seemingly invincible, for as long as Brad could remember. They were also blatantly and viciously racist. Leaving Eden Valley after losing every game had always been a relief; today's victorious departure resembled a skin-of-your-teeth escape.

The Eden Valley team and spectators had greeted Brad in particular with ugly catcalls. Their pitcher loudly called for volunteers to steam-clean the dugout after the nigger team left. Brad's first time at bat, the pitcher beaned him on the head with a fast ball, denting his helmet. Their catcher, pretending to help Brad up, whispered loudly, "That's just for starters, nigger boy."

In retaliation, George Lawson had pitched a no-hitter. It was not a pretty game, certainly not a victory to savor, Brad thought. Unable to hit George's pitches, the Eden Valley team simply disintegrated, allowing run after run on fumbles and errors. By the fifth inning, behind 11 to zero, they had turned their rage on each other. In the top of the seventh, their shortstop punched out their pitcher when he dropped a pop fly.

Eden Valley defeated was a frightening sight. As their left fielder swung wildly at George's final pitch of the game, the Eden Valley team erupted from the dugout and descended on the hapless batter, punching and kicking. Brad saw the plate umpire go down, saw Coach dragging their own catcher from the fray. Spectators poured onto the field to join the fight. With the rest of his team, Brad ran for the bus.

The driver didn't wait for everyone to find seats. He spun out of the parking lot, spitting gravel, and raced down the landscaped access road, slowing only when he reached Main Street. No one spoke. Brad stared out the window at the faux leaded windows of store fronts, idly noting the number of BMWs parked outside them.

When the last of the matching lawns and picket fences were well behind in the foothills, Coach stood up. He pulled his cooler from under a front seat and opened a soda.

"Men," he said, his face solemn. The bus swung around a steep curve and he steadied himself against George Lawson's seat.

"Men," he started again. "Oh, hell, I'm so proud of you I could just…." His face couldn't hold the laughter back. "I could just shit!"

With a happy roar, he poured the soda over George's head. Dripping and laughing, George passed sodas to the team and poured one on Brad. In the soda-spattered uproar that followed, no one noticed the bus slowing. Silenced finally by its abrupt stop, they saw a row of flashing police vehicles blocking the road. Two cops were directing traffic into the wide turnout and viewpoint for Keller's Falls. Two log trucks, a mobile home, and assorted cars and pickups were already parked in the turnout, their occupants milling restlessly about. Coach got out and spoke with the traffic cop. Two cops armed with shotguns and riot gear opened a portable barrier between the highway and turnout. Coach climbed back in and held up his arms for silence while the bus was maneuvered into the turnout and backed up alongside a log truck.

"A slight delay for the pizza party," Coach said. "They're closing the highway all the way to the coast…No, not a tsunami, and not an accident. National security, he says. You can get out, but no one's to cross that police line. Got it?"

Soda-soaked and happy for action, the team piled out of the bus. Brad put his shoes on and followed. The bus driver and George Lawson were talking with one of the truck drivers, a huge man wearing a grease-stained, faded Grateful Dead t-shirt. The cap covering his nearly bald head had a Marines eagle on it, and his lopsided stance, Brad suspected, was due to a prosthetic leg.

"Hey Brad!" George yelled. "It's not a bomb, it's your mom! A whole convoy!"

"Not a bomb! It's your mom!" the team echoed. Some kids among the crowd took up the chant. Brad froze on the steps of the bus. The DA had announced a gag order on when Molly would be transferred to the coast hospital, hinting that eco-terror groups planned another escape attempt.

"He thinks he can gag doctors and nurses?" Bullhead had said, laughing. "Hospitals run on gossip! Every news outlet in town will know when that ambulance leaves."

Catching the stares of strangers and remembering the silver SUV, Brad stayed close to the bus. The rest of the team joined George, talking to the large truck driver and pointing out Brad to him. A small crowd gathered. The trucker addressed them angrily, waving his fist. More cars were shunted into the turnout, and the crowd around the truck driver grew. Families with children left their vehicles and wandered over to hear. Brad watched nervously. His teammates stayed with the crowd, nodding their heads at the trucker's words. Coach listened for a few minutes, then caught Brad's eye and swung his arms out in a "safe" signal.

There was no time to figure out what Coach meant. A cop stood in front of the barrier to the highway with a battery-powered bullhorn, shouting orders.

"Everyone back in their vehicles, please. Back to your vehicles, please. Remain in your vehicles until told to proceed."

A few families drifted toward their cars and stopped. The throb of a helicopter echoed through the steep hillsides, drowning the bullhorn's repeated orders. The large truck driver limped toward Brad, the team and large crowd following. He held out a massive, scarred hand.

"You're the fiddling fool," the man said. His grin split a bristling hedgehog face. "'Ccording to Howie, you could fiddle rocks from the sea," he added, pulling Brad along with him. With Brad in tow, he led the crowd toward the police barrier.

The din of chopper blades was deafening now, rebounding and amplified by the hills. The cop with the bullhorn backed away from the advancing crowd, yelling unheard orders. One arm around Brad's shoulder, the trucker lifted the police barrier aside and led the crowd to the highway. The roadblock cops spoke into radios and unholstered their weapons. For some reason, the trucker found this amusing and laughed.

The chopper thundered into view around a curve to the east, an ABC News helicopter, swinging dangerously between steep hillside and tall trees. A cavalcade of satellite vans appeared, leading a string of flashing state police cars and emergency vehicles, trailed by two ambulances and black, unmarked armored trucks. The cavalcade ground to a stop fifty yards from the trucker and his crowd, the helicopter hovering overhead.

Cops poured out of the police and armored cars, wearing Star Wars helmets and pointing assault weapons at the crowd. Reporters tumbled from the news vans, aiming lenses and microphones at the cops, panning the crowd. Brad felt the trucker's hand tighten on his shoulder and wondered if his body would be shown on the six o'clock news.

The helicopter shot upwards suddenly, perhaps to get a wider view. In the relative sound vacuum, a little girl squeezed past Brad into the roadway. She wore a pink dress and had Shirley Temple curls. Ignoring the rank of weapons aimed at her, she gazed rapturously at the cameras.

"Look, Daddy! We're on TV!" she yelled, waving and dimpling at the reporters.

In the horrified silence that followed, one cop lowered his riot gun and laughed. One by one, the rest lowered weapons, smiling sheepishly at the pink, joyful child.

* * *

For the second time that evening, Joey trotted up the alley behind the funeral home and vaulted the low fence into the old lady's yard. It was dark. The streetlights were on, and the team bus had still not returned, but his urgency about the videotape had been replaced by a new worry.

Earlier, he had brought four cans of Iams to the old lady's house, stacking them neatly on the back porch. As always, the cat watched him from its window, but something had felt wrong. Joey had shrugged off his uneasiness, anxious to return the bike and meet Brad's bus. Not until well after dark, when he had given up on the bus and headed up the ridge for home, did he think of the old lady again. Pausing at the old hospital site, he had looked down on the lights of the town and realized what was wrong about the old lady's house. The cat in the kitchen window had not been backlit by the glow of a TV screen.

The old lady kept that TV on day and night. Joey figured it was company for her. In his nocturnal ramblings, its glow was a beacon to him, signaling that the old lady was safe, but when he'd brought the cat food, the room behind the cat was dim and unlit. Old ladies fell down sometimes, he knew, or had heart attacks. He thought of her lying unconscious or in pain on the floor, all alone. Panicked, he had run back down the hill to town.

He stood now in back of the darkened house, frightened and uncertain. He knocked on the kitchen door, then the front, pressing his cheek and hand against the glass panels, trying to detect any motion inside. Nothing. The house across the alley was well lit, and a Chevy Suburban stood in its driveway. Joey ran across the alley. As he raised his fist to knock and ask for help, a big Lincoln town car pulled to a stop in front of the old lady's house. Joey crouched beside the Suburban and watched in astonishment.

The driver's door opened, and Mrs. Robinson climbed out, leaving motor and headlights running. Joey shrank back behind the Suburban, recalling her cruelty to Brad over a fifty-cent Hershey bar. In the light of the street lamp, he saw her grim face clearly. She unlocked the trunk and lifted out the old lady's walker, carried it to the passenger door, and helped the old lady out. Together, they inched up the three steps to the porch. Mrs. Robinson waited, tapping her foot impatiently while the old lady fumbled at the door and switched on the porch light. The old lady was smiling happily. Mrs. Robinson didn't smile back. She nodded briskly at something the old lady said, then got in her car and drove off.

Joey watched the old lady's house come to life again. One by one, in very slow motion, the windows of the small house lit up. The front porch light was switched off. From the alley, Joey watched the old lady pick up the cans of cat food stacked on the back porch. Leaning on her walker, she could carry only two at a time. He should put the cans in a bag, he realized. He saw the glowing TV screen through the open door. Relieved of his fears, he ran for home and his own hungry cat.

When Brad's team bus finally rolled in long after dark, Joey was snug in his bed with the last chapters of Harry Potter awaiting him. The black cat was curled up beside him. Only a small hairless patch above its eye remained from the gruesome infection, and its purr rumbled contentedly through the bedding. Joey thought of the old lady and how much younger she had looked when she smiled. In fact, she wasn't old at all, just flimsy or wounded somehow. The mystery was what she had been doing with Mrs. Robinson, of all people.

Joey liked mysteries, but the conversation between Dinkum's landlord and the DA's flunky was more than a mystery, it was a major crisis. As soon as the DA heard about it, Molly's videotape would be found and destroyed. Joey imagined the three men who had killed Howie laughing while the Decaf Monster burned the tape. Not even the Hardy Boys could save Molly then, he thought.

Leaving Harry Potter tucked under his blankets, Joey eased himself from the bed without disturbing the cat. He switched off his reading light and climbed out the van windshield into the night.

Chapter Twenty-Three

Howie says the reason people write books is so we don't have to read cereal boxes. Ha-ha. When he was a kid, he says, cereal boxes were actually interesting. The one he liked best was shredded wheat, 'cause it had cardboard dividers with Red Indian *lore for camping in the woods and tracking animals. He saved them all even though there were no woods in Brooklyn. But there were birds, and because of those cards, he started watching the birds to see what they were up to. Then when he was in Vietnam he says the birds were the only sane things in sight, different from Brooklyn birds but they made him feel less far away from home.*

That's all he's ever said about Vietnam except about the hospital afterward. He must'a been wounded but he didn't say how, just told about this dude whose arm and leg and balls were blown off by a landmine. Howie said he was one of the funniest people he ever met, always ready with a joke or one-liner and drawing cartoons of everyone in the ward. Howie asked him how the hell he kept on going, and the dude showed him pictures of his folks and his dog back home and said he was lucky, 'cause he still had the three things you can't do without – something to love, something to do, and something to look forward to. I think for Howie, birds are all three of those things.

—*The Oreo File*

Molly woke up in a tranquilizer fog, wondering where she was. But for the familiar IV stand, the traction rig, and the bedpan chrysanthemums next to her mended penguin mug, the room had the impersonal class of a spendy motel suite. Wherever she was, she thought, it was a distinct improvement over the security ward in Portland.

The walls were finished, painted a soft ivory and hung with watercolors of sea-scapes and fishing boats. Through a large window she could just see the ocean beyond the roof vents of a fast-food restaurant and a steam-belching dry cleaners. Curtains printed with pastel sea horses and kelp framed the window. Beneath the window was an upholstered daybed stacked with neatly folded blankets and pillows. In one corner, an oversized door opened on a spacious bath and shower, and a large TV set was mounted near the ceiling opposite her bed. Best of all, Grandma Rose sat in the bedside chair, beaming at her.

"Howdy, neighbor. Welcome back!"

"Back?" Molly drank gratefully from the penguin mug. "Oh, yeah. But this room – where are we?"

"Branscombe County General," Grandma Rose said, laughing. "Our VIP suite."

"Your what?"

"That's what we call it. Specially endowed – for Fallwell CEOs and hotshots. Just for you, it's now Branscombe's national security ward, thanks to our puffed-up DA."

"At least it has a floor," Molly said.

"And two fat cops outside." Grandma Rose refilled the penguin mug. "So much gear hangin' off 'em, their butts must be dented. I made sure they got hard plastic chairs. The super drew the line at machine guns, and Doctor says if they stick their noses in here to knock 'em out and lock 'em out."

"Doctor?"

"Dr. Kahn, your personal surgeon."

"Oh, Bullhead! You know he's Mac's old logging buddy?"

"So he tells me," Grandma Rose said.

"Where is he?" Molly asked.

Grandma Rose grinned. "With his other patient. The Admiral. VIPs up the Yazoo today. He's taking the cast off. Said he'd pick up pizza on the way back." She nodded toward the daybed. "Him and me's taking turns staying over here. Keep the Gestapo out. He was fit to wring that DA's neck, you know."

Molly knew, all right. The ambulance had been a four-hour nightmare. With every stop and turn she'd felt her breath cut off, and the traction bar holding her newly reconstructed wrist nearly pulled her arm from its socket. Bullhead, doing his best to keep too many rigs stable, had raged furiously at the DA's refusal to shell out for a helicopter.

"Asshole wants a goddamn parade – federal marshals, SWAT teams, riot guns, can't fit all that in a fucking chopper."

He had given her something when the retching started, soon after leaving the freeway for the winding slopes of the coast range. A helicopter had joined them then, its incessant pounding the last thing she remembered. Almost the last thing.

"Brad!" she said, looking puzzled. "Brad. I saw Brad. Or did I dream it?"

The ambulance had stopped, the chopper throbbing overhead. She was gratefully fading under whatever drug Bullhead had injected when he woke her with a yell.

"You're not going to believe this," he said, and lifted her to the side window. The roadway was lined with people, a contingent of them in baseball uniforms. Blocking the window suddenly was Brad's anxious face. She saw a large, scarred hand holding him up, and then he was gone, and so was she.

"You weren't dreaming." Bullhead carried a large pizza box into the room. He set it down and grabbed the TV remote. "Your boss says don't miss the six o'clock news."

* * *

Tired, sticky, and desperately hungry, Brad summoned energy to run up the driveway. Barely noticing Mort's Lexus parked in the yard, he dashed for the back door. The pizza shop had been closed by the time the bus returned, and Coach had dropped him off after repeating his promise of a victory pizza at the next practice. As if conjured by his own hunger, a teasing whiff of pepperoni and mushroom sauce met him even before he opened the door.

Two extra-large pizzas, half-eaten, were spread out on the table. Bullhead had been and gone. The Admiral, free of his cast and bandage, slept on Howie's boot by the door. "He can lift his wing almost all the way," Sal crowed, "and he only limps a little."

Scarfing pizza, Brad crouched beside her to inspect the sleeping penguin. The Admiral looked naked without his cast and bandage. "But can he swim? Get his own food?"

"Bullhead says he needs to practice – get his muscles back. We'll take him to the tidepool tomorrow, no one can see it from the road. Oh, I forgot ..." Sal jumped up. "This is Mom's new lawyer. I mean, she never had an old one, but..."

Brad rose to his feet and gaped. A tall black woman in a sleek suit stood with Mort next to the stove. Behind them, in the living area, Mac and Sara were dragging the TV set from Molly's room.

"Eleanor Thomas," Mort said. "Molly's son, Brad."

"I've been anxious to meet you," Thomas said.

Brad took her hand and stared at her, puzzled, then incredulous. "Gurdieff," he blurted, remembering. Tómas Gurdieff, a Chicago-born violinist who vanished after a concert in Budapest. Eleanor Thomas had tracked him down in a secret CIA prison in Poland, barely alive a whole year after the agency realized they'd snatched the wrong man. His hands had been smashed beyond repair. Brad, watching the scandal unfold, had thrown up all night after seeing those mangled fingers on the screen.

Eleanor Thomas nodded, and glanced at Brad's soda-soaked uniform. "Must have been quite a game," she said.

Brad didn't answer. He stared at his own intact fingers, then at Eleanor Thomas's eyes. "And you're Mom's lawyer? We saw her. On the road. After the game. They closed the whole highway...."

Mort looked at his watch and interrupted. "Turn on that television," he said, "and see her again. The networks were there, but it's my clips they're all showing."

It was like those out-of-body experiences you read about, Brad thought, watching himself on the screen from another plane entirely. Mort was either lucky or extremely astute and quick-footed. His opening shot panned the cavalcade of ambulances and armoured trucks slowing to a stop, then zoomed in on the police blockade, the team bus, the log trucks and other vehicles. The camera angle changed, showing the truckdriver and Brad's team leading a crowd of families and kids past the toppled police barrier. Then a wide-angle view of helmeted assault teams pouring out of armored trucks, weapons trained on a Little League team and assorted small children.

Brad hadn't felt the full horror of that moment until it unfolded on the screen. Suddenly there she was, the child in the pink dress darting past Brad into the middle of the road. A close-up of the trucker grabbing Brad as he hurled himself after her. Damn, he didn't remember that part at all. A man's voice called frantically in the distance, "Jessie! Jessie!" The camera froze on a foreshortened shot of the child waving happily into a dozen shotgun barrels.

Abruptly, the face of the district attorney filled the screen, a replay of his press conference last week. "The eco-warriors are armed and dangerous and will stop at nothing to thwart justice."

The district attorney's face was replaced by the blond-haired child, the line-up of Star Wars weapons trained on her, and then a single figure lowering his weapon and smiling. Then a wide-angle view of the cavalcade moving past a cheering Little League team, waving children, a trucker standing at attention, the same trucker lifting Brad to the ambulance window.

"You were there?" Brad asked. "You put this together?"

"Keep watching," Mort said. "The best comes last."

On the screen, the truck driver stood on the step of his cab, the diesel engine rumbling. The team bus moved slowly past in the background.

"So I ask you, who's the [beep]ing terrorists here?" the trucker asked the camera. The screen jumped to a close-up of his hedgehog face, the

Marine eagle glittering on his cap. "Look, I don't know nothin' about the woman. But I do know one hell of a lot about Howie – Howard Borstall – and he sure as [beep] wasn't no [beep]ing FBI agent." His voice continued over a close-up of a pant leg pulled back from his prosthetic limb. "That dude save my ass twice over in 'Nam, we been beer buddies ever since. And if he's FBI I'm the [beep]ing queen of Brazil."

Mort switched off the TV, grinning.

"You got that man's name?" Eleanor Thomas asked.

* * *

Joey headed slowly past the lumberyard, his pockets empty. He had reached the Sinkhole just in time to see the teal-blue pickup pull out and head toward the coast highway. Too discouraged for further requisitioning, he had turned for home.

It was too dark to see the sign outside the driveway of the new historical museum, but lights showed in its upper windows and a flashlight bobbed in the darkness near the building. Someone looking for something, Joey thought. A small, floppy projectile careened into his legs, knocking him off balance. He reached down and a wet tongue licked his fingers, furry paws scrabbled at his arm. He scooped up what felt like a wriggling ball of fluff with a wet nose and soft, silky ears. A puppy.

Joey hugged the pup, stroking it, and looked toward the museum. The flashlight still bobbed aimlessly, farther from the building now. Carrying the puppy, he headed toward it. The light wandered still farther, and he tripped over a low hedge.

"Bark? Bark?" he called hesitantly, not sure if puppies barked. "You looking for a puppy?"

The light swept toward him, bouncing closer in the dark. Blinded by the glare, he could see only a figure with a mane of frizzy hair, holding the light on the puppy. Joey hugged it close and waited. The figure gestured with the light and turned toward the house. Joey followed.

In the brightly lit kitchen, he recognized the light-bearer. He didn't know her name, but she came frequently to Dinkum's music nights. She set the flashlight and a leash on the table. The broken buckle of a woven collar told its own story.

"I just stepped out the door with him and he was gone," she said. "Thank god you found him!"

"He's hurt," Joey said, holding out the pup's paw. His hand and jacket were dotted with blood. "It's a splinter, I think. See?"

She touched the paw, and the pup shrank back in Joey's arms.

"Tweezers," the woman said. "The bathroom's upstairs. Can you help?"

Joey nodded. She seemed to see him for the first time.

"I know you from somewhere," she said.

Joey smiled. "Dinkum's."

"Ah. That's it."

Hugging the puppy, Joey followed her up the stairs and stopped in surprise. The stairway led directly into a large, carpeted room. Flanking two windows on one wall were banks of floor-to-ceiling library stacks filled with books. Partially completed shelves leaned against the opposite wall, surrounded by uncut lumber, a table saw, and tool boxes. Encircling the stairwell were neatly stacked cartons of books, each labeled. At the far end of the room, a TV set was on, an armchair in front of it, next to a playpen spread with newspaper and puppy toys.

Joey stood on the top step and held his breath, afraid to move lest the room disappear. In books, kids walked through a cupboard or mirror into magic realms fraught with treachery, betrayal, and danger. This stairway was the reverse, he thought. From a perilous real world it led to a place Joey had never dared to think of calling home.

In the bathroom, Tess Campbell took tweezers and a bottle of rubbing alcohol from a cluttered drawer in the sink cabinet. "Found them!" she called. "Bring him in here, the light's better."

There was no response. Turning, she saw his motionless figure on the top step, facing the wall of books.

"In here," she called again. No reaction. Wondering uneasily if he might be epileptic, she moved to his side and saw his face. The puppy was licking a tear from his cheek. She touched him lightly on the shoulder. Startled, he turned to face her.

"Did you find them? The tweezers?"

No, not epilepsy, Tess Campbell thought, and then she understood. "Yes," she said. "Bring him in the bathroom, the light's better."

* * *

"Joey," he told her later, when she asked his name and told him her own. The puppy slept contentedly on a slipper in his playpen, the trauma of a monster thorn extraction already forgotten. Joey sat on a cushion beside the pen, sipping hot chocolate and feeling sleepy himself. He glanced at the wall of books dreamily, then at Ms. Campbell's attentive face.

"I have a book," he said. "And a cat but it has no name. What's your puppy's name?"

"He doesn't have a name yet. He's not even mine."

"Oh. Whose is he, then?" asked Joey.

Ms. Campbell sighed. "It's complicated. A friend bought him for a boy's birthday, and then – well, the friend was killed the day he was to pick up the puppy. This morning the kennel called to find out what happened, so I went and got him myself. But the boy's mother is …."

She had lost her audience. Joey was staring past her at the eleven o'clock news roundup on the television screen.

"That's Brad!" he said.

Chapter Twenty-Four

I like girls, but music is easier. To relate to, that is. Like violin. A lot of girls – more girls than guys, actually – take violin, and some of them could be really good, but just when they're about to be really good they drop out to go cheerleading or to some boyfriend's football games. You can see it coming. They've always come to lessons or orchestra rehearsal dressed like everyone else – jeans, sweats, t-shirts – and all of a sudden they show up wearing makeup and hairstyles and the latest cool clothes, and next thing you know they're through with violin.

I don't get it. I liked them fine the way they were. Like this girl Ellen. In third grade she used to hide in the library and read Zane Grey because she was fat and everyone teased her. I was there to get away from the smear the queer mob, so we had something kind of in common. We talked about books and adventures and explorers and space travel and thought we were best friends for life. Now she's skinny and made up and hangs out with a bunch of other skinny, made-up girls that scream a lot and she won't even say hi to me.

Is it being black or is there something wrong with me? Howie laughed at that. "You're just not a sheep," he said. And Mom said I was lucky, it takes some people way too long to find out they don't have to be sheep. She meant herself, I think, but I don't know why.

—*The Oreo File*

Brad and Sal sat in the moonlight on the porch steps, arguing about John Philip Sousa. Next door, Mac's house was dark. A soft northeast wind bathed the coast in leftover heat from sunbaked inland marshes, tainted by occasional whiffs of diesel exhaust and for some reason, a hint of vanilla. Brad could hear Joe idly chewing hay in his shed. He wondered if horses ate in their sleep.

Brad's violin and bow lay across his lap. Sal held Howie's guitar, its neck propped against the Admiral's gate. They had worked up what Brad thought a prime set of Nigger Lew tunes when Sal insisted on adding a Sousa march.

"Sousa wrote those in the eighteen-eighties and nineties," Brad said. "Way after Lew was playing to earn his freedom."

"He lived 'til 1917. He didn't stop playing, did he? And 'Handsome Molly' wasn't 'til 1909," Sal pointed out. "Sousa was real popular, Lew would'a loved him!"

Brad looked at her face, stubborn and radiant in the moonlight. He didn't care if they added every march Sousa wrote, but she was enjoying the argument. He hadn't seen her so happy since Molly's arrest. As far as Sal was concerned, Molly was almost home, only twenty miles away in a hospital VIP suite, with Bullhead and Grandma Rose faithfully carrying messages back and forth every day. Eleanor Thomas, her new lawyer, had flown back to Philadelphia to assemble an investigative team and collect affidavits from Mort's former associates in D.C. The district attorney, according to courthouse gossip, had blown a gasket over the cavalcade newscast. Sara had taught Brad the secrets of making piecrust. And the entire glorious weekend had been devoted to Nigger Lew's music and the Admiral's swimming therapy.

Three or four times a day, depending on the tides, they had led the Admiral down the trail to the beach north of the house, Sal carrying Howie's boot, the Admiral lurching along like an old sea-dog on shore leave. Joe followed behind. Where the trail forked at the base of the cliff, Joe continued toward the beach, while the swimming party followed the left fork through seaweed-draped boulders to the tidepool.

The pool was a magical, secret place, hidden by rocky outcrops from the coast highway that skirted the bay and shielded from seaward by a huge muffin-shaped chunk of stone – aptly named The Muffin – that became an island at high tide. A deep basin sheltered from wind and flooded twice a day by the tide, the pool was home to crabs, anemones, sea urchins, and ever-changing populations of small fish. At low tide its surface was a clear lens on busy lives at the bottom. For three days, they had watched the Admiral's strength return, his first lopsided dives quickly gaining balance and grace. Twice, Mort had come along to try out his new toy, a submersible digital video camera.

"Look at that resolution!" Mort had crowed that evening, replaying his latest footage for Bullhead.

"Look at that wing – full mobility!" Bullhead watched again the Admiral's triumphant leap from the water. "And what a landing – full weight on both feet."

Mac had laughed. "Not bad for chainsaw surgery."

"Hey!" Bullhead held up his hands. "The only bird I ever carved before was a damn turkey."

A good weekend, a Sunday dinner flavored with hope. Sal's tongue was still purple from Brad's successful huckleberry pie. Grinning now at her earnest defense of John Philip Sousa, he picked up his violin and played the opening bars of "Stars and Stripes Forever."

"No, no!" Sal said. "'Liberty Bell.' That's the one Lew would've loved. Besides, it's the one I know best."

"You and Monty Python." Brad laughed and stood up, bow poised.

He played hard to meet Sal's overenthusiastic chords, his foot pounding march time on the wooden step. Sitting sideways to support the guitar, Sal didn't see what happened next until Brad nudged her with his knee. She almost missed a beat, staring at Joe.

At the first bars of "Liberty Bell," he had high-stepped out of his shed, neck arched, tail high. Keeping perfect time, he marched in place through the first repeat, while invisible troops fell in behind him. Then he stepped out, marching in a precise circle, mane and tail flying, hooves rising and falling to the beat. Round and round in the moonlight he pranced while Sal and Brad held their breath and played. On Sal's final, exaggerated chord, he froze in place, ears twitching.

Brad raised an eyebrow at Sal. Tentatively, on a hunch, he played the opening bars of a waltz, "The Blue Danube." Joe tossed his head and resumed his circle, his hooves flashing in a complicated, side-stepping waltz pattern. At the closing note, he stretched out his front feet and bowed. He trotted swiftly once around his invisible ring and continued offstage to his shed.

"Wow!" Sal breathed. "If only he could play at Dinkum's, too."

"It's Nigger Lew's show, remember?" Brad, laughing, put his violin to bed in its case. "Besides, that's an act no one could follow."

*   *   *

"I'm an historian, not a cook," Ms. Campbell said. "But spaghetti's easy."

His mouth full, Joey smiled. The 1950s paperback they had found, Cooking for Two, lay open on the counter. From the spattered burners of the formerly pristine gas range, blobs of tomato sauce dripped down the front, mingling with starchy streaks where the pasta had boiled over.

Ms. Campbell laughed. "Well, the spaghetti's easy. What they don't tell you is how to clean up the mess."

She lived mostly on salads and oatmeal, she had told Joey. "I make a mean bowl of oatmeal, but that's the extent of my culinary skill."

The dinner was to celebrate their weekend's work. Together, they had built bookshelves, arranged and indexed thousands of books. The big upstairs room now had the comfortable feel of a real library. The heaps of bulging boxes were gone, their contents tidily shelved. Beneath each window was a small table with a chair and reading lamp between ranks of library stacks. In the open center of the room, under the skylight installed by Howie, they had placed an ornate, drop-leaf mahogany dining table with matching chairs, a two-seater horsehair couch, and several shabby but comfortable overstuffed chairs. Next to the stairwell railing was their greatest triumph, a glass-fronted apothecary cabinet filled with index cards for every book.

They had hauled the furniture, much of it antique, from the huge old barn behind the house. Joey sighed happily over his spaghetti. As if the books upstairs weren't miracle enough, the barn had stunned him with more surprises.

"It's a mess," Ms. Campbell had warned him, throwing a switch in the breaker box mounted inside the door. "None of it's catalogued yet, just piles of stuff people have donated or bequeathed to the society over the years. Howie was going to finish the wiring here, but...."

A string of drop lights, wired directly to the breaker box, illuminated shadowy, angular mountains rising in places to a hayloft piled with boxes. Armed with flashlights, they had navigated narrow canyons between these slag-heaps of history, climbing precarious piles in search of library furnishings. Peering through tangles of bed frames, oars, disembodied water closets, organ pipes, butter churns, and other debris, Joey detected a sense of order overwhelmed by quantity. The bottom layers had originally been arranged by function: cookstoves and other kitchen equipment; bedroom, dining, and parlour furniture; harness, buckboards, carriages. Against the back wall, behind layers of slate blackboards and rows of cast iron school desks, he had found the equivalent of Aladdin's cave.

Ms. Campbell, alarmed by metallic crashes, had found him there, frantically heaving rolls of carpet and theatre seats from a row of vehicles lined up against the wall. He emerged from under one of them with his flashlight, dust-smeared and grinning.

"A Model T," he told her, inarticulate with excitement. "A little rust – well, a lot, actually. Tires gone. But it's all there. And look at that one, it's got – what are they, train wheels?"

"We've got photos of one like that," Ms. Campbell said. "There were no roads out here then. They drove on the tracks of the logging railroad."

Half crawling, he led her past the collection of vehicles, rattling off models and dates up to 1936. At the end of the row, still half buried, was something even he couldn't identify. All that was visible were broad, steel wheels and part of a bulbous metal structure. Ms. Campbell laughed, recognizing it.

"That's a steam tractor, one of the earlier ones – the first that John Deere ever made."

Joey gazed at her in admiration. "Wow. There's another one, with treads, in there next to it. More cars, too, and look at this!" He wheeled from the shadows what looked like a cartoon bicycle, with an enormous front wheel and tiny back one. "There's all kinds of bikes buried in there."

Dragging chairs and tables out to Ms. Campbell's pickup to haul up to the house, Joey looked around the huge barn with new eyes. "If we got all the junk out, this could be a car museum," he said eagerly. "Cars, tractors, those bikes. I bet I could even get that T running again, some of the others, too, maybe."

Ms. Campbell set down her end of the heavy mahogany table, smiling. "There's something else," she said.

She led him around a stack of church pews to a walled-off corner room and opened a door, flipping a switch. Inside was an orderly sanctuary sealed off from the chaos of the barn. A heavy workbench, variously sized vices bolted to it, ran along one outside wall, lit by two windows. A lathe, a table saw, and a guillotine miter stood on the floor, power cables carefully coiled. Peg-board hung with hundreds of tools covered one interior wall, and a drafting table just right of the door caught the light from a corner window. The fourth wall was fitted with racks holding boards and moldings of different kinds of wood.

"Howie's workroom," Ms. Campbell said, "just as he left it. He built all the cabinets for the museum right here. But this is what I wanted to show you."

From behind the drafting table she wheeled an elegant, narrow-wheeled bicycle. Joey stared.

"It's made of wood!"

"Bamboo," Ms. Campbell said. "Pick it up – it hardly weighs anything."

Joey lifted the bicycle, astonished. The frame, wheel rims, and curved handlebars were made of polished bamboo. Only the hub, sprockets, chain, and front fork were metal. He set it down and wheeled it back and forth. The tires looked new and were fully inflated.

"They called it the fishing pole bike," Ms. Campbell said. "It was made in Wisconsin in 1897 – the main use of bamboo back then was for fishing poles."

Joey thrust the bike back to her in horror, afraid it would turn to dust in his hands. "It's over a hundred years old!"

Ms. Campbell laughed. "Don't worry, it's in beautiful shape. It was hidden away in an attic most of that time. Howie helped me clean it up, we had to put a new chain on it. The hard part was finding those narrow tires, they had to be special ordered. Go ahead, take a spin. I've ridden it to the store a few times, it's sturdy as hell."

Joey finished the last of his spaghetti, thinking of the amazing fishing pole bike. Riding it was almost like flying, it was so light, and it had felt alive in his hands. He had ridden it to Dinkum's that day, proudly parking it on the stage while he worked. He had ridden it to the not-so-old lady's house, with four cans of Iams in a bag. And twice he had ridden it to Brad's, only to find no one home.

"I'd give it to you, for all your hard work," Ms. Campbell had said, giving him a key to the barn, "but it's not mine to give, it belongs to the museum. Machines die if they're not used, though, like violins. So use it whenever you like, you'll be performing a service."

Joey didn't need a key to get into the barn, but he hadn't told her that. He had hung the key proudly around his neck on a stout length of baling twine. Watching Ms. Campbell dish out the cake and icecream she'd bought, he traced the metal outline through his t-shirt with awed fingers. Like the Harry Potter receipt, it accorded him a legitimacy as gratifying as it was undeserved. Momentarily assailed by an imposter's worst fear, he glanced at Ms. Campbell. She met his eye and winked.

"Oh – I talked to Mort Holland today," she said, placing cake plates on the table. "Dinkum's landlord?"

Joey nodded. He stared at her, ignoring his cake.

"He put up most of the money for the new museum," Ms. Campbell explained. "That woman you saw him with? She's not the DA's flunky. She's Molly Matthissen's lawyer. From Philadelphia. Mort hired her."

"Oh." A slow smile spread over Joey's face. So Molly's tape was safe. So far, maybe. He hadn't seen the teal-blue pickup all weekend and had feared the worst. The penguins, too, seemed to have vanished, gone to sea or holed up somewhere, though Greenpeace and party boats still patrolled the coastline. But a pickup couldn't vanish out to sea, it had to be somewhere. Joey's hand went to the key around his neck.

"Tomorrow – I can use the bike?"

"All week if you want," Ms. Campbell said. "Any time!"

* * *

Tess Campbell watched the small figure trot up the driveway in the moonlight, his bag of cat scraps swinging jauntily from one arm. The puppy strained at the leash in her hand, whining to follow. She picked him up, fighting an insane urge to run after the boy herself.

Her partner would have taken the child in, Tess thought, like the three-legged rabbit, the blind pony and geriatric dogs and cats Myrna had dragged home from her veterinary practice. Tess had tended them faithfully after Myrna's death; by the time the last weary critter succumbed to age and infirmity, she had barricaded her solitude behind impenetrable kindness, a friend to all and needing none. Somehow this kid had slipped through the razor wire, an alarming thought.

The puppy wriggled in her arms and licked her neck.

"Not you, too!" Tess shut the door before putting him down. "This week, pal, we'll get you where you belong."

Chapter Twenty-Five

When Mac found out they had a baby coming he was so excited he ordered a baby carriage. I don't mean your basic Walmart baby stroller, this is the real thing, a Rolls Royce of a carriage with big rubber tires and leaf springs. The carriage part is all satin and leather, with a special clear hood you can snap on for rain. He ordered it from New York or Boston or somewhere, and no one could talk him out of it, never mind the nearest sidewalk is four miles away and the only pavement is the coast highway. He had this picture of Mary Poppins in his head, and had to have something straight out of Kensington Garden. Except for the army, where instead of Vietnam they sent him to Okinawa to guard a weather balloon and shoot it if it escaped, Mac's never been anywhere but here in the woods. I don't know where he heard about Kensington Garden, but it sure gave him a powerful idea of what his kid had to have.

Mac's so big he could hold Baby Craig in the palm of his hand at first, but he can change a diaper like he's done it forever. Sometimes him and Howie sit on the steps with a beer after work and watch Baby Craig sleeping in that perambulator, not talking, just drinking their brew and watching the baby like he's the best tv show on earth. Sal doesn't have much use for babies. She says he'll be more interesting when he learns to swim.

—The Oreo File

"I'm almost human again!"

Leaning on Grandma Rose, Molly emerged from the VIP bath and made a wobbly circuit around the room. Bullhead had replaced the cast on her leg with a removable, steel-reinforced Velcro wrap. The bandage over her eye was gone. Her hair, wet from her first shower in weeks, drooped rakishly over a shaved eyebrow replaced by a bulbous purple and yellow swelling, seamed like a football with stitch scars. Her right arm, its cast wrapped in a plastic bag, hung in a padded sling.

"Don't count your blessings afore they hatch," Grandma Rose said. "That slimeball DA's just itching to haul you back to jail."

Out of breath, Molly collapsed on the daybed and lifted her still-swollen ankle onto a pillow. She frowned at the hospital bed, where Rose began dismantling traction and IV rigs. Even a leaky jail was better than being half blind and trussed up in traction, breathing by machine.

Rose carried the bedpan chrysanthemums to a table by the daybed and placed a small collection of photos on the windowsill: Brad at a recital, oblivious to camera or audience; Sal on Joe's back, splashing in the tideline; a rare shot of Howie, holding the fawn he'd raised last year after setting its broken front legs.

Molly stared at the third photo. For the first time, she could look at it without shoving it quickly out of sight and groping for the oxygen. Bewildered, she gazed now at the familiar figure with only a dull ache of tenderness.

When Brad was little, he would close his eyes against the death of Babar's mother, blindly flipping the awful page to keep Molly from reading it; he wouldn't open his eyes again until Babar, the unthinkable behind him, discovered the thrill of driving an elevator. Molly smiled. A drop of water from her wet hair dribbled down her back and she almost laughed. It was the shower, she thought. The shower – and the thrill of regaining an eye and a leg – had rescued her from some lifeless event horizon.

Molly had taken the photo herself. She eyed it critically. She hadn't adjusted for the light, and Howie's battered Dodger cap shadowed his face. The fawn in his arms had been the real object of the lens. Its bandaged front legs dangled over Howie's forearm, its head nestled trustfully against his shoulder, facing the camera with eyes and ears alert.

Howie's hand supporting the fawn's middle was in perfect focus. She could see the scarred knuckles, the thickened fingertips, the veins and tendons standing out in taut relief – a hand at home with rope or cable, climbing ax or hoof pick. Leaning over the photo, she could see tiny rainbow glints of sunlight on fine, dark wrist hairs. The long fingers, as nimble fine-tuning a chainsaw as cross-picking a guitar, splayed over the fawn's belly in support and gentle restraint.

The day they'd first met, it was his hands she'd noticed first. The fingers then were splayed over the borders of a large topo map, the light from the window in front of him glinting on the wrist hairs just as in the photo. He was sitting cross-legged on the table like the Tailor of Gloucester, his back to her, leaning over the map.

That morning, the doctors had announced that Sal's leukemia was in remission and they were sending her home. Molly and Brad had driven back from Portland, singing all the way, celebrating with icecream cones. Pulling into Mort's parking area, they were still singing. "Inch by inch, Row by row, Gonna make this garden grow…." She was late for the job interview and hardly cared.

The door of Mort's office was open. Molly had never met Mort, only seen him on the screen. The man leaning over the map was whistling the Garden Song they'd just been singing; she and Brad grinned at each other.

"Hello? Mr. Holland?"

"Not here."

Molly and Brad grinned at each other again. He sounded exactly like My Cousin Vinnie.

The man turned slightly, keeping his hands on the map. Under a faded Brooklyn Dodgers cap, his seamed, tanned face beamed at her. "You're Molly? C'mon in. Mort's in Florence with the governor. Said to tell you welcome aboard, we start next week."

"Um – no interview?" Molly asked.

"What you sent was good enough, he said – and the governor got him out of the interview."

He slid off the table to introduce himself. "Howard – Howie – oops!"

The map, freed of his hands, lifted into the breeze from the open window and sailed across the room. Brad jumped and caught it before it blew out the door.

"Good catch!" Howie grabbed a stapler and an unmounted spotlight to weight the map.

Brad looked at the topo map, and at a Triple-A map pinned to a makeshift easel on the table. "What are all the marks?"

"Owls," Howie said. "Spotted owls. The red's an occupied nest, blue's a sighting, yellow an unconfirmed nest. Green is old-growth not surveyed yet." He pointed to the road map on the easel. "I'm transferring the field observations – from all the topo maps – to the highway map."

Brad studied the two maps and pointed. "That one should be blue, shouldn't it?"

"Bingo. My eyes are fried. Here, help me finish this last one." Howie hopped up on the table again. "Just call out the nearest coordinates and what color, okay?"

"Okay." Brad checked the maps. "R-ten. Blue. Just like Battleship."

Molly smiled at them and stared around the absent Mort's office. It was more like a warehouse, a large room piled with crates, boxes, tripods, a mike boom, and something that looked like a golf cart with a camera mounted on it. Against the back wall was the nominal office: filing cabinets, shelves of labeled tapes, a table heaped with papers amid a telephone, ashtray, computer, and fax/printer. A row of flat-screen monitors sat on stout crates, facing the desk table. Molly took it all in with the giddy disbelief of a shipwrecked sailor washed up on home shores.

Here, in Mort's haphazard, breezy office with no fanfare, a long, terrible year of running on empty came to an end. She had watched Sal dying bit by bit before her eyes, and now Sal was going to live. On a few meagre song royalties from another life, she had managed to give Brad clean soil and the best violin teacher in the state, but barely enough to eat. And now she had a job. A job she loved and could do well, so why did she suddenly feel so utterly boneless?

Molly shook off the strange mood and began rolling the maps stacked to one side of Howie's table. "And my job is….?"

"These are last year's surveys," Howie told her. "We'll revisit each nest site, film any active ones, look for new ones. And if we're really lucky, spot a murrelet nest."

"K-twelve. Yellow. That's the last one," Brad said. "What's the road map for?"

"Logistics. You see how few and far between these sites are. The road map's to plot each day's route – cover as many on each trip as possible. Starting next week, we have only six weeks or so."

"My sister comes home next week," Brad said.

"Oh," said Howie politely. "From where?"

"The hospital in Portland. She's coming home as soon as the doctors find a horse trailer."

"Uhhh … Your sister's a horse?"

"No, a salamander." Brad laughed and looked to Molly for help. She explained about Sal, the leukemia, Joe the mystery horse. Howie's eyes, green and deep as glacier melt, registered the fears behind her words, the relentless dread mounting day after day, night after night. His instant understanding unnerved her. Trying to describe the doctors' wonderful news that morning, her voice broke and she found herself sobbing, reaching blindly for Brad's shoulder. Embarrassed, she glanced at Howie. She shouldn't have worried. A huge smile had engulfed his knowing eyes. He leapt to his feet, scattering maps and easel and pens, and hopped to the floor.

"And you just found out today? The fuck're we doin' in here, then?" He grabbed their hands and rushed them out the door, bellowing, swinging their hands high. Crows and gulls raiding a dumpster in the parking lot scattered and took off in flapping confusion.

"Yo, birds! Listen up!" Howie let go their hands and cupped his into a megaphone. “Salamander’s coming home!” The crows and gulls wheeled overhead, shrieking back. Molly and Brad dropped to the ground, laughing. With wild gestures, Howie peered into the trees for snipers. “Hear this, Dow Chemical! Monsanto! Fallwell! All you Fuckers! You lost this one, assholes! Wanna know why? ’Cause Salamander disdains to die!”

He collapsed beside Molly and Brad. “Disdains to die! Good line, eh?” he said, grinning. His amazing hands rolled a cigarette by themselves. “Not mine, though. The guy who started the Civil Air Patrol wrote it, about a tree, but it could’a been for Salamander – she damn right disdains to die. Shit, I forgot to ask you,” he turned to Molly. “I hope you like climbing trees.”

“Lord, who are these ruffians?” Grandma Rose, carrying a stack of mail, nudged the picture of Howie aside and added another photo to the row. It was a Polaroid, taken in Portland. Four black teenagers, identically posed in belligerent, heavy-browed attitudes, stood next to a uniformed cop. The shop front behind them had a cracked window, the faded sign over the door only legible with the magnifying glass Molly had borrowed from Bullhead.

Molly took the photo, smiling. “It’s the Fairly Honest Eddies.” She pointed. “That’s Mel on the left, the guard who gave me the harmonica. And that’s his kid brother Gaspar next to him. The others are Andrews, Mog, and Bricker. Gobi took the picture, so he’s not in it.”

“Hate to run into any of ’em in a dark alley,” Rose said.

“They’re musicians!” Molly laughed. “Or trying to be. Mel’s bringing them down next weekend – to see the penguins. And hear Brad and Sal play at Dinkum’s – the Not-A-Memorial-For-Howie night.”

She set the photo carefully next to the others. “Mort said he’d tape it for me. If Bullhead can keep me out of jail ’til then.”

* * *

“Every time someone puts a scalpel in my hand, I panic.”

Bullhead had come to see the Admiral’s progress first-hand. Hiking back from the tidepool, he studied the Admiral's gait with approval. Not a trace of a limp, even after a strenuous swim. The Admiral plodded sturdily after Sal and Howie's boot. Beside Bullhead, Mort tracked the bird on camera.

"I'm a fraud, see," Bullhead went on. "A fuckin' logger in surgical scrubs, a bad joke." He waved an imaginary scalpel at the Admiral. "When it all works – like Molly and that little guy – it's the gods on call deserve the credit."

"Gods?" Mort looked up from his view screen. "How many are there?"

"Dunno." Bullhead laughed. "Never seen any, myself. But someone's workin' miracles, and it ain't me."

He stopped abruptly at the top of the trail. Brad, following behind, nearly walked into him. Sal stood, grinning, pointing at the house. Four penguins stood in a row on the porch next to the open gate. The Admiral hopped up the steps and waddled past them to the railing, where Bertha waited with a beak full of fish.

Chapter Twenty-Six

South of here there are black sand beaches where Mac takes us on picnics sometimes. He grew up here, and going places with him is a trip. He showed us secret tunnels through the rocks that he says were built by Chinese people after the railroads didn't need them any more. So they came here and dug the tunnels to sift gold out of the black sand. And at full moon he took us there, smelting. Smelt are these little fish, no bigger'n your hand, that come onto black sand beaches to spawn at certain high tides with a full moon. Somehow they come in on a wave and lay their eggs and fertilize them and then ride back out on the next wave. There used to be billions of 'em, Mac says, so many the whole beach'd be quilted with them. It's not like that any more, but it's pretty amazing even so, going out in the moonlight and seein' the beach flashing with fish between each wave. You can scoop them up with buckets or coffee cans, whatever you've got, and people fry 'em up whole – and eat 'em whole – or freeze them in buckets of water for later.

We ate our life quota of smelt, I think. Then this old couple that would've froze to death last winter gave Mac some ice-blocks of smelt after he brought them dry firewood and split it for them. He didn't want nothing for it, but he said they had their pride so he took the smelt. It's still there in Sara's freezer waiting for us to feel like eating smelt again.

—*The Oreo File*

Mrs. Frederick J. Robinson had successfully evaded jury duty for eighteen years. When both luck and connections failed her that spring, she had been ignominiously assigned to the grand jury. A trial jury at least had a chance of glamor in it, the possibility of a nice death penalty or terrorism case with jurors interviewed afterward on national television. A grand jury offered no glory whatsoever; nobody even knew it existed, no reporters were allowed, and it didn't matter what you wore, because there was no judge or audience to impress. It was also excruciatingly boring.

Further testing her peevish martyrdom, Mrs. Robinson's fellow jurors had asked her to drive a disabled jury member to and from jury sessions while her usual driver recovered from pneumonia. The juror, a mousey young woman with a steel leg brace and scarred throat, could speak only in a whisper and needed a wheeled walker to get about; the other jurors had appointed her clerk, to take notes of their sessions. Mrs. Robinson had no tolerance whatever for cripples and would as soon share her elegant Lincoln with a real rodent.

"She's only four blocks from the bridge," the foreman had said, "right on your way."

"This is the first she's been out of the house in two years," another juror added, "since the accident, you know. Of course we all want to encourage her."

Mrs. Robinson remembered the accident vaguely. A log truck had overturned, crushing the woman and killing her husband and baby. Disgusted by the woman's frailty and disfigurement, Mrs. Robinson privately thought she should have been put out of her misery. She had grudgingly agreed to the driving only when the foreman added that if the cripple withdrew, they would appoint Mrs. Robinson clerk. Clerk, indeed! The proud businesswoman in her gagged at the thought.

The grand jury met every Tuesday and Thursday in the basement of the county courthouse. The windowless room, previously a storage area for janitorial supplies, smelled of chlorine and synthetic pine scent. A table large enough to seat nine people nearly filled the room. In one corner was a television monitor for viewing evidence tapes; a small shelf held a jug of water, a bowl of stale pretzels, and on occasion a box of day-old Safeway donuts. Before each session, the district attorney taped on the wall a schedule of cases to be considered, often too many to fit in a nine-hour day.

There were seven grand jurors and two alternates, who were likely to be needed, Mrs. Robinson thought, as three of the regular jurors were in their seventies; one of these, unaccountably appointed foreman by the court, carried a portable oxygen tank. The cripple was the youngest; the only other female juror under age sixty was a thirty-five-year-old hair stylist whose appalling hair advertised a different color and style every day; she also chewed gum and wore spike heels with sequined straps. Worse still, one of the three male jurors, a gaunt internet consultant with greying hair pulled back in a long pony tail, actually wore an earring. A day with this jury, Mrs. Robinson thought, was worse than being trapped in an elevator full of shoplifters.

The sessions themselves were an endless parade of depravity, one case after another of methamphetamine production and distribution, child abuse and neglect, or domestic violence, often all of these combined. Mrs. Robinson's belief that most of humanity should be strangled at birth hardly needed such reinforcement. By association, her fellow jurors, the prosecutors, and the police witnesses became as subhuman as the crooks.

There was neither time nor opportunity for the jury to engage in soul-searching or even superficial inquiry in what was an assembly-line routine. The prosecutor – an assistant or deputy district attorney, the difference never explained – would summarize the evidence in each case, calling arresting officers and showing police videos to prove particular points. The prosecutor then withdrew, leaving the jurors to determine whether the evidence was sufficient to support the charges and go to trial. With only the prosecutor's side of the story available, and ever mindful of the list of cases tacked to the wall, the jury simply rubber-stamped each case, usually within minutes.

The only occasional relief in this stultifying routine was the testimony of undercover cops in drug investigations. Mrs. Robinson generally approved of police, who were her bastion against shoplifters, but her approval was put to the test by the undercover cops, who she found to be B-movie caricatures, overweight hulks with pea brains, drunk on their own power. For her, the real high point of grand jury duty was the guided tour of the new county jail, where they were treated to a jailhouse lunch: sandwiches of dry white bread filled with a wilted piece of iceberg lettuce and a sliver of highly suspect meat product, accompanied by a brown, wrinkled wedge of apple. While her fellow jurors picked wanly at such fare, Mrs. Robinson ate every bite and declared it too good for prisoners, a waste of taxpayers' money.

On the Tuesday morning of the fourth grand jury session, Mrs. Robinson's limited patience was further taxed when she found cat hairs on the Lincoln's passenger seat. Convinced that the entire grand jury process was a waste of public money and of her time, she had brought an Anne Rice paperback to read. She barely looked up when the District Attorney himself entered, to present the case of State v. Molly Matthissen.

* * *

Sal stood in the doorway, watching the Admiral gulp Bertha's catch. In the driveway next door, Mac's pickup started up. She returned his wave half-heartedly. He had put off leaving for work until the last minute, hoping to see the Admiral join his crew in the ocean, but everything seemed to be happening late this morning. Bertha had been slow bringing the Admiral's fish, and the penguins seemed in no hurry to leave.

Sal watched the birds idling in a row at the closed gate, preening, staring up at the sky. She would open the gate when the Admiral was finished. If he were well and truly healed, this might be his last breakfast here.

Behind her, Brad glanced at Sal's hunched shoulders and clenched fists. It wasn't worry about the Admiral that upset her, he knew. It was fury over the paper in his hands, returned by her teacher with the week's assignments. The vague instruction for the paper had been to "write one page about your favorite fruit or vegetable." Sal had worked two nights on it, consigning draft after draft to the kindling box; the finished product had not a single misspelling. At the top of the paper, the teacher had scrawled a huge red D-minus. In disgust, Brad handed it to Mort, who sat with Eleanor Thomas, grinning over the contents of the file she'd brought from D.C.

"Read that, will you?" Brad said. "Tell me that's a D-minus third grade paper."

Mort glanced apologetically at Ms. Thomas. He adjusted his glasses and read aloud in his news anchor voice.

"Apples. Apples are my favorite fruit. Apples are very good for you and an apple a day keeps the doctor away is no joke. So everyone should eat an apple every day. There are eighty-four billion pounds of apples grown in the world every year. There are about four apples in a pound so that's three-hundred-thirty-six billion apples a year. There are six point five billion people in the world so there are enough apples for each person to have an apple only fifty-one point six days of the year. Some people eat a lot more apples than that and a whole lot of people don't get any. But even if every person got equal shares there would not be enough apples for everyone to eat an apple every day. So we need to grow a lot more apples or make a lot less babies or have a lot more doctors.

"Addendum, teacher's note at bottom," Mort added. "'This was a writting' – spelled with two T's, mind you – 'a writting assigment, not a math quiz.' Assig-ment! And this person calls itself a teacher?"

Brad nodded, too angry to speak. Mort scanned the paper again and winked at him.

"Sal," Mort said to her stiff back. "Did I ever tell you about my work for the BBC, the London Economist, and Le Monde, among others? What I did for many years was read every sort of submission under the sun, and I'm well qualified to tell you this is as concise and articulate a piece of writing as anything I've ever read. With your permission, I'd very much like to share it with a few people."

Eleanor Thomas was reading the paper now. "I concur. And there are a few folks I'd like to share it with, too."

"Whatever." Sal turned, still glowering, but Brad saw her shoulders straighten. "Brad helped with the spelling, though. And I forgot about commas. And the Admiral's ready to go."

Carrying Howie's boot, Sal opened the porch gate. The Admiral and his crew and Joe followed in line behind her, Mort darting off the trail to film the procession. Sara grabbed her Polaroid camera and trotted after them. Brad, carrying Baby Craig, walked slowly, well in the rear. He had little wish to see the Admiral swim away, possibly forever. Beside him, Eleanor Thomas kept pace gingerly, her high heels sinking in the moist dirt.

At the head of the line, Sal stopped and pulled off her shoe to shake a pebble out of it. The Admiral and his crew marched stolidly on and disappeared one by one over the cliff edge. Sal hopped after them on one foot, waving her shoe in one hand and Howie's boot in the other. Brad burst out laughing, and Baby Craig gurgled. Brad looked down at the round, toothless smile.

"Hey, man, you're turning into a real live person!"

Sal's scream broke the momentary connection. He thrust Baby Craig into Eleanor Thomas's arms and ran.

Just below the cliff edge, Mort held Sal's arm to keep her from leaping down the rocks. Farther down, the ebbing tide was still high, flooding the penguins' ledge. Brad saw the last bird bellyflop into a wave, saw the heads of the others above the foam – and two party boats roaring down on them. Farther out, two Greenpeace zodiacs raced toward them. Sal screamed again. As if in response, the Admiral turned north, toward the sheer cliff of the Muffin, and dove. All four penguins disappeared after him. The party boats swerved sharply, following.

At low tide, the Muffin was connected to the mainland by a causeway of jagged rocks and boulders, from which driftwood logs protruded like monstrous pickup sticks. At high tide, rocks and logs were submerged with too little clearance for any but a very shallow draft boat; on the ebbing tide, waves concealed the danger only inches below the surface. The first party boat slammed into the causeway at full speed with a sickening crunch, its ruptured bow thrust skyward. The second boat, veering to avoid running into the first, ran full tilt into the vertical wall of the Muffin. The Greenpeace zodiacs converged on the wrecks cautiously. Beside Brad, Joe whinnied.

Sal broke free from Mort's grasp and clambered back to Brad.

"The tidepool! Boost me up!"

Brad lifted her knee and tossed her onto Joe's back. Joe wheeled and shot off in a clatter of hooves, heading back toward the beach trail. Brad glanced at the drama below. The zodiacs were fending off the upturned hull of the second boat, their crews pulling swimmers from the waves. They would have to take the survivors seaward, around the Muffin, to the beach. If Sal was right and the Admiral was headed for the safety of the tidepool, the birds would be trapped there. Brad tugged Mort up the rocks and ran.

From the north end of the long curve of highway above the beach, the Muffin and its drama were clearly visible. Vehicles were already stopped, traffic along the entire stretch coming to a halt. Brad barely noticed. He plunged down the beach trail, eyes only on Sal. At the bottom, she slipped from Joe's back and slapped him toward the beach, then disappeared among the rocks sheltering the tidepool.

* * *

Mac drove his old pickup mercilessly over the ruts and potholes and small saplings of a neglected fire road across Boone's Ridge. He had been halfway to work, just biting into one of Sara's raspberry-filled donuts, when Mort's cell phone had shrieked its electronic travesty of the 1812 Overture. He'd forgotten the damn thing was still in the cab and bit too hard in reaction. Like a squashed sea slug, the donut had spurted raspberry jam over the steering wheel and up his sleeve. Pulling into a turnout, he had groped for the phone with a jam-smeared hand. Three minutes later, he was headed home, a crimson blob of jam dripping unnoticed from his ear.

"Forget the highway," Mort had said. "It's backed up miles already. Nothing's getting through."

The fire road crested the ridge overlooking a vast clearcut, blanketed with late spring growth of tansy ragwort and fireweed. One glance through the cosmetic strip of trees bordering the highway far below confirmed Mort's call. Vehicles were stopped bumper to bumper north and south. Recklessly, Mac swerved onto a skid trail gashed diagonally down the steep slope toward the southern boundary of the clearcut. Leaving the pickup at the bottom, he ran through the tree belt, emerging on the highway opposite his and Molly's driveway. Through a press of people and vehicles, he made his way to the driveway and vaulted the locked gate.

At the top of the beach trail behind Molly's house, he found Sara, sitting on a log with Baby Craig at her breast. Beside her sat Eleanor Thomas, her bare feet stretched out, her shoes and nylons in her lap. On the beach below, people swarmed in the tideline, surging back and forth with the waves. Far up the beach he could see tiny figures pouring down the broken eighty-seven steps, a few tumbling and falling. Others clambered down the cliff from the mobbed highway, where a TV crew was lowering camera equipment on a rope. Joe galloped back and forth across the mouth of the trail, kicking out at anyone trying to enter or climb the rocks.

Above the roar of surf, Mac heard the crowd yell. A zodiac churned into sight around the Muffin, moving ponderously and low in the water. Brad emerged from the track to the tidepool and climbed a boulder, watching a Life Flight helicopter hovering over the beach. Something on the highway beyond the helicopter caught his attention. He spotted Mac and waved a frantic, unintelligible signal.

"Sal's at the tidepool," Sara said. "I think the penguins are, too. Go on, they need you!"

Mac kissed the top of her head and ran.

"Mac, your ear!" Sara called after him. He paused, wiped his ear, and licked his fingers.

"Jam!" he yelled back.

Brad met him halfway down the trail. Breathless, he pointed to the highway just north of the trees bordering their driveway. A teal-blue pickup was parked crookedly on the highway shoulder, hemmed in by a bread truck and a Pontiac sedan. Below it, three figures were clambering down to the beach, clinging to rocks and using oyster-catcher nest holes for toe holds. One had a camera bag slung over his shoulders.

"Sweet Jesus," Mac said.

"Joey's there. Look!" Brad pointed farther north, where Joey, holding a bicycle over his head, flitted among the stalled vehicles and wove through the press of spectators.

Mac glanced at the crowded beach. The zodiac had pulled up on the sand, its dripping passengers staggering ashore. The zodiac pushed off to return to the wrecks. Mort stood on a boulder near the tidepool, filming. No one had yet broken through Joe's hooved defense.

"Get going," Mac said. "I'll see to Sal."

Chapter Twenty-Seven

Howie told us there were two reasons he quit the Forest Service. The first was when he blew the whistle on a special agent who was supposed to be investigating pot growing and timber sabotage. The guy was finding pot and selling it instead of turning it in, and spiking trees himself to make his job look good and get publicity against environmentalists. Then Howie realized something worse. All his field reports, showing where endangered species were so they wouldn't be logged, were getting leaked to Fallwell and other timber companies so they could bid and cut those places before anyone found out what nested there. By the time copies of Howie's reports made it to the decision offices, the trees were cut and gone. He was handing them the birds on a platter, he said, and didn't know how to fight it so he quit.

I got so mad hearing that, I wanted to go punch out a few Forest Service dudes, but Sal doesn't get mad, she just thinks everything over and then asks Howie which saved more birds, working for the Forest Service or working for Mort. He says there's no way to know for sure, but the films he makes with Mom have won four lawsuits so far, saving seven or eight nest areas, and the only ones the Forest Service saved were a couple units that couldn't be cut anyway for other reasons.

—*The Oreo File*

Joey's pink backpack thumped unevenly against his ribs. Harry Potter, now residing with the Dinkum's crew, had been replaced by puppy and cat treats. The beef shank bone and bag of chicken scraps, both double wrapped, shifted with every turn and pothole. Joey hardly noticed.

Giddy with the unexpected fortunes of his morning, he sailed the bamboo bicycle down the long hill south of Dinkum's, reciting the Declaration of Independence into the wind.

Joey loved the Declaration of Independence, especially the bitchy list of grievances. The book lady at the detention center, horrified at his ignorance, had taught him to read with it, explaining the lurid history behind each provision. Joey knew the whole document by heart; its precise, unequivocal language steadied him when events proved overwhelming, though the phrase "pursuit of happiness" still puzzled him. In his experience, pursuit was something cops did to you. Nobody, not even cops, could pursue happiness; it was something that just washed over you unannounced, like when the cat's eye healed or Mex handed him the Harry Potter out of the blue.

"He has made judges dependent on his will alone for the tenure of their offices…" Joey swept around a curve, his momentum carrying the bike up a small rise. For the second time that morning, happiness had sneaked up on him. The Dinkum's crew had not only approved Ms. Campbell's puppy plan, they had improved on it.

"A puppy!" Mex had exclaimed. "Too perfect! Howie would love this. What's its name?"

"A cake." Harpo's eyes gleamed. "We'll have to have a cake!"

They would make party hats, raid the tip jar for silly favors, embellish Ms. Campbell's plan to present the puppy to Brad at the Not-A-Memorial-For-Howie party. Joey pedaled hard up curves and small hills. He'd never planned anything beyond a shoplifting list, and suddenly plans swarmed in his head like mayflies – for Brad's puppy, for building his own bamboo bicycle, for compost toilet construction.

"What do you think?" Ms. Campbell had said that morning over printouts of compost toilet specs. "Can we do it ourselves?"

"Why?" Joey had asked. "I mean, why do you need one?"

"Well, if we're going to clean out that barn and set up the car and tractor exhibit, we can't be running all the way to the house to pee. And this is a lot cheaper than sewer lines."

Joey stared at her, speechless. A real exhibit! Visions of Model T's and steam tractors nearly eclipsed what she said next.

"Look, Joey, I don't know where you've been living. I don't want to know. But that shop of Howie's is insulated and heated, there's a water line out there already, too. So whenever you're ready, it's yours. And we need a cat," she added. "I found rat poop in some of those cabinets."

Plans. Joey was dizzy with them. He was to be paid money for what he loved to do – care for books and rebuild cars. She would teach him to use the computer, had already helped him find bamboo bicycles on the internet. The internet! He could find anything – how to make a solar water heater, a wind generator, a cat door. Joey pedaled harder, recited faster.

"A prince whose character is thus marked by every act which may define a tyrant is unfit to be the ruler of – oh, shit!"

Joey skidded to a stop. Ahead of him, the highway was packed with stalled vehicles in both lanes. Between the cars and on both shoulders, people walked, ran, pushed strollers up the sloping highway. Joey picked up the bike to spare its tires from the gravel shoulder; carrying it over his head, he followed the crowd. Penguins. How could he have forgotten the penguins? Abashed, he abandoned pipe dreams and looked for the teal-blue pickup. Wedged among log trucks, SUVs, motor homes, semis and cars, the lights of an ambulance and a cop car flashed uselessly.

At the top of the hill, the road curved along the cliff above a long stretch of beach before cutting inland through the trees by Brad's driveway. Clutching the bike, Joey fought his way through jostling people backed up behind the Eighty-Seven Steps. Below, people surged over the beach toward the headland, where a horse reared and kicked, driving them back. Westward, a zodiac weaved into wreckage at the base of the Muffin. A red Coast Guard helicopter swung low over the beach and out over the wrecks. Joey scanned the long curve of highway ahead. At the far end of the long curve, he saw a teal-blue pickup among the packed vehicles.

Joey almost dropped the bamboo bike. Grasping it tightly overhead, he ran, weaving through clumps of people, dodging around vehicles. Far ahead, he saw Brad scramble up a boulder behind the horse. Another zodiac swept toward the beach. Brad glanced up at a Life Flight helicopter circling low over the crowd and spotted Joey, waving. Joey set the bike down and pointed frantically toward the pickup. He saw Brad stiffen, then jump off his boulder.

Joey picked up the bike and began running again. When he looked down, Brad had vanished.

Eight feet below the highway shoulder, the crumbling pavement of the old coast road protruded from the cliff, undercut by tides and wind. A large section of it had broken away completely just north of the teal-blue pickup. Hugging the cliff, Brad scooted along the old pavement, placing his feet carefully. Joey was waiting for him near the broken end, leaning over to pull him up. The teal-blue pickup faced them six feet away, tilted onto the soft gravel shoulder behind a bread truck.

"They're down there." Joey pointed at three men scrambling down the rocks to the beach. He shoved the bike at Brad. "Hold this. And be careful, it's Antique."

Brad stared at the peculiar bicycle, amazed. When he looked up, Joey was already crouching at the driver's door of the pickup. The pickup door opened, blocking Joey from view. Beer cans, chip wrappers and McDonald's cups tumbled out. Then the door closed and Joey stood, triumphant, holding up a McDonald's bag and video case. He bent to pick up the spilled beer cans and trash, and Brad screamed. Directly behind Joey, running up the shoulder, was the cop, Dumb Darryl.

"Joey!" Brad yelled. "Behind you!"

Oblivious, Joey scrambled to collect more beer cans and cups.

"Joey!" Brad screamed. "Run!"

Too late, Joey straightened up, just as Dumb Darryl's hand closed over his arm. He turned an agonized look at Brad, and then they were gone, the cop hauling him into the mass of spectators still flooding the highway.

Lifting the bike, Brad tried to follow, then stopped. Above the roar of surf and helicopters and the yelling crowd came the piercing, high scream of a horse. Brad turned and pushed his way to the cliff edge.

On the beach, people converged on the second zodiac. Its crew had carried two limp figures ashore and were crouched over them, attempting to revive them. The Life Flight helicopter descended, scattering the crowd. Uniformed EMTs jumped to the ground, carrying litters and ducking under the rotor blades. Sodden shipwreck survivors huddled in separate groups nearby, gesturing angrily at each other. The Coast Guard helicopter hovered over the Muffin causeway, where a rescue craft secured lines to the second party boat.

Unnoticed, the other Greenpeace zodiac floated quietly just off the rocks concealing the tidepool. Brad saw Mac crouched on a boulder, fending her off. Behind him, Sal emerged from the tidepool, carrying Howie's boot. The Admiral plodded behind her, followed by his crew. Sal slid into the water beside the zodiac, the Admiral and other penguins plopping in one by one after her. Brad saw her bald head crest a wave, saw Mac jump into the zodiac. The Greenpeace crew rowed steadily, keeping abreast of Sal. Penguin heads bobbed up behind her.

On shore, only Joe saw them go. With another ear-splitting scream, he abandoned the trailhead and galloped into the waves, swimming hard. As the zodiac rounded the Muffin and slid out of sight, Brad saw Sal clamber onto Joe's back, still trailing Howie's boot.

The crowd on the beach parted, allowing the EMTs to carry two litters to the Life Flight chopper, and Brad saw that at least one person had noticed the penguins' departure. Far up the beach, away from the densest crowds, a small private helicopter was landing. Brad recognized it. Molly and Howie had ridden in it often; Mort kept it on standby at the airstrip for breaking news coverage. Running toward it in a crouch was Mort himself. He was pulled into the cockpit and the helicopter took off, flying past the Muffin after Sal and her escorts.

The Life Flight helicopter lifted off a minute later, its rotor wash knocking pebbles off the cliff. Brad held onto Joey's strange bike to keep it from blowing away. Down on the beach, the crowd milled restlessly, and on the highway around him, Brad saw people heading for their trapped vehicles. The show seemed to be over. He wondered how long it would take for the highway to clear, and how the hell he could tell Sal he'd been six feet from Molly's tape and lost it. Furious, he wanted to hurl the bike over the cliff, punish Joey for getting caught. Why hadn't he run? With Brad screaming practically in his ear, the little shit had grinned and gone on picking up beer cans.

Brad stared at the teal-blue pickup, at the beer cans still strewn beside it, and his anger dissolved. A sudden, horrible suspicion crystalized into certainty. He tucked the bike gently under his arm and headed for home.

"He's deaf," he told Sara, explaining what had happened. "Stone fucking deaf! I never knew it. Jesus, no one ever told me."

"Maybe no one else knew, either," Sara said. "Especially if he didn't want people to know. A good lip reader can fool a lot of people."

She had binoculars to her eyes, watching the horizon. Brad paced beside her on the headland, holding Baby Craig. Mort had phoned from the helicopter. A mile or so out, the penguins had abruptly veered north as if back on track. The Greenpeace zodiac was ferrying Mac and Sal home, a Coast Guard cutter standing by in case Joe's stamina failed him.

"There they are!" Sara handed Brad the binoculars and took Baby Craig.

Brad's eyes misted the lenses of the binoculars; he could see better without them. The zodiac was moving slowly, keeping pace with a tired horse. The Coast Guard cutter followed a quarter mile behind, and far beyond them, the Greenpeace ship bobbed on the sunlit water. Mort's helicopter dipped low over the zodiac and clattered shoreward. It circled the headland once, Mort waving cheerfully, then veered southeast toward his studio. Brad and Sara headed back to the beach trail to meet the zodiac.

"I just can't believe it," Brad said. "I've known Joey at least four years, you'd think I'd have noticed!"

* * *

Mrs. Frederick G. Robinson stared at a page of Anne Rice. Too angry to read, she swore to campaign against the district attorney in the next election, even if it meant electing a Democrat. She glanced at her watch. Almost two o'clock. The man was an idiot. He'd kept them here since eight in the morning, waiting for his stupid witnesses to show up.

There had been some promise to the day at first. State v. Matthissen was their first murder case, and the jury had gaped at gory crime scene and autopsy photos with appropriately horrified fascination. The video of the arrest of Molly Matthissen had caused a minor commotion when the pony-tailed consultant with the earring blurted, "You call that resisting arrest? She walked right into their arms, no need to throw her down in the dirt!"

Stiffly, the district attorney had reminded him that they were to review the evidence without comment until he withdrew. He called the interrogating detectives and the jury listened to a long, boring tape of the questioning session; even Mrs. Robinson smiled when Molly advised the cops to try Atkin's diet, and the crippled juror laughed out loud for the first time. Furious, the DA had turned on her.

"What, are you brain-damaged, too?" he snapped, a singularly cruel remark that reduced her to tears. That was his first mistake. His second was to lecture the whole jury as if they were half-witted children about the seriousness and brutality of the murder.

Oblivious to the jury's growing hostility, he had then informed them that his eyewitnesses and evidence officer were delayed in a traffic jam. Perhaps as punishment for their levity, he ordered them to suspend consideration of the Matthissen case and take up other matters until his witnesses arrived. In retaliation, the jury unanimously refused to return indictments on two assault cases presented by nervous, unprepared deputy prosecutors. Mrs. Robinson was amazed to find herself enjoying the rebellious spirit of what she had thought a despicable group.

Having exercised their anger so boldly, the grand jurors nervously prepared to address the Matthissen case with due solemnity, but the eyewitnesses, when they finally arrived, proved too tempting a target. There were three of them, each dressed in brand-new clothes; the first witness's flannel shirt still had an Eddie Bauer tag hanging from one sleeve. Separately, one at a time, they stood in front of the jury table and answered the DA's questions with exactly the same well-coached answers, telling the same story with almost the same words. They were Fallwell loggers, they said, who had been working with the victim, an FBI agent investigating timber sabotage. None of them got much further than this point in their story.

The foreman with the portable oxygen tank started it. In a surprisingly strong voice, he asked the first witness what the victim's name was.

"Uh." The man looked at the DA. "Uh, whose name?"

"The victim's name!" the old man barked. Mrs. Robinson remembered that he was a retired Navy officer.

"Uh," the logger said again, staring helplessly at the DA, who mouthed a word at him and he brightened. "Borshal. Yeah. Agent Borshal."

"First name?" The foreman was wheezing now, groping for his oxygen.

"Uh. Dunno," the witness aid. "Agent Borshal. Just Agent Borshal."

Next to Mrs. Robinson, the sequined hairdresser looked up from her nail file, snapping her chewing gum. "So how'd ja know he's an agent? Like, he showed you ID?"

"Uh, yeah ..." Seeing the glower on the DA's face, he stammered, "I mean no, no ID, it was just – uh – he just told us. Yeah, he just told us."

Phonier than a shoplifter's alibi, Mrs. Robinson thought. For this they'd been kept waiting all day? It got worse. The jurors took it in turns, peppering each witness with questions. After blatant prompting by the DA, the second logger got Howie's last name right, but said his first name was Harry and of course he'd shown them ID, a fancy FBI card with his photo on it and all. When Mrs. Robinson took her turn and asked the third witness how they'd known Howie was an FBI agent, he nodded toward the DA and said "He told us."

"Agent Borstal, you mean," the DA snapped.

"Oh. Yeah. Him."

The damage was done. The jurors groaned openly when the DA ushered in his last witness, followed by two clerks wheeling a cart stacked with evidence boxes.

The witness seemed no happier than the jurors. His uniform was disheveled, its collar askew, and he carried a filthy McDonald's take-out bag under one arm. A dark smudge streaked one side of his face, his hands, encased in latex gloves, looked wooden. Charlie McCarthy, Mrs. Robinson thought, he looks like Charlie McCarthy. He smiled vaguely at the jurors, a dazed, haunted smile. The DA introduced him as Lieutenant Denson, assigned the maintenance of evidence in the Matthissen case.

Mrs. Robinson looked at her watch. It was almost four o'clock.

Chapter Twenty-Eight

Howie says science tries to make sense of the universe but music and art make sense of existence. I sorta know what he means, but I wonder if music doesn't tap into some sense that's already out there. My violin teacher knew what I meant when I asked her. She said isn't it wonderful that there are things like music and gravity that we can measure but never explain. She's the only person named Fern I ever met and the best teacher I ever had, in music or anything else. I don't know anything about her except every lesson is like plugging into a recharge unit. For a whole hour you are the absolute most important thing on earth and no matter how much shit's happening in the rest of your life, you always leave that room feeling good about yourself.

Violin lessons are in a church meeting room that they rent out during the week. One time I was early for my lesson and this piano tuner was there, tuning the piano. He showed me what he was doing, which was cool, and said I had perfect pitch. By the time my teacher showed up we were playing ragtime and marching tunes together, and Fern joined right in. When he was leaving the tuner dropped that he was coaching Little League that year and said to drop by the field, it would be fun. I did, and it was. That's how I met Coach and started baseball. He tunes pianos and shoes horses for a living, and coaches baseball for fun. Howie says that's what makes him such a good coach.

—*The Oreo File*

In order to appear before Oregon courts, out-of-state attorneys must associate with an Oregon lawyer. Ernest Carlson, Mort's friend and tax lawyer, had happily agreed to join Eleanor Thomas in the Matthissen case, presuming that little more than his name would be needed. An afternoon logging thirty-two phone calls proved him wrong.

"The IRS is a cakewalk compared to cops and prosecutors," Carlson told Thomas cheerfully. "Now I know why I avoided criminal law."

She thanked him and snapped her cell phone shut, one hand resting lightly on Joe's halter. Brad and Sal had been alternately walking and rubbing down the horse for hours. They looked at her eagerly.

"Not much to report, I'm afraid. He finally located the DA and Lieutenant Denson, but they're both in a grand jury hearing. Those can go on into evening sometimes, he says. As for Joey, he's not in custody, either in the shelter or detention. No booking record today. And no one, it seems, knows where he lives."

"Shit, no one knows he's deaf, either." Brad rubbed savagely at hot muscles in Joe's foreleg. "Cops 've probably burned the damn tape by now."

Joe ducked his head and tugged Brad's hair, slobbering down his neck.

"Dammit, Joe, what'd you do that for?"

"He's telling you to lighten up," Sal said.

Brad wiped the back of his head and neck in disgust. "Oh, yuck! Did you feed him more damn marshmallows?"

"He needs high energy food," Sal said.

"We gave him bran mash and sweet grain, for chrissake." Brad tossed his rub-rag onto Joe's back. "I gotta go clean this gunk off."

On the porch, Joey's bamboo bicycle leaned against the wall. The ice mountain was gone, the floor hosed clean, the old fridge unplugged. Brad kicked the gate angrily on his way inside.

"I'm sorry." Ms. Thomas patted Joe absently. "I didn't mean to start a fight."

"He's just scared," Sal said. "About the Admiral, about Joey. And he blames himself for losing the tape, and not realizing Joey's deaf."

"Not a good day," Ms. Thomas said. "I can't reach Mort, either.

And the judge bought the DA's arguments, they're moving Molly back to jail tomorrow. I'm going to the hospital to tell her. Will your brother be all right?"

From the house came the opening bars of "The Devil's Trill." Sal listened. He'd never played it so furiously, or so well. She nodded. "He'll be fine."

* * *

"You have to speak up." The prosecutor glared at the crippled juror with the scarred throat.

"She said perhaps the witness would like a chair," bellowed the foreman.

The prosecutor looked at his watch. He needed Denson only to support his theories about the missing video camera and the many videos of trees and birds seized as evidence of eco-terrorist conspiracy. "This won't take long."

The pony-tailed man was already out of his seat, pulling apart a stack of plastic lawn chairs against the wall. The first was cracked down the middle, the second missing a leg. He found a whole one and carried it to the table. Darryl Denson sat down and nodded gratefully. Avoiding the district attorney's eyes, he answered with a weary yes or no to questions about the search of the Fisher Creek site.

"Those tire tracks," the pony-tailed juror interrupted, "the ones you found the day after the murder – you ever figure out who made 'em or what they were after?"

"It had rained that night," Denson said, welcoming the interruption. "The tracks were too indistinct to identify. One theory was that some person or persons searched the area during the night for the murder weapon – a splitting maul, the witnesses said."

No, he answered, they had not found the weapon. The DA tried to return to his agenda, but an elderly female juror asked what other theories the police had about the tracks.

"We thought someone might have been searching for the defendant's camera, video camera, that is. Or a videotape that might have been in it. The battery pack for the camera was found in the defendant's car, but the camera was not found."

To the DA's question about the search warrant, he described the search of the Matthissen house, neglecting to mention the pelican's fish attack. Mrs. Robinson noticed his blush, though, and wondered what he was leaving out.

"And the camera that matches the battery pack was not found in defendant's house?"

"No, sir."

"And no videotape relevant to the Fisher Creek incident was found?"

For the first time, Darryl Denson looked directly at the prosecutor, then at the jury. "Not in the defendant's house, or at that time, no."

"Thank you, Lieutenant Denson," the DA said, moving quickly to his agenda. "But news videos were found…."

"'Scuse me," the hairdresser pounced, waving blue fingernails at Denson. "D'ja find a tape like that anywheres else, like, any other time?"

"Yes, ma'am," Denson said, looking her in the eye. "This morning, in fact."

The DA, taken unaware, gaped at him. "But …"

"Cool!" the hairdresser said.

"All right!" Mr. Ponytail added, and even Mrs. Robinson leaned forward, interested at last. "Where is it?"

"Um, this morning, yes." The DA pulled himself together, trying to regain control. "Yes. Could you describe the circumstances in which it – uh, the tape?—was found?"

Darryl Denson dug in his back pocket for a grungy notebook and opened it, licking his finger to turn pages. He glanced at the page he wanted and looked up, describing the traffic backup that had delayed his appointment with the grand jury. Unable to maneuver his car through the stalled vehicles, he had gotten out to assess the situation.

"I proceeded on foot to the cliff above the beach known as Eighty-

Seven Steps," he said, describing the scene briefly. "Parked on the shoulder was a Ford pickup known to me as one registered to Craven T. Mallory, one of the eyewitnesses in this case. It was the same vehicle I observed parked at Fisher Creek the morning of March the Twelfth."

The DA frowned impatiently. "Was anyone in the vehicle?"

"No, sir. But I observed Mr. Mallory and his two companions on some rocks at the base of the cliff. Mr. Mallory was holding what appeared to be a video camera, apparently filming the two wrecks."

The DA interrupted again. Mrs. Robinson thought he looked relieved. "And is that the film you found?"

"No, sir. I'm getting to that, sir. When I looked again in the direction of the Ford pickup, I observed a young white male who appeared to be picking the lock of the driver's door. As I made my approach to the vehicle, the young person emerged from the cab holding a McDonald's bag and an empty beer can." Denson looked at his notebook. "Budweiser, Bud lite. He opened the bag and took out a videotape, at which point I apprehended him and confiscated the items."

"So who was the kid?" asked the hairdresser.

Darryl Denson glanced again at his notebook. "He identified himself as – uh – Ronald Weasely, ma'am. But I have reason to believe he was not completely truthful."

The man with the ponytail burst out laughing. The hairdresser and the crippled woman joined in. Mrs. Robinson had no clue what was so funny.

Nor did the DA. He glared furiously at the laughing jurors. "And was the identity of this Ronald Weasely later established?"

Darryl Denson, blank and deadpan, said, "No sir. He got away, sir."

"Ah, so he got away." The prosecutor nodded, back on solid ground again. "And how did that happen?"

"It was while I was leading the suspect – young Mr. Weasely, that is – back to my vehicle. Before we reached it – the road was completely jammed with stalled traffic, see – a young man grabbed me in a state of agitation. His wife was in their vehicle in the northbound ditch." He looked at his notebook again. "A sixty-nine Stanza wagon. She – the wife—was in – uh – in labor, and they were on their way to the hospital when they got stuck in the traffic jam. He had tried to drive around the stalled traffic and broke an axle. The woman was in the back seat, in considerable – well, discomfort."

The prosecutor was definitely looking relieved now, Mrs. Robinson thought. "And the young thief slipped away while you offered assistance?"

"No, sir. It wasn't like that. I called for backup and an ambulance, but they couldn't get through that section of highway, and the Life Flight helicopter was occupied with shipwreck victims. It was obvious the baby was going to – uh – arrive before any help came, and the father was too agitated to be useful, so I – um – we…"

"Holy cow!" the hairdresser exclaimed. "You delivered a baby? Right there in the car?"

Darryl Denson closed his eyes for a moment, then shrugged. "Yes, ma'am."

"Jesus, give this man a drink!" the hairdresser said.

"Certainly understandable the thief getting away, then." The DA stood straighter, ready to wrap things up.

"Oh, no, sir." Darryl leaned forward, all his weary stiffness gone. "He was – young, uh, Weasely, that is – he was remarkable. Truly remarkable. I couldn't have done it, see. I mean, I didn't know…."

He's not testifying any more, he's spilling his guts, Mrs. Robinson thought, listening breathlessly with the other jurors. Not even the DA tried to interrupt.

"First of all, the father's in the way, he's so frantic he's upsetting his wife. So this Weasely as he called himself, he sends the father off to open any unlocked vehicles he can find and get blankets or newspapers, lots of 'em. I wouldn't have thought of that. Then he, Weasely, he kneels on the seat behind the young woman's head and props her shoulders up, telling her how to breathe. I never seen the like, never. I mean in training we saw videos, but this was nothing like they showed us, I wouldn't have known what to do, see? How to help her stop screaming? But this kid is breathing with her and telling her when to push, and then there it was in my hands. The baby, I mean."

Denson held his hands out, cupped under an imaginary infant. "Only it's not like the training videos. It's not breathing or nothin'." He looked down at his hands. "It was so small. I – I could see its skin turning blue."

Darryl shook his head and looked wide-eyed at the DA. The jury groaned collectively. The hairdresser clapped her hands over her mouth.

"I mean, I shook it a little, tapped its bottom like in the movies, but – nothing. I'm holding it and it's not breathing. It's dying."

Denson's eyes pleaded with the jury not to blame him. "And then this young, uh, Weasely, he grabs it from me and puts his mouth right over its nose and starts sucking out mucus, spitting it in the ditch, and he's running his thumb down its spine over and over. And would you believe, the little thing starts breathing. Starts breathing and squalling like any normal baby."

The jury sighed. The hairdresser sobbed openly. Darryl grinned at the DA. "He saved the baby's life, sir. Absolutely. Said he learned it from goats. Then the young man, the father, came back with the Coastal Linen Service driver, they're both carrying stacks of tablecloths, so we kept the mother and baby comfortable until the traffic moved and the ambulance made it through. It was after the EMTs got done and drove off with the new family, that's when I noticed he was gone. Ronald Weasely, that is, or whoever he was."

Darryl Denson stopped talking. He looked at the waiting jury, then at the DA, then stiffened back to his deadpan posture. "Oh. It was a girl, sir."

The jury murmured approval. The crippled woman hugged the sobbing hairdresser. The DA pulled himself together.

"Thank you, Lieutenant. I presume the videotape disappeared along with Mr. Weasely?"

"Oh, no, sir. I mean, I have it with me, sir. As evidence."

The DA frowned. "A tape stolen from a truck. And what suggested its relevance to this case?"

Darryl Denson lifted the dirty McDonald's bag from his lap and set it on the table, pulling out a videocassette with his gloved hand. "Its relevance was suggested to me, sir, by its imprinted label. It says KWOL, and is identical to labels on news tapes collected in evidence from the defendant's home – the tapes in those boxes." He gestured toward the evidence cart.

"There's also a handwritten label underneath that says M.M., that's the defendant's initials, and after that it says merlet – uh, that's spelled M-U-RR-E-L-E-T – merlet nest Fisher Creek March Twelve." He paused, then added unnecessarily, "That's the date and location of the alleged crime, sir."

"So let's see the thing, eh?" The man with the ponytail said.

Denson held up the tape. "You can look, but please don't touch it. It hasn't been fingerprinted, hasn't been logged in as evidence yet."

"We don't need to touch it, just slap it in the machine there," the hairdresser said. "Let's see what's on it!"

"No!" The DA looked positively fearful now. "I mean, that would be highly irregular. You heard him, it hasn't been logged in yet." He reached for the tape.

Darryl hastily slid the tape back into the McDonald's bag and held it under his arm. "Sir, with respect, I ..."

The foreman's Navy commander voice cut him short. "When the grand jury has reason to believe other evidence exists, it shall order such evidence to be produced," he boomed, turning to the DA. "O.R.S. one thirty-two dot three twenty. Correct, sir?"

Defeated, sweating now, the DA nodded and retreated to stand by the door. Lieutenant Denson removed the tape from the bag and slid it into the VCR in the corner. Mrs. Robinson lumbered to her feet to switch off the lights. She glanced at her watch.

It was four thirty-two.

At five-twenty, Mort Holland turned the ignition of his Lexus, parked at a copy shop opposite the courthouse. With a six o'clock newscast to wrap up, he could wait no longer. As he stopped for traffic at the copy shop entrance, a disheveled figure dodged around a bus shelter and slid into the passenger seat.

Darryl Denson, pale but smiling, handed Mort a slightly smudged sheaf of paper. "Public record. The entire jury signed it."

Mort pulled around the block and parked illegally in a bus zone, studying the paper and listening.

"I kept the boy out of it the best I could," Denson finished, getting out of the car. "You'll see he gets his bike back? He's specially worried about it, says it's an Antique."

Chapter Twenty-Nine

You have to go down a steep trail to get to the beach north of our house. The beach is almost a mile long, with steep cliffs going up to the highway, and at the far north end a smaller spit than ours where there used to be a house that fell into the ocean along with a big chunk of land. All that's left there is a rickety set of wooden steps that used to go from the yard to the beach. There are eighty-seven steps, or there were until some fell apart, so locals call the whole beach Eighty-Seven Steps. They're so flimsy now most people don't dare use them, so we almost never see anyone on the beach. Before Sal came home, Mom and I would hike down there sometimes, especially after that long drive from the hospital, and walk or run all the way to the steps and back, sometimes splashing in the tideline, but I never went in the water. I can swim, but the ocean's too big, and has sharks and rays and other big things in it.

At low tide, though, there's a really cool tidepool hidden in the rocks at our end of the beach. It's big and deep and so clear you can watch the crabs running around the bottom, and you never know what kind of fish you'll find between tides. On hot days we would jump in and pretend to be dolphins.

When Sal came home and saw the ocean she couldn't wait to get down there. She wasn't strong enough to hike down, so I put her on Joe's back. She never learned to swim before she got sick, but she ran into the water like she'd done it all her life and I had to run out there and swim with her. I was so scared of that ocean and it was cold as hell, but it was like coming home for her and it made her strong again faster than any doctors could. When she could hike through the rocks we started going to the tidepool, which wasn't so scary, and when winter came Mom signed her up for the county team so she could keep swimming. She racks up blue ribbons but just stuffs them in a drawer, it's being in the water she loves and winning don't mean shit. Maybe it's something natural to the way she was born with gills and that salamander heart.

—The Oreo File

"This one, I think. The balance between bow and bat is clearer." Molly, propped on a crutch, leaned over sketches of heraldic designs strewn over the VIP hospital bed.

Harpo, in chef's cap and apron, picked up the preferred design and grinned. "Good. I think so, too. And the cake – you said chocolate?"

Molly nodded. In the bathroom doorway, Eleanor Thomas rummaged in her purse for a ringing cell phone, frowning at Molly and her visitor. The total lapse of security alarmed her. She had arrived to find no cops on duty at Molly's door and this strange young man in Molly's room.

"Filling?" Harpo asked, taking notes. "We could do raspberry or cherry. Or a walnut cream….?"

"Pecans – he loves pecans," Molly said. "Can you do a pecan filling?"

Ms. Thomas found her phone and glanced at the caller ID. She retreated into the bathroom to answer it. Moments later, she flung the door open and ran to the TV in the corner.

"How do you turn this on? Quick! It's almost six."

Molly pointed to the remote, lying on the daybed. Harpo picked it up and clicked it.

"Channel Four," Ms. Thomas said.

* * *

"What now?" His violin and bow under one arm, Brad stood in the doorway of Molly's room, where Sal had dragged him, protesting. "Didn't he tell you?"

"There wasn't time," Sal said. "He just said turn on the news, quick."

"Oh, great." Brad rolled his eyes. "How many more things can go wrong?"

Sal didn't answer, busy plugging in the TV. Sara and Mac, Baby Craig in his arms, squeezed past Brad and sat on Molly's bed. Her alarm clock still flashed its red POWER OFF light. Mort's face filled the TV screen.

"The case against Molly Matthissen, charged with the murder of alleged FBI agent Howard Borstal last month, took a surprising turn today," Mort said solemnly. He glanced at a sheaf of paper in his hands and looked into the camera. "A Branscombe County grand jury has unanimously rejected the prosecutor's indictment of Ms. Matthissen. The grand jury's 'not a true bill' statement, filed with the court late this afternoon, effectively dismisses all charges against Ms. Matthissen...."

Sal screamed and hurled herself against Brad. He held the violin away from her shrieking embrace and stared blankly at the screen, too prepared for bad news to process the good. Mort's trademark bow tie was askew, he noted.

"Shhhh!" Sara said. "There's more."

"...further surprising development, the same grand jury – on its own initiative and also unanimously – endorsed murder indictments against three prosecution witnesses, who were immediately taken into custody without incident. The three men...."

On the screen, Mort's mouth continued to move, his voice drowned in the general uproar. Sal bounced on Brad's feet, shouting "Yes! Yes!" Mac laughed happily. Sara sang "Halleluliah!" over and over. Baby Craig woke up and howled. Brad stared at the TV screen, the news finally registering. A huge sob choked him and he slumped against the door frame. Sara gently took the violin and bow from his hand.

In the kitchen, the phone rang, unheard.

* * *

Joey crouched by the bamboo bicycle, wiping sprockets and chain with a dry paintbrush. Mort crouched next to him, his long legs folded like a grasshopper's. In a corner by Ms. Campbell's stove, the puppy growled over his shank bone, warning the bicycle off.

"That's quite a bike," said Mort. "Never saw one like it before."

Joey grinned at him. "Thank you for bringing it back.'

"He's been worried about it all day." Tess Campbell poured coffee at the kitchen table and set out a plate of cookies. "I'm a sucker for Girl Scout cookies, especially the peanut butter. How did you know Joey was here?"

"Lieutenant Denson," Mort said. "He made me promise to return the bike."

It was after midnight. He'd had a long day. They all had, he thought. He poured cream in his coffee and drank from the spoon.

Joey dunked a cookie in coffee and slurped the soggy end. "We saw you. On the news," he told Mort. "Do I still have to hide out here?"

"No, sir. It's over. Lieutenant Denson wanted you out of sight in case he had to tell your real name." Ms. Campbell looked at Joey curiously. He hadn't told her much about his morning, just that he had found something important and the cop who dropped him off had told him to lay low.

"What name did you give him?" she asked.

Joey choked on his cookie, spattering soggy crumbs. "Ron," he sputtered. "Ronald Weasely."

Mort thumped his back, laughing. "Oh, too good!"

Their laughter mystified Ms. Campbell. "Ronald Weasely?"

"Harry Potter's best pal," Mort explained, still laughing. He turned to Joey. "Did Lieutenant Denson know?"

Joey nodded. "He said he's read all the books to his kid. And you know what? He knew where that tape was all along!"

"But how?" Mort looked worried.

"His kid. Pete. I fixed his skateboard. He heard Brad tell about the tape and he told his dad."

"Why didn't he just get a search warrant, then?" Ms. Campbell wondered.

"From what he told me," Mort said, "he didn't trust the DA. That's why he brought it to the studio first – wanted me to copy it for insurance – before he took it to the jury."

"That DA's a crook," Ms. Campbell said. "Molly should sue his slimy socks off."

Mort grinned. "Eleanor – Molly's lawyer – is already drafting a complaint. Says her first discovery request will finish his career…."

Joey lost interest when talk turned to lawyers. He grinned at the puppy. It had dragged the bone under the stove in case the bicycle attacked. Joey turned to Mort. "Where's Brad? He okay?"

Mort laughed. "They're all at the hospital, raising holy hell in the VIP suite."

"Good." Joey's smile stretched into a yawn. He slipped his pink backpack onto his shoulders and picked up the bike. "I'll put this away," he told Ms. Campbell. "I got a cat waiting for scraps."

Mort and Tess Campbell caught each other in simultaneous yawns and laughed. He stood up, taking the bicycle from Joey.

"Best be off myself," he said. "I'll carry that for you."

Ms. Campbell followed them down the dark path to the barn. Joey ran ahead to throw the breaker for the lights. She heard Joey describe their plans for a car exhibit, then unlock the door of Howie's workroom.

"This is my room," she heard him say proudly. "Or it will be soon as we build the toilet."

* * *

Brad led Joe slowly along the trail to the headland, a last walk before sleep. The lights winked off in Mac's house as he passed. They had left Sal asleep in Molly's hospital bed, Molly beside her, smiling drowsily. Bullhead had gone home to Portland after delivering a stack of pizzas and promising to release Molly in two days. She had wanted to come home tonight.

"Two more days," he'd said. "By god, the state's paying for it, live it up!"

A waning quarter moon hung low over the ocean. Brad stood, watching the water, the riding lights of fishing boats on the horizon. Joe rested his head on Brad's shoulder. Sal had tied her quilt around him with baling twine, and he looked ridiculous. Brad scratched his ears. Howie's voice repeated a refrain in his head: "Midnight has gone, and the Pleiades…." He couldn't remember the rest, or where it was from. The matching beat changed it to Howie has gone, and the Admiral….

Howie was gone forever, and so was the Admiral. Midnight would come again, he thought. So would the Pleiades. Somehow, there was comfort in that. He fed Joe a carrot and turned for home.

Chapter Thirty

I'll never finish this stupid Autobiography. We're supposed to write how we see ourselves in the future, like what we'll be when we grow up. That's easy, Sal says, "You'll be a famous violinist and I'll have a camera and save birds when Mom and Howie are too old to climb trees."

I put my violin in its case. We've been practicing Boccherini for my recital and Howie's still holding his guitar. He looks like Norman Blake without the glasses, his fingers making soft arpeggios on the strings.

"I don't wanna be famous," I tell Sal. "And what good's violin if all the glaciers are melted and the subways flooded and there's no newts left and only a few stupid humans, starving and killing each other?"

Howie's hand bangs a horrible discord that hurts my teeth. "Ah, but will they still be human without music? Why are you putting that away? It's Sal's turn, remember?"

He plays and sings a tune I love but secretly hate 'cause it makes me think of Sal dyin' in that hospital. Sal comes in with her perfect harmony:

> *"Little birdie, little birdie,*
> *Come sing to me your song,*
> *I've a short while to be stayin' here*
> *And a long while to be gone…"*

I pick up my fiddle and play. But I still don't know what the hell I'll be when I grow up.

—*The Oreo File*

Before dawn on the morning of the Not-A-Memorial-For-Howie celebration, Mac dragged a heavily laden sheet of tin roofing out to the headland. Maneuvering it onto the look-out slab, he began untying ropes from a large bundle wrapped in feed sacks.

The day before, Mac had taken Eleanor Thomas to the bank, to open Howie's safe deposit box with the key left in an envelope full of owl feathers. The box contained Howie's will, along with a sheaf of bank documents. One of these established a trust fund for Brad, Sal, and Baby Craig. Mac still shook his head at the other. It was the deed to the property where his and Molly's houses stood; for the past year, their rent checks had been deposited to a second trust account, its interest to be used for taxes and upkeep. In his will, Howie left the property jointly to Mac, Sara, and Molly, and explained that he had finally found a use for the estate he had inherited from his parents.

Mac had told no one about the will yet. He had a self-imposed task to complete first. Carefully, he slid the heavy bundle from its makeshift sledge onto the rock and cut the cords binding the feed sacks. He tossed rope and sacks onto the tin roofing and pulled it quickly back up the trail without looking back.

Behind him on the rock ledge, Howie's massive cedar Rana Madonna nursed her pollywogs and smiled serenely out to sea.

* * *

The Fairly Honest Eddies looked younger than Molly had expected, and more vulnerable. They slouched against Dinkum's wall like a juvenile police line-up, their cool attitudes wilting. Fish out of water, Molly thought. Their usual armor on white turf was no defense against a crowd so mixed as this.

First two old blues idols and a jazz drummer had welcomed them like long-lost children, and a hit rap artist from New York had slapped their hands and called each "my man." Eleanor Thomas, whose idea of informal wear ran toward the castaway, had undermined their last ramparts of indifference. Dressed in cut-offs that threatened crotch seams, a tie-dyed tank top, and gold sandals that glittered against her black skin, she had actually hugged each of them, her warm touch and lingering perfume leaving them breathless.

At Molly's side, Mel grinned at the Eddies' discomfort. He had raided thrift shops for jeans that wouldn't show butt cracks and crisp button down shirts in shades of blue and grey. The clothes alone made them strangers to themselves, Molly thought. She had recognized each from the Polaroid photo and greeted them by name, trying not to laugh at their awkward handshakes and mumbled, "Pleased to meet you." Mel had worked hard to impose some manners, too.

Gobi, the boy who had taken the photo, was a surprise. He was considerably shorter than the others, a year or two older, and he was shaped like a kite. His broad, flat shoulders tapered to a waist and hips an anorexic would die for. Mel's luck with blue jeans had apparently ended at Gobi; he wore black velveteen slacks held up by green suspenders, and a smock with a fierce-looking goat emblazoned on the back. He was the only one at ease in his finery, though, and the only one who made eye contact, his bird-like innocence a shade too genuine. Molly remembered Mel saying some of these kids had criminal records and decided she didn't want to know which, or for what.

Dinkum's was crowded well beyond its occupancy limit. Not that anyone would report the violation, Molly knew. She sat on the back of a battered armchair, her braced ankle propped on its arm, and leaned against the wall by the fireplace.

The Dinkum's crew had prepared a serve-yourself array of sausage rolls, croissants, cheeses, sauces, breads, raw vegetables and fruits on a long table, bright with displays of edible flowers and stacks of Lion King napkins from a warehouse sale. Geordie and Mex swept in and out, replenishing supplies.

Harpo remained in the kitchen, putting finishing touches to the huge cake he had proudly shown Molly earlier. Except for its size and a border of grace notes, it was exactly as she had first imagined it in that bleak interrogation room the day Howie was killed. Looking at the crowd, she wondered now if Harpo's cake was big enough. Brad's coach and baseball team were carrying in stacks of rented chairs and unfolding them. There had been no announcement of the event, yet people had come from as far as Canada and New York – musicians, biologists, veterans, a congresswoman, a well-known poet. Molly had met many of them before, or knew who they were. Not surprisingly, there were also some total strangers.

One of these, a burly, tattooed man wearing a greasy U.S. Marines cap, had limped up to shake her hand. Howie had saved his life in 'Nam, he said. He introduced his magnificent, tattooed Valkyrie of a wife and their two small daughters, dressed in identical flowered pinafores, with ribbons in their hair.

On the other side of the fireplace, two women shared a table, one a flamboyant redhead with blue fingernails, sequined shoes, and hair piled into a rhinestone-studded Leaning Tower of Pisa. Molly recognized her: the only barber in town who could cut Brad's hair without mangling it. With her was a pale, mousey woman, her throat scarred, a walker parked by her chair. Molly felt a wave of sympathy on seeing the walker, having just graduated to a crutch herself. She had no idea who the woman was.

Near the stage, she saw Bullhead, kneeling with Mort Holland over some recording equipment. Mort wore an appalling orange and green plaid suit, complete with purple vest and red bow tie. Sal had told him he looked like Mr. Boomschmidt, and then had to explain about the circus man in the Freddy the Pig books. Mac and Sara, holding Baby Craig, were sitting with the brown-eyed cop who had told her not to say a word. Dumb Darryl, Mac called him – yet but for him, she'd be in a leaky jail cell right now. On his lap sat Pete, his young son, gazing starry-eyed at Brad on the stage. Molly found his hero worship endearing.

"Brad talked to me and hit a home run," he'd told her when Mac introduced them. Then, noticing Molly's ankle brace, he added, "My dad has a wart on his foot."

Brad stood alone at the front of the stage, his violin under his arm. Inexplicably, he wore his white shirt and black slacks, bought but never worn for recitals, with a black bow tie borrowed from Mort. Behind him, her orange cap bearing crudely embroidered penguins, Sal sat with Howie's guitar propped against a paint-spattered stepladder. The buzz of myriad conversations faded, and the room was silent. So was Brad. His eyes scanned the room, looking for someone who would never be there again. His right hand moved to the bow tucked under his left arm.

"Brad!" hissed Sal.

Brad pulled his hand back. Molly tried not to laugh. They had argued all afternoon about an introduction to Nigger Lew's songs. Beside Molly on a kitchen stool, Mel grinned. The Fairly Honest Eddies shuffled uncertainly. Brad shifted his feet.

"Um," he began. "This isn't a memorial for Howie, because he would've hated it. Me, too. I mean … well, actually, I – I thought I could never play here again…."

His voice broke. Molly felt every throat in the room tighten. She fought the urge to run to him, comfort him, spare him all the grief he'd already suffered.

Sal had a more practical impulse. Leaning forward, she goosed Brad with the neck of her guitar. He jumped, and the crowd laughed.

"And then something happened." Brad made a face at Sal. "Something else, I mean. It happened because of Howie. A lot of things happened because of Howie. Like tonight. All because of Howie…."

Brad's voice started to falter again. His violin was sneaking up to playing position. Sal coughed loudly. Brad tucked the violin firmly under his arm.

"Okay. What happened was I needed some ancestors for a school project. And Howie helped me find some."

The Fairly Honest Eddies lapsed into stone-faced boredom. They hadn't known Howie, and the word school was a total downer. Molly felt sorry for them.

"One of the ancestors he found me was a guy named Lew Southworth," Brad went on, his voice stronger. "You prob'ly never heard of him. I sure hadn't, even though I'd seen the creek named after him a thousand times. It's called Darkey Creek. Lew named it himself. Back in the eighteen hundreds, he was the only black person on the coast here. He called the creek Darkey Creek, and he called himself Nigger Lew."

Even the Eddies jolted to attention. Molly forgot them and listened, fascinated, to her son's tale of a slave who bought his freedom and built himself a homestead on the bay.

"That's all Howie knew," Brad was saying. "We were gonna find out more at the Historical Society, but … well, I had to do that myself. And what I found out – what Howie never knew – was how Nigger Lew earned a thousand dollars to buy himself…."

The Fairly Honest Eddies succumbed, spellbound as four-year-olds at story time. On the stage, Brad paced unconsciously, his violin now a precious relic in his hands, and told of Nigger Lew as if he'd grown up at the old man's feet. He brought to life a young slave with his fiddle, playing for white folks' barn dances and weddings, charming hardrock miners and loggers to earn his freedom; the free man's loneliness in a white backwater; his love of Abraham Lincoln, whose war was fought over again at every polling place; his battle against a storm to exercise his right to vote; his refusal to give up the fiddle denounced by the church; his gift of land for a school and election to the school board. He painted in words the haunting portrait of Nigger Lew, an old man in his rocker before a mantelpiece where his most prized possessions, a fiddle and a photograph of Abe Lincoln, shared pride of place.

"Howie didn't know any of this," Brad concluded. "He didn't even know about the fiddle. He was just finding me fake ancestors 'cause I was adopted and didn't have any real ones. He didn't know how many songs we used to play here were the same tunes Nigger Lew played. He didn't know, no way he could've known, the fake ancestor he found me turned out to be as real as chromosomes. He would've loved it."

Brad looked in mild astonishment at the bow in his right hand. The violin had crept unnoticed to his shoulder. He kept it there.

"So because of Howie – because he would've loved it – and because of Nigger Lew – because someone has to care – we put together some of the songs Nigger Lew played." While he spoke, he played double stops, twisting the fine-tuners. "You'll recognize a lot of them. Some we know Lew played because he said so, some are slave songs he would've played, and some are dance tunes real popular at the time."

Bow poised, he gestured mischievously at Sal. "Sal did all the research – a lot of research – on the songs, so if you want to know more, ask her."

He stepped back and nodded at Sal, tapping his foot. Molly's surge of pride gave way to familiar panic. The bow meeting the strings would take him where she could never follow. And this time, Sal would go with him. In a single beat she saw her children as through a retreating lens, their image dwindling to vanishing point.

"The way I see it, raising a kid is like setting a swallow's wing," Howie had said once. They were scuffing the forest floor, searching for fumets, the regurgitated pellets of fur and bone discarded by owls. "The point of caring is to turn the little bugger loose."

Brad's bow met Sal's opening chord to "Handsome Molly." The confident, playful harmonies and somewhat reckless ornamentation sent a shiver down Molly's spine. Behind the lilting melody, she heard Howie's voice as clearly as if he'd joined them on stage.

"Sailing across the ocean, sailing across the sea, I think of Handsome Molly, wherever she may be…."

"Sometimes they'll come back," Howie had added, "but only because they want to, not because they need to."

Molly smiled. Maternal crisis passed, she gave herself up to the magic of Nigger Lew's music. Even the stone-faced Eddies were tapping their feet.

"Shit, that mother can play," Bricker muttered, staring at Brad. And Gaspar, mesmerized by Sal's fingers, nudged Mel furiously. "How the fuck's she doin' that?"

The final song, "Liberty Bell," brought everyone to their feet, laughing at the familiar Monty Python theme song. From her perch beside the fireplace, Molly saw Tess Campbell work her way toward the stage. Tess beckoned toward the kitchen, then winked at Molly. Joey emerged, carrying the puppy. It cringed in his arms, frightened by the noise. Joey stood between the food and drink tables, concealed from the stage by coffee urns, waiting for Tess's signal.

The plan, Tess had told Molly, was to catch Brad on stage, before he could flee, and present him with Howie's belated birthday gift. "He'll be furious, but wouldn't Howie just love it?" Tess had laughed.

Like most best-laid plans, this one didn't account for the unexpected. Molly heard a chair scrape the floor beside her, a stunned voice saying, "Shit! It can't be!"

Gobi climbed onto a table, waving his arms, his hands weaving arcane patterns across his mouth and chest. For a horrified moment, Molly feared an eruption of gang warfare. Then she saw the object of his frenzied signals.

Next to the coffee urns, Joey stood, staring over the laughing, stomping crowd. His eyes were fixed on Gobi, his mouth open in a classic "O" of surprise. His hands lifted reflexively in response to Gobi's sign language.

The puppy, released from his grip, sprang onto the food table, its yips of terror punctuating the last chord of "Liberty Bell." Toppling vases of edible flowers, wading through cheese plates and dip bowls, scattering Lion King napkins and croissants, the puppy skidded into the sausage rolls and rode the platter over the edge with a frightened howl.

Joey saw nothing of this, nor of the chaos that followed. A trail of yells and leaps marked the puppy's progress through the startled crowd. On the stage, Brad and Sal watched in bewilderment, still holding their instruments. Harpo hastily drew the cart holding his enormous cake back into the kitchen. Joey had scrambled onto the wreckage of the food display. Tears streamed freely down his cheeks. Silently, joyfully, his hands answered Gobi Webster, the foster brother who had taught him to hot-wire cars.

Their nonstop hands went on talking as the noise slowly subsided. At the table near Molly, the puppy had found safety in the mousey woman's lap, its head burrowed under her arm. Tess Campbell and the hairdresser helped her to her feet. Hugging the pup and smiling shyly, a helper at each elbow, she made her way through the parting crowd toward the astonished Brad.

* * *

Propped on her crutch, Molly stood in comforting solitude by Dinkum's fireplace. Inconsequentially, she thought of penguins she'd never seen, plunging unguarded into strange seas, new adventures, likely but not uneventful extinction.

Nearly empty now, the big room had the unnatural stillness of a drained swimming pool. Small, bold sounds of clean-up and weary farewells rang out randomly and faded. On the stage, Harpo and Mex gathered Lion King napkins and discarded forks beneath the empty cake cart, where Mel and Dumb Darryl swiped fugitive globs of icing with their fingers and traded cop lore. From the kitchen came small bursts of talk and laughter, the clink of dishwasher trays, Geordie whistling "Pajama Game." Joey and Gobi, an apron wrapped over his velveteen trousers, wiped tables between bouts of rapid-fire hand talk.

Sara and Mac had taken Baby Craig home after the cake, before the musical free-for-all started. Bullhead had also slipped away, a long drive and early morning shift ahead of him. Molly's arm and ankle throbbed, and the stitch scars on her face ached, over-stretched by laughter. She heard Mort's Lexus splash softly to a stop outside the open door, waiting to take them home. A vision of bed – her own dear bed in her own dear room – beckoned. Molly hobbled forward to round up her brood.

She found Sal, sitting with Gaspar at the foot of the stage, Howie's guitar across their laps. Sal was asleep, leaning against Gaspar's shoulder. He sat rigidly, afraid to move, and looked up at Molly, embarrassed.

"She was showin' me that cross-picking – and then she just faded out, like," he whispered.

Sal didn't wake when Mort picked her up and carried her to the car,

Gaspar following with the guitar.

Molly found Brad by ear. In the corner behind Harpo's shrouded instrument, the puppy slept in Brad's violin case. Beside it, Brad sat with young Pete, holding the violin up for him and guiding his hand on the bow. Eyes shining, Pete drew the bow shakily across each string, singing the notes: "G-D-A-E."

"Perfect," Brad said. "You're a natural, kid. Now you're ready for a tune. You know 'Aunt Rhody?"

Softly, Molly backed away, placing her crutch with care on the wooden floor. She was sitting in a chair by the window when Mort returned, her chin resting on the crutch, eyes closed. Had Mort ever seen Howie's cedar Rana Madonna, he would have recognized the smile glowing through her battered, stitch-scarred face. The notes she hummed were just audible over the hiss of rain on the window:

"G-D-A-E."

Made in the USA
Charleston, SC
16 February 2017